J.B. raced up the gangplank

He traveled its length in heartbeats, covering left as he sprinted past the cabin, but nobody lay in wait for him. He let the Uzi drop to the end of its sling and waved Mildred to follow from cover.

As she started up the gangplank, J.B. kicked aside the dead pirate sprawled behind the Browning and took his place.

A few seconds passed before Ryan appeared, running flat out, his longblaster slantwise across his chest. As he headed west from the street, a mob of pursuers burst onto the waterfront behind him.

Roaring in triumph, they leveled their blasters at Ryan's fleeing back.

**Other titles in the
Deathlands saga:**

JAMES AXLER

DEATH LANDS®

Crimson Waters

A GOLD EAGLE BOOK FROM

WORLDWIDE®

TORONTO • NEW YORK • LONDON
AMSTERDAM • PARIS • SYDNEY • HAMBURG
STOCKHOLM • ATHENS • TOKYO • MILAN
MADRID • WARSAW • BUDAPEST • AUCKLAND

Recycling programs
for this product may
not exist in your area.

First edition September 2012

ISBN-13: 978-0-373-62616-8

CRIMSON WATERS

Printed in U.S.A.

Nothing in the world can take the place of persistence. Talent will not; nothing is more common than unsuccessful men with talent. Genius will not; unrewarded genius is almost a proverb. Education will not; the world is full of educated derelicts. Persistence and determination alone are omnipotent. The slogan "press on" has solved, and always will sólve, the problems of the human race.

—Calvin Coolidge,
30th President of
the United States

THE DEATHLANDS SAGA

This world is their legacy, a world born in the violent nuclear spasm of 2001 that was the bitter outcome of a struggle for global dominance.

There is no real escape from this shockscape where life always hangs in the balance, vulnerable to newly demonic nature, barbarism, lawlessness.

But they are the warrior survivalists, and they endure—in the way of the lion, the hawk and the tiger, true to nature's heart despite its ruination.

Ryan Cawdor: The privileged son of an East Coast baron. Acquainted with betrayal from a tender age, he is a master of the hard realities.

Krysty Wroth: Harmony ville's own Titian-haired beauty, a woman with the strength of tempered steel. Her premonitions and Gaia powers have been fostered by her Mother Sonja.

J. B. Dix, the Armorer: Weapons master and Ryan's close ally, he, too, honed his skills traversing the Deathlands with the legendary Trader.

Doctor Theophilus Tanner: Torn from his family and a gentler life in 1896, Doc has been thrown into a future he couldn't have imagined.

Dr. Mildred Wyeth: Her father was killed by the Ku Klux Klan, but her fate is not much lighter. Restored from pre-dark cryogenic suspension, she brings twentieth-century healing skills to a nightmare.

Jak Lauren: A true child of the wastelands, reared on adversity, loss and danger, the albino teenager is a fierce fighter and loyal friend.

Dean Cawdor: Ryan's young son by Sharona accepts the only world he knows, and yet he is the seedling bearing the promise of tomorrow.

In a world where all was lost, they are humanity's last hope.…

Chapter One

"Smoke!"

The cry penetrated the fog of ache and confusion that enveloped Ryan Cawdor's brain and body.

"Need go! *Now!*"

Jak Lauren. He recognized the albino youth's voice.

Also his urgency. Jak said little, even less than J. B. Dix, the group's armorer. When he did speak, it was even more to the point.

Ryan made himself sit up. He wobbled. His head spun like a gyroscope. The mat-trans unit swirled with the usual jump mists, but the stench of ozone and burning insulation was cutting through the physical haze as well as that in his brain now. It made his eye water and his stomach feel even worse.

Jump sickness, he thought. The jump had been a rough one. Jumping outside normal space via mat-trans gateway was always a wrenchingly disorienting experience, but it seldom hit him as hard as this one had.

Someone tugged his arm. By sheer iron will he forced himself to *move,* despite the pain and nausea. He lurched unsteadily to his feet.

Another hand clutched the back of his coat. Before he could get his balance, he felt himself being towed forward. He had to speed-stagger to keep from falling on his face on the hard floor.

He tried to fight off his assistant. "Krysty!" he cried.

His voice came out a croak. Dense brown smoke watered his eye and scorched down his throat like lye.

"I'm fine, Ryan!" he heard her call. Her hoarseness didn't encourage him to believe she was exactly telling the truth.

But the fact that she was awake and aware enough to respond reassured him. He put a hand down briefly to keep from collapsing despite what he was pretty sure was the wiry strength of Jak—a young man half his size—holding him up. Then he banged his left shoulder on the frame of the six-sided chamber's door and was out.

At once the air cleared. He fell to his knees, coughing hard enough to bring up a lung. Jak let him go.

When the hacking fit passed he shook his head to clear it, then raised it to look around.

They were in the gateway's antechamber. A few feet away his redheaded mate, Krysty Wroth, stood with one arm around the shoulders of Mildred Wyeth, helping her keep her feet.

Mildred was a black woman in her late thirties, with hair worn in beaded plaits. She was stocky, but after a few years of hiking across the Deathlands very little of that was fat. Despite Mildred's weight, Krysty didn't have much trouble holding her up. Mildred was also a freezie from predark.

Ryan became aware of Jak hovering at his side nervously. "Thanks," he said to the youth, whose white hair had fallen forward to almost obscure his face. "I'm fit to fight. Help the others."

"At last you rejoin us, my dear Ryan," a deep voice said. "Welcome back to the land of the living."

Dr. Theophilus Tanner stood by a darkened bank of camp consoles, looking dapper, and surprisingly hale for a man who normally looked as if he were on his last leg after a jump. A tall stork of a man with silver-white hair hanging down to the collar of his old-time frock coat, he carried a black swordstick with a silver lion's head.

His head still feeling as if it might go spinning off his shoulders at any moment, Ryan looked back at the mat-trans. The walls of the chamber were made of arma-glass tinted a dull, nasty-looking mustard color. Smoke of a similar but darker hue still snaked out into the ante-chamber of the redoubt that housed the mat-trans.

"Not good," he muttered, rubbing the back of his neck.

"What do we have here?" Doc asked.

"Looks like a map," J.B. said. He was a little banty rooster of a man, in a battered, dusty bomber jacket, steel-framed specs and a fedora. In addition to being the group's armorer and general gadget master, he was also Ryan Cawdor's oldest and best friend.

It was a map, Ryan saw. Or at least part of one, any-way, hung on a sheet of particle board that showed a mess of holes. Some were small and precisely round. Others were more irregular.

"Somebody blasted the map for some reason," J.B.

said. "Bullets ricocheted off the wall behind. They tumbled and deformed. That's why the funny holes."

"Maybe it wasn't the map they were shooting at," Mildred said. "Maybe there was somebody standing in front of it at the time."

J.B. shrugged. "Triple-stupe idea, either way. The ricochets were as like to chill the shooters as whoever they were shooting at."

"From the scrap of map," Doc said, reaching up to almost touch the faded colors of the paper with the tip of a finger, "we would appear to be here, in the Leeward Islands—the northern segment of the Lesser Antilles, in the Caribbean."

"How you reckon that, Doc?" Mildred asked.

"Behold the symbol here," he said. "An ocher hexagon. Does that suggest anything to you?"

He smiled, his winter-pale blue eyes dancing, and nodded toward the gateway.

Ryan stepped close. "So mebbe this one in the mountains is another mat-trans gateway?" he asked.

"It would certainly appear so. If that is indeed the case, my dear Ryan, then it would seem to be located on the island of Puerto Rico."

He frowned. "Curiously, the mat-trans in San Juan we jumped to once upon a time isn't shown. Perhaps it postdates this facility and the map was never updated."

Ryan shrugged, uninterested. Knowing, not knowing—wouldn't feed him, either way.

"So where are we now?" Krysty asked. She smoothed back her hair from her flawless face.

Doc shook his head. "Alas, dear lady, that I cannot say. The geography of the region was never of more than passing interest to me."

"Well, let's get rolling, people," Ryan said. "Finding some kind of supplies in this rad-blasted redoubt is of more than passing interest to *me*."

"WHAT COULD DO?" Jak asked.

A quick search had showed the redoubt's stores were well looted, so empty they might never have been stocked in the first place. But that wasn't what had them all standing and staring openmouthed in awe and surprise.

The albino youth asked a good question, Ryan judged. The walls of a redoubt could shrug off blaster bullets like spit, and it would take a powerful blaster to seriously scratch them.

The corridor ahead of them was pinched shut, like an old length of hose with a swag-bellied sec man standing on it.

"Seismic activity, at a guess, dear boy," Doc said.

"Talk plain, Doc!" Jak admonished.

"Earthquakes," J.B. said.

"I thought most of the really massive quakes happened along the Pacific Rim," Mildred said.

"The West Indies and Central America have been traditional hotbeds of such upheaval," Doc said, used to Jak's outbursts.

While he could sit stone still for hours on guard or on a hunt, Jak wasn't known for patience where his fellow humans were concerned, particularly the time-trawled professor. Still, Ryan eyed the old man closely. He also had a habit of drifting in and out of reality.

Mildred grunted. "Oh. That's right. I remember back in the early twentieth century there was a terrible eruption that killed tens of thousands of people. Mount Pelée, the volcano was called. Wiped out the city of Saint-Pierre the way Vesuvius did Pompeii."

"On the island of Martinique, then," Doc said. "That would lie south and perhaps somewhat east of here, if my reading of that map fragment was correct."

J.B. rubbed the back of his neck. "We sure got bellies full of eruptions when we were in Mex Land," he remarked.

"Gaia is restless here," Krysty said, frowning. Her emerald-green eyes were pointed at the crushed corridor, but Ryan saw they were focused on nothing in particular.

He shook his head. "It doesn't matter. We need to find a way out of here."

"Find food," Jak said. "Hungry."

"How can you even think of food?" Mildred demanded. "My stomach's still doing slow rolls from that damned jump."

J.B. squinted critically into the dark depths of his upended canteen. "I wouldn't sweat the grub, Jak," he said. "The water's about gone. Dehydration'll chill us before hunger gets a proper start gnawing our vitals."

"So," Ryan said. "Out."

"I hope the doors aren't blocked by the same forces that did this," Mildred said. "Whatever they were."

Jak shook his head. "Open. Air fresh."

Mildred eyed him. "You sure about that, Jak?"

"Power's still on," J.B. added. "Or didn't you notice we're not stumbling around in darkness blacker than twelve feet up a stubbie's bowels?"

Jak shook his head irritably. "Air *fresh*," he repeated. "Not filtered. Not smell?"

J.B. drew in a deep breath. "Mebbe not," he said, "compared to you."

Ryan grunted. "So lead the way," he said to Jak. "Get us out of here."

J.B. SQUINTED THROUGH his minisextant at the sun, which was about halfway up a blue sky free of chem clouds. "You were right about the map," J.B. said, lowering the device. "We're in the Caribbean, all right."

The companions stood on the highest point of the island, which was as bare as a baby's backside and not a whole lot larger, if not nearly so smooth. In fact, the rock beneath their feet was black, hard and porous—lava. Though it didn't rise more than forty or fifty feet above the dancing green water that surrounded it, its regular shape unpleasantly suggested that it was the cinder cone of an actual volcano.

The breeze up the west side of the island, off a beach where stretches of white sand alternated with rusty-brown, smelled of salt and decaying sea life.

"What now?" Krysty asked.

"We could try the mat-trans," Mildred said. "It hasn't exactly taken us a long time to find out there was nothing but rock and sand on this damn island. Might be able to get back inside the time limit of the LD button."

The gateways had a feature that allowed a user to return to the originating point by pressing the "last destination" button within half an hour of a jump.

J.B. frowned at his wrist chron. "We'd be crowding it," he said. "Anyway, I'm not rightly sure I want to trust a malfunking machine."

"Do you like the idea of dying of thirst here, with water, water everywhere, and not a drop to damn well drink?" Mildred asked.

"Not starve, anyway," Jak said. "Sea here—food always."

MILDRED GLARED AROUND at the others. "Why *not* try the gateway? We can always jump to a random destination. It got us here, after all."

J.B. shook his head. "Bad idea, Millie. There's something wrong with it. I don't think it's safe."

"Safe?" Doc whinnied the word like a laughing horse. Mildred noted the way his blue eyes rolled. He was losing his grip on reality, which was never rock solid to begin with. "Jumping through time and space by such unnatural means is never safe, J.B.! Never safe at all."

Doc slumped suddenly, his face crumpling like an old newspaper. Mildred knew he was remembering his lost family and life, before he'd been time-trawled away from everything he knew or held dear by the scientists of Operation Chronos.

"We're not trying the mat-trans," Ryan said. He

wasn't a man who minced words; while he might consult his friends on decisions, once he spoke in that tone, as flat and hard as slate, it was final. "We're getting off this nuke-withered rock. *Alive.*"

Krysty had walked down toward the beach to the northwest. It wasn't a long trip.

"There are islands off this way," she said. "Some of them have trees."

"Might be game," J.B. added.

"Trees mean fresh water," Jak said.

"Not necessarily where we can get at it," Ryan said. "But yeah."

"This is an area, as our youthful friend so astutely points out, that abounds in edible sea life," Doc said. He seemed to have snapped back to the present; he tended to do that when confronted with a problem he found interesting, Mildred had noticed. "That suggests humans live here, too."

"That's so," Ryan said. "People go where there's chow. So we start working our way from island to island. Only question is, how?"

"Nearest island's a good mile, mile and a half off," J.B. said. "Anybody feel like a swim?"

"You've got to be kidding me, John Barrymore," Mildred said. The armorer was her lover. "I can't swim that far. We don't know what the current's like, anyway."

"Sharks," Jak stated.

"Just joking, Millie," J.B. said.

"Down here!"

Everybody looked to where Krysty was standing on the beach with her back to the sea. She was waving.

"I think I found a way!"

Chapter Two

"What way?" Jak said. "Only see water."

Ryan stood at Krysty's side on the white coral sand. The others had gathered nearby.

"You have to learn to look below the surface, Jak," J.B. said.

Ryan was doing so, and frowning. The water close to shore was shallow and as clear as glass, but he wasn't sure what it was he was seeing.

"It would appear to be a road," Doc said, bending over like a feeding crane to peer into the water. "Made out of cyclopean blocks. Limestone, I would say."

Mildred's forehead creased into a frown. "That sounds like the Bimini Roads," she said. "Except aren't they off the Bahamas? And I don't think the Bahamas are all that near to here, are they?"

Ryan polled the others with his eye. They looked as blank as he felt.

Doc blinked at Mildred like a newly hatched baby bird. "Dear lady," he said, "I fear the rest of us have little idea what you are saying. Except that, yes, the Bahamas lie far to the northwest of here, beyond the island of Hispaniola. Quite near the east coast of Florida, in fact."

"So, what would subsurface blocks like this be doing here?" Mildred demanded.

"Who knows?" Ryan said. "Why care?"

"The road, if that's what it is, seems to lead right past that next island," Krysty observed. She flashed that smile Ryan loved so well, as dazzling as late-morning sun breaking bright off the wavelets.

"If the road leads to the next island," Ryan said, "it's the closest thing to a way off this sorry bare-ass rock that we've got. I'm going."

Doc straightened and shot the cuffs of the white shirt he wore beneath his frock coat. "And we shall follow," he said. "As usual."

"Ow! Shit."

"What is it, Mildred?" Krysty asked.

They were wading through thigh-deep water, following the big oblong blocks of pale stone. Ryan led, holding his Steyr Scout Tactical longblaster at the ready. Behind him marched J.B., cradling his Uzi. Then Mildred, Krysty and Doc, who flourished his swordstick in the hot air with every sloshing step. Jak brought up the rear, scowling around at the water as if expecting something to dart through it and bite them.

As it appeared, something just had. "My leg," Mildred said. "Something stung me just now. Right above my right boot."

Jak pointed. "There!"

What he was pointing at moved fast, but Krysty had good reflexes. She looked in time to see something like a silver shadow, long and slim as the concealed blade of Doc's sword, dart away through the water.

Looking back at Mildred, she saw a dark cloud puff into the water by her leg.

"'Cudas!" Jak shouted.

"Barracuda," Doc said doubtfully. "I didn't think they were known for attacking humans. Swimmers, perhaps. But certainly not walking ones. Or even waders."

Balancing precariously on one leg against the slow ocean current, Mildred hoisted her right leg out of the water. "Somehow I don't think this one got the memo, Doc," she said.

Evidently not. Krysty saw a red slice, vivid against the coffee-with-cream skin of Mildred's calf. Blood flowed freely to drip into the water.

"Ace on the line," J.B. said. "That blood could draw sharks."

"Screw sharks!" shouted Jak. "More 'cuda coming!"

Quickly Krysty looked around. Sure enough, the shallow Caribbean waters, so deceptively peaceful on the surface, swarmed with sinister shiny shapes just below. Some circled just out of range. Others…

Mildred jumped one-legged straight out of the water. "Fuck!" she screamed. Through the roiling water Krysty saw a lean shape lance past, just where the woman had been standing.

With a rattling roar J.B. cut loose a burst from his machine pistol. Water spouted in an arc twenty feet from where Mildred was splashing back down. She came down on both feet but teetered. Krysty grabbed her wrist and kept her from toppling.

The fall itself was no danger, obviously, but to be floundering around, depending on her own modest human swimming abilities, while contending with a shoal of killer fish could be deadly.

A corpse bobbed to the surface. Its belly was white and showed the tips of black tiger stripes. Jaws filled with razor-edged teeth gaped. A round eye stared blankly. An inky cloud surrounded it.

"Good shooting." Ryan hefted his Scout but didn't find any targets worth a precious 7.62 mm round.

"Strike, more like," J.B. called. "I was mainly looking to scare the nuke-suckers off. Or at least back. Bullets don't travel for shit in water, anyway."

"These barracuda seem unnaturally large," Doc said. He had his sword drawn and pointed toward the water. "I do not recall them growing significantly longer than six feet, yet yon specimen is a good nine or ten feet long, and some of his kindred seem longer still."

"Mebbe muties," Jak said with a snarl of distaste.

"Keep moving, everybody!" Ryan said. "They'll chew us to bits if we just stand here gaping like a pack of stupes!"

They moved into a slow-motion run, raising hip-high waves. Krysty held her snub-nosed Smith & Wesson Model 640 in her hand, but their wakes made it difficult to spot the finny horrors close by.

Then again, if they were that close it was probably too late to do anything about them, anyway. Seeing a shape arrow at her from about thirty feet off to her right, Krysty snapped a shot at it. The .38-caliber slug kicked up a foot-tall jet of water. Whether the bullet hit the 'cuda, or even came near, she didn't know. The fish sheered away.

And she felt an impact against her own left calf. She looked down to see another ten-foot fish whip away from her. By reflex she looked down. It had ripped the tough denim of her jeans, but she saw no blood and felt no sting of salt water on a fresh wound.

"Go!" Jak shouted from right behind her.

J.B.'s Uzi snarled again. Ryan's Steyr went off with a hard crack that seemed to hit the water and skip like a stone; Krysty felt the shock wave on her cheek as she started into forward motion again.

"They don't like the bullets hitting near them," Mildred said in satisfaction, letting her big, ZKR-551 handblaster settle back online from a shot.

"Yeah," J.B. said. He fired a single shot from his mini-Uzi. "But when I said we had plenty of cartridges, I didn't mean enough to keep blasting them into the ocean all day to frighten fish."

Jak snarled a curse. His handblaster roared. Lighting off right behind Krysty, its muzzle-blast made her ears ring, and the shock slapped the back of her head like an open palm. A .357 Magnum revolver had the nastiest blast of any handblaster she'd encountered, nearly as bad as Ryan's 7.62 mm longblaster.

"Fucker bit!" Jak said, evidently meaning it bit *him*. He uttered a scream of triumph as another barracuda bobbed to the surface. It had the front part of its head and whole upper jaw blown away.

Though it made her stumble slightly as she continued to run through the warm water, Krysty glanced back. She saw the floating corpse bounce as one of its fellows hit it from below.

"They eat their dead," she called.

Ryan had slung his longblaster now in favor of his 9 mm SIG-Sauer handblaster. Its cartridges were far more common than the big bottleneck rifle rounds, and if anything, the pistol's handiness and quicker firing gave him a better chance of hitting one of the slim, elusive targets. "But I think we got a bigger problem than these little fuckers."

"Why, Ryan?" Doc asked. Swirls of dark blood trailed from both his legs now. But his upheld swordstick ran red halfway down its blade, indicating he'd at least gotten some vengeance. "The blighters appear to be fleeing."

"'Cuda got bigger problem, too!" Jak yelled. "Look!"

Thirty yards to their left, a big triangular fin cut the surface. As Krysty watched, at least half a dozen more appeared behind it, gray and unspeakably sinister.

"Sharks!" Jak shouted unnecessarily.

"Bull sharks, I do believe," Doc said. "Known for their highly aggressive natures. And for their proclivity for extremely shallow water."

Krysty spun and lunged. She caught Jak and yanked him up out of the water in a huge gout of spray. She winced at the way the nasty sharp bits of metal sewn to his jacket bit into the flesh of her arm, meant to discourage just this sort of bear hug.

A foot-tall fin slashed past beneath him, barely two feet from Krysty's own legs.

Krysty managed to pump three quick shots after the departing bull shark.

"Looks bad, here," J.B. said, racking back the charging handle on his Uzi after slamming in a fresh thirty-round mag.

"All this blood in the water is drawing them," Doc said. "It will induce a feeding frenzy, no doubt."

Ryan had holstered his SIG-Sauer to whip up the Steyr. He fired a blast. Water gushed into the air just in front of another fin carving toward him. The big shark turned away not five feet from Ryan's legs, red foam marking its wake.

"Ryan, behind you!" Mildred shouted.

Ryan spun with remarkable alacrity despite the water's drag. Holding on to his longblaster's forestock, he whipped his long panga from its sheath, sidestepped and swung upward.

Horrified, Krysty saw a great dark shape like a fat gray torpedo blast out of the water to fly with its open jaws aimed right at Ryan's face. Or where it had been an instant before. She saw his heavy knife blade score a long gash from the gill slits back along the water-streaming side of the killer fish. Trailing a pennon of bright blood, the shark dived back into the water in a huge shower of spray.

In an eyeblink Ryan had the panga sheathed again and

his longblaster shouldered. Taking a flash aim through the flip-up ghost ring sights, he fired, but not at the shark that had so narrowly missed biting his head off. Nor at any of the others swimming horrifyingly close by to the eight-foot-wide path of submerged stone slabs. But at a fin moving at the back of the pack, almost a hundred feet away.

A pink-tinged jet greeted the shot, and the fin began to move away. Ryan cranked the bolt and fired again, at another of the more distant sharks.

"They're turning away!" Mildred shouted.

"Got bigger food," Jak said as Krysty let him back down into the warm embrace of the sea. Her bare left arm streamed blood from a dozen gashes into the water.

"You're hurt, Krysty," Mildred said.

"Not as bad as I will be if those big bastards come back," Krysty said. "Let's move while we've got a chance! We might actually make the island."

They ran clumsily. The water pulled at Krysty. Strong as she was, it sucked the strength right out of her. She was bleeding, too—not fast, but enough that it would sap her energy in a short time.

Doc ran high-stepping, water flashing by his up-raised knees. But the effort quickly took its toll. Mildred cruised past him, grabbed him by the coat and towed him behind her as if she were a tugboat.

Most of the sharks were distracted by the bigger feasts offered by the three of their kinfolk Ryan had chilled. Especially the one that was thrashing on the surface, sending prisms of water flying and causing a tremendous commotion. Which apparently was exactly what sharks liked, because the other fins in sight were making a beeline toward their flailing comrade.

Most of them. J.B.'s Uzi loosed off another burst as one came close from the far side. A beat later, Ryan's longblaster boomed.

Then, before Krysty even realized the island was nearby, Ryan was standing in water to his shins, shouting at them to power on as he swung up the Steyr to put another shot into a charging shark. J.B. stopped to stand beside him and lay down covering fire with his machine pistol. The pistol slugs might or might not actually hurt the sharks underwater, but the tubby gray monsters sure didn't like the impacts in the water nearby.

Then they were on a white beach. Krysty toppled and fell forward.

"HOW ARE YOU DOING?" Ryan asked, squatting beside Krysty where she sat in the shade of a palm tree near some brush.

She smiled wanly and gripped his offered hand with hers. Mildred knelt on her left, clucking in dismay as she did her best to tend the cuts Jak's boobied jacket had left in her arm.

"Better now," the redhead said. "Thanks to you, lover."

"We're not home free yet," Ryan said, standing. "Just on a different island."

"Jak and Doc think they might find fresh water," J.B.

said. "Plus the road keeps going to the next island, whatever that's worth."

Ryan rose and peered into the distance. About half a mile to the north stood yet another island. This one was large, at least a couple hundred yards by about a quarter mile. The next one looked larger still.

"Still got to get there," he said. "And those 'cudas are still around. Sharks, too. Even if that last bunch got bellies full of each other, there are still lots of sharks in a whole bastard ocean."

"Well, see now, Ryan," J.B. said. "I aim to do something about that."

He had one of their precious few blocks of C-4 moldable plas-ex and was breaking it into quarter-kilo chunks and stuffing those into detonators. The explosive had been scavvied from a recent find.

"Shock waves propagate better in water than in air, John Barrymore," Doc said, walking back along the beach. "Would not those bombs you are so cleverly improvising pose as great a threat to us as to the sharks?"

"Find any drinking water?" Ryan asked.

Doc sat down in the shade of some kind of bush and mopped his forehead with a handkerchief. "No. Jak was circling the other way. Perhaps he'll have more luck. He has a better nose for such things than I."

"There," Mildred said, cutting off the end of a roll of gauze she'd wound around Krysty's upper arm and standing up. "That ought to keep you from bleeding to death."

"Thank you, Mildred," Krysty said.

Mildred grunted. "Glad to help. Makes me feel useful."

She looked at Doc. "I'm no expert on underwater blasts. But I believe shock waves in water pose danger mostly to internal organs. And mainly through bodily orifices."

"So if we keep our bungholes out of the water," Ryan said, "we should be green."

"Not exactly a medically precise description," Mildred said, "but close enough for the Deathlands. Of course, good thing we don't have lawyers anymore, so you can't sue me for malpractice if I'm wrong."

Doc smiled sadly. "No lawyers indeed," he said. "Ah, it just goes to show. Even a war taking billions of innocent lives has a bright side, if one looks closely enough!"

Chapter Three

"Yonder she lies," the old one-legged black boatman said grandly. "Nueva Tortuga. Or NuTuga, as the folk who live there like to call her."

"If I am not mistaken," Doc said, "this is the island of Nevis we see before us."

"So 'tis," the boatman said.

"Call me Oldie of the Sea," he'd told them. "Or call me Ishmael. Just don't call me late for supper." Then he'd laughed and laughed, so hard it was infectious despite the fact the joke was older than Doc and twice as worn-out. He'd appeared out of a sun falling into a brownish-black bank of clouds on the western horizon, rowing his little skiff, towing a net full of writhing silver-sided fish.

Ryan frowned out across water that danced with midafternoon sun-dazzle at a hilly green island to the north and east of the little boat. A shiny white ville with neat orange-and-red-tile roofs tumbled down some of the hills to a harbor crowded with boats. None of them was as much as a hundred feet long, as far as he could tell.

It looked like the last place on earth settled by, inhabited by and run exclusively for the benefit of the coldest-hearted pirates in the West Indies.

He and his companions had found an inhabited island

late the previous afternoon. Actually, they'd found the boatman's camp, which consisted mainly of a firepit and a shanty made of warped, sun-silvered planks and a roof of ancient corrugated plastic, a mottled cream color with little hints of original orange remaining in the troughs. Ryan couldn't see it surviving the next stiff breeze, to say nothing of the next hurricane.

A quick search of the island, which wasn't much bigger than the one they'd jumped in on, showed no one else was currently on it. But the fact that there were ashes and burned wood chunks visible in the fireplace, instead of drifted sand, showed somebody had been there recently. After a brief conference they agreed to hide in the brush. Except for Ryan, who sat to see who showed up by boat.

"So…Oldie," Mildred said reluctantly. "You sure you're going to be okay here?"

"Sure," he said. "Ever'body's safe as houses in Nu-Tuga. Houses're safe, too. Syndicate don't let anybody act out. Ever'body's equal before the law."

He was a wiry guy of medium height, just a finger or two taller than J.B. His skin had started black and gotten blacker from constant exposure to the Caribbean sun. It made for a startling contrast with his hair and beard, full despite his years although cut close to his skull, and white as the snow he'd likely never seen. His face was a mass of wrinkles, as much, Ryan reckoned, from habitual good humor as age or sun.

He'd haggled briefly and halfheartedly before agreeing to feed them, refill their canteens from his hidden water cistern, let them sleep rough on his island and ferry them to the nearest port in the morning for three 7.62 mm rounds from Ryan's Steyr Scout longblaster. Ryan got the impression he only accepted payment because his new friends would naturally suspect him of plotting something if he hadn't—and that what he was really after was some company, however brief.

His skiff, named the *Ernie H,* was well kept but seemed as ancient as Oldie was. Right now, the little vessel ran on a broad reach across a breeze from the northwest, using a single triangular sail on the mast. Oldie had a pair of oars locked up under the gunwales for calm seas.

He also had an Ishapore 2A longblaster clamped under a tarp by his seat in the stern. It was the reason he'd been willing to take the 7.62 mm rounds in exchange for passage, since the Indian-made rifle had been built to fire those rounds. Though the forestock was secured by windings of bright red copper wire, Ryan had seen how the steel of the barrel and receiver shone with a faint coating of oil. It was a piece both well used and well maintained.

"So truly," Doc said, peering toward the near ville, "the city is ruled by a council of pirates?"

"Right as rain," Oldie said. "They started using the place soon as the quakes settled down after the war. Much as they ever settled down, that is. Wasn't much commerce to raid in those days, but a lot of richies tried to weather the nuke-storm at sea on their yachts. They made pretty ripe plucking."

The wind died as they approached the mouth of the

harbor. Oldie calmly stood and began furling the sail, easily shifting his weight to accommodate the boat's rocking.

"Pirates did a lot of coastal raiding in those days, too," he said. He was clearly doing something he did every day. It didn't take much conscious attention on his part. "These days, too, of course. Anyway, what with one thing or another, this side of the island wound up with a double-cherry natural harbor—if you could call what made it 'natural,' speaking rightly.

"Since the quakes and storms and whatnot had pretty much leveled Charlestown, which was pretty much the only town that counted, here or on St. Kitts just off to the north, there—" he nodded his white-bearded chin at a humpy green line lying off on the horizon as he lowered the sail "—the place tended to attract folks. Took hold right quick as a place to trade. 'Course, being as the only folks with much to trade—or at least, the means to insist on getting *paid* for what they had to trade, if you catch my drift—were pirates, pirates it was as settled it. Some got *so* successful they decided they could do better by staying put, keeping things running smooth and taking their cut off the top, than by sea-roving. Less work, and a shitload safer."

"So they sell rum, gaudy sluts and beans to the gangs that bring in loot," J.B. said. "Good income, if you got the weapons to hang on to it."

Oldie grinned. "Told you, they was pirates to start with. They may put on airs and strut around cocky, but they didn't forget their roots. They call their sec men Monitors. People as run afoul of them live to regret it."

He got out his oars and set them in locks to either side of the bench that ran across the bow, then sat and began to pull with strong, practiced strokes. Muscles bunched and corded on arms left bare by the sleeveless burlap-sack blouse he wore.

"No engine on this thing?" Mildred asked in apparent surprise.

"Won't have one." He turned his head and spat into the water. "Don't hold by the things. Don't need gas. Get all the fuel I need, growing from the ground or in our sister the sea. And don't need replacement parts."

He grinned and thumped the hand-carved wood stump that replaced his lower left leg. "Not since I whittled this one to replace the pin that mutie eel bit off for me. More-ay we call 'em—'a' for *ass,* 'cause those are some big-ass eels!"

Jak scowled suspiciously. "Thought said shark bit off," he said.

"Did I?" Oldie laughed. "One of them things. See, son, man gets to a certain age, trivial little details just naturally start to slip out of his mind. Great white, mutie more-ay—whichever. It got my leg and I don't have it any longer."

Jak lapsed into sullen silence, as the crusty old bastard laughed at him. But Ryan had seen the end of the stump beneath Oldie's left knee. *Something* with big jaws and big teeth had taken it off; he knew that much from the marks. If the ancient half-crazed mariner wanted to make a joke out of something like that, good for him. Ryan had to smile in acknowledgment of his balls.

"Sweet yacht, there," J.B. said, pointing.

J.B. was no nautical man—far less than Ryan, anyway, who'd at least grown up with small boats as a baron's son in the rich and powerful East Coast barony of Front Royal. But J.B. was a skilled mechanic and tinkerer, not just an armorer. He knew wags of all sort, land and sea alike. He had a feel for them, and an eye.

Ryan nodded. He admired the clean lines of the vessel, although she had a funny prow: straight up and down, not angling up from the sea. She had to run ninety feet over waterline, with a smooth white coat of paint, unlike many of the other vessels in the harbor, whether masted or motor craft. Most were dilapidated and didn't look well maintained at all.

Ryan also appreciated the machine gun on the pintle mount rising from the foredeck. He judged it was .30 caliber, which made it a Browning 1919. An oldie but goody, even by the time the balloon went up on the Big Nuke. But if it was maintained properly, as he reckoned this one had to be, it would still be capable of dealing out serious hurt. It even sported a splinter shield welded together from thick steel plates. The gun could kill a small craft's engine, or just shoot the crew out of a larger vessel, without doing much damage to cargo or hull.

"Not bad," Oldie admitted, "even if she has an engine in her belly. That's the *Wailer*. Don't burn your eyes on her too long, boys and girls. Like about half the hulls tied up here right now, she belongs to the Sea Wasp

Posse, out of Ocho Rios over to Jah-Mek-Ya. Biggest, meanest pirate bunch working the Antilles and northern Gulf since that giant-ass 'cane took down the Black Gang some time back. The Blacks were cocks of the walk before that."

J.B. caught Ryan's eye and gave him a quick, tight, closemouthed grin. It hadn't been a hurricane that took down the most feared pirate crew in the West Indies. Although not one but two hurricanes had helped. The real cause of their demise had been the companions.

It wasn't a fact Ryan felt the need to advertise. Especially not closing in on a place that was the main pirate trading, refitting and recreational port. Odds were, the Black Gang had been NuTuga's best customers in their time. The Syndicate might not look kindly on people who took that big a bite out of their business.

Quays had been built out into the NuTuga harbor out of broken-up volcanic rock, mostly a dark, rusty redbrown. The tops had been boarded over with planks. Some of the craft, such as the *Wailer,* were tied up to them. Others rode at anchor in the harbor itself.

As they entered the harbor Krysty pointed off to the left. "What are those?" she asked.

Squinting, Ryan saw what appeared to be half a dozen steel cranes standing by the shore, which was brown volcanic sand shored up by bigger chunks of lava. Four of the arms were swung out over the harbor. Something that looked like a curiously shaped duffel bag hung from a chain from each into the water. A seagull perched on the rounded top of one, bending forward to peck at it.

"Oh, no," Krysty said in a small voice.

Frowning, Ryan looked closer. Those were humans hung from the chains, waist-deep in water with steel bands under the armpits. Their sun-blackened bodies were nude. At least one seemed to have been a woman.

One twitched. The seagull spread slate-backed wings and flew away. It had been pecking at the victim's eyes.

"Is that one still alive?" Krysty asked.

J.B. shrugged. "Not much wind stirring," he said.

"Oh, God—" Mildred emitted a strangled cry. Turning away just in time, she vomited noisily into the harbor.

"Lady got a delicate disposition?" Oldie inquired solicitously.

"She possesses a certain sensibility," Doc said, with irony Ryan could make out distinctly even though he wasn't sure their guide did. "Which fits not altogether comfortably with the exigencies of our modern world."

Oldie shrugged. "She's probably not gonna find Nu-Tuga much to her taste, then."

"Punishment is harsh," Ryan rasped.

"Told you," Oldie said with a certain gloomy satisfaction. "Syndicate runs a tight ship, even if they don't tread the decks themselves much anymore. These poor folk broke the law. So they got their legs slashed and hung into the harbor to think things over."

"Legs slashed?" Krysty said. She wasn't a delicate flower, by any stretch. She was Deathlands born and bred, like Ryan himself, like everybody but Doc and the vigorously puking Mildred. It took a lot to shock her.

But this had done the trick.

"Doesn't that bring 'cudas and sharks?" she asked. The way her emerald-green eyes flashed the instant the words were out of her mouth showed she got it.

"Reckon that's the point," J.B. said. "Right?" He took off his glasses and began to polish the lenses with a stained handkerchief.

"Best keep your noses clean while visiting lovely Nueva Tortuga, folks," Oldie said. He continued to row.

"What manner of crimes," Doc asked, "would occasion such stern punishment?"

Oldie managed to shrug without missing a stroke. "Could be a lot of things. Theft. Vandalism. Cheating at cards. Welshing on a debt. Brawling."

J.B. frowned and fitted the glasses back on his nose. "Reckon those things're pretty much what pass for recreation among pirates," he said.

"There're limits, see," Oldie said.

"What are they, precisely, my good man?" Doc asked.

Oldie laughed. "You sure find out once you cross 'em," he said, nodding to the dangling, half-submerged bodies.

"So the one real rule is don't piss off the Syndicate," Ryan said. He grunted.

Krysty knelt on the sideboard next to Mildred. She helped the shorter woman turn back inboard and wiped her mouth with a rag.

"Are we sure we want to visit this place, Ryan?" she asked.

"We do got a habit of pissing off the powerful, Ryan," J.B. said.

"It's not like we're here on a pleasure cruise," Ryan said with a bit of a rasp. "We got to find passage back to the mainland. Or some kind of paying gig. Triple-fast. Otherwise we'll be boiling the shirts off our back to make soup of the sweat—if we could find a way to pay for fresh water, that is."

"Oh, there's work aplenty to be found in NuTuga," Oldie said, "if a body's got the stomach for it."

"We got the stomach for a lot," J.B. said. But he was frowning at the dangling bodies as he did it.

The body that had had the seagull pecking its eyes jerked. Ryan guessed something big had hit its legs underwater. He still couldn't tell if any kind of living muscular reaction contributed to the motion.

He didn't really want to know. He was a hard man, but he had limits, too.

"So the ville's actually run by pirates?" Mildred asked. Her skin was the color of the ash in Oldie's firepit. "They must be monsters."

"They turned into something worse," the old man said. "Government."

And he laughed and laughed.

Chapter Four

Oldie pulled the *Ernie H* up next to the end of an unoc-cupied wharf. "You folks make it ashore without I tie up?" he asked.

"Reckon so," Ryan said. "Why?"

J.B. went over the side to stand knee-deep in water on the slope of the busted-rock mole to help the others across.

"Don't wanna pay their fee. Not my kind of place, NuTuga. Not my kinda crowd."

"That speaks well for you," Mildred said.

"Don't they try to stick you, anyway?" Ryan asked. He was surprised that the Syndicate, as Oldie described it, would let loose of the smallest chance at income. It was standard operating procedure for barons every-where, whatever they called themselves.

Oldie laughed again. "The Monitors let me slide if I don't technically land. They're not too keen on splash-ing around in water where all the big fish and most of the little ones got a taste for human flesh."

J.B. was just handing Mildred across to the slanted rock face of the pier. He cocked an eyebrow.

"Get your fool ass out of the water, J.B.," Ryan said.

The armorer grinned, but he scampered up to the boardwalk with a vigorous splash just the same.

Ryan sat on the outboard gunwale to counterbalance the others as first Krysty, then Doc leaped to the rock. Contemptuously, Jak jumped into the water, then waded the couple of steps up out of the sea. At the last, he yelped and jumped clear.

"Something bumped leg!" he said, then glared as the others grinned at him.

Ryan tossed everybody's pack and weapons over to them. After Krysty fielded his own, he took the leap. He wasn't going to go wading with sharks and killer 'cuda.

"Word to the wise, Ryan," Oldie called after him.

Ryan looked down at the man where he sat in the prow with his oars cocked up in their locks.

"Mind your steps here, folks," the old man said. "Walk careful, especially around the Sea Wasps."

"I thought you said theirs was an egalitarian society," Doc said.

"Yeah. Whatever that is. The Syndicate is law." He chuckled. "Just remember that people are basically dogs. They always got them a pack order. The more folks talk about everybody being equal, the more some're more equal than others."

"Talk sense!" Jak grumbled.

J.B. clapped him on the shoulder—gingerly, to avoid the sharp bits.

"He is, son. He is. Someday you'll appreciate the fact. If you happen to live, that is."

Ryan nodded to Oldie, and the old man pushed off

with an oar. Ryan shouldered his pack and headed up the pier.

A party of men materialized at the inland end. There were six of them. Some were burly, some were wiry. All were hard. All were armed.

"Monitors?" J.B. asked as he swung along by Ryan's side.

"Reckon so," the one-eyed man replied.

The waiting six all had shaved heads and black T-shirts. Bloused over their boots, they wore baggy camo pants with many pockets and sundry patterns. Each had a hefty truncheon of polished black wood hanging from his belt. Counterbalancing the sticks were sawed-off scatterguns, either pump or double-barreled, with grips cut down to pistol size.

"Cute touch about these matching armbands," J.B. murmured from half a pace behind Ryan's left elbow.

Ryan knew Krysty was walking just behind his right elbow. He could smell the clean woman scent of her. She'd bathed in the sea off Oldie's little beach the previous night. Both before and after lovemaking with Ryan.

"How you mean?" Ryan asked, making no effort either to be heard by the waiting sec men, or not to be.

J.B. jutted his chin at a jackstaff mounted above a solid-looking blockhouse made of brown lava chunks that stood back across an esplanade from the waterfront. A flag swung in a rising but still sluggish breeze. Ryan could tell it had some kind of black figure on a white field. So did the armbands, he saw.

"Yeah," Mildred said from behind. "That's cute. Photonegative skull and crossbones."

Looking closer at the welcoming committee Ryan saw the armbands did indeed show a black skull over crossed bones.

"They look like event security at a rock show in the nineties," Mildred said cryptically, then snorted. The notion seemed to amuse her.

"Welcome to Nueva Tortuga," said the man in the middle. He stood a little ahead of his flankers. He was on the lean side, and an inch or so less than Ryan's own six foot two. His skin was tanned dark, although his coal-smudge eyebrows and black beard made his tan look paper-pale.

"NuTuga, as we call it," he went on. "We're Monitors. We keep the peace. That's all you need to know. Except you got to pay the entry fee."

"Entry fee?" Ryan said, halting about ten feet short of them.

The leader provided several options in trade goods, ammo, gold or local jack. Ryan felt his cheeks tighten and his skin prickle as though he'd caught a touch of sunburn.

"No exceptions," the squad leader said, pleasantly enough. "You don't pay, you don't stay."

"What," Mildred said truculently. "Or you'll hang us off one of those derricks?"

Ryan felt his jaw tighten. Mildred's predark outrage was building a healthy head of steam.

The leader only smiled wider. His teeth were white.

Both men and clothes were clean, an unusual touch even in a relatively well-off ville on the mainland. The leader's boots were cowboy pattern, obviously handmade of sharkskin. They may even have been built since skydark.

"Only if you make your way back here," he said, "after we take you out a mile or two and toss your asses over the rail."

Ryan looked back at his companions. He noted right off that Oldie was still hovering right off the end of the pier, keeping his skiff in place with light sculling of his oars. Even at this range the old sailor managed to catch Ryan's eye. He cocked his head in question.

Ryan raised a hand to the boatman and nodded just once. The white-bearded old man shrugged expressively. Your funeral, Ryan could all but hear him say. He began to row back out among the ships rocking gently at anchor.

"All right," Ryan said, emphasizing the words just enough to let his friends know his mind was made up. "We pay." He handed over the requisite number of rounds.

"Must hurt like a nuke when you light those puppies off," J.B. said conversationally.

"Not half as much as when you're on the other end," said the shortest member of the crew, an Asian whose flat, fringe-bearded chin sloped outward along with his neck, which in turn simply got wider and wider until it became shoulders. He had a surprisingly mild voice. Ryan reckoned the Syndicate's strongarms didn't need to bluster much.

"One more thing," the leader said, tucking the ammo away in a pouch at his web gear belt. "We need to peace-bond your weapons."

"Peace-bond?" Ryan asked.

"Yeah. We won't try taking them away from you, but we don't want you using them in our fair ville."

"What's the point of letting us keep them, then?" Mildred demanded.

"Would you rather we confiscate them? Look, it's for your protection. You shoot or cut somebody, that *will* get you hung in the harbor with a few cuts down your legs to rile up the fish."

"What if the other guy starts it?" J.B. asked.

The enforcers, not so subtly, had settled into braced positions, suggesting they were considering the chance the newcomers might try resisting. Ryan wanted to assure them that nothing could be further from their minds. But that wasn't the sort of thing it did much good to say, he'd found.

It wouldn't be true, of course. All of them, even the unusually squeamish Mildred and the spirit of mercy herself, Krysty, were imagining what it'd be like to shove those scatterguns up the Monitors' uptight asses to the breech-locks and light them off. He knew that. Just as he knew his friends also calculated that the odds weren't with them on that play.

"Just how do you mean 'peace-bond,' anyway?" Ryan asked.

"We wire the breeches open on your blasters," the

squad leader said. "Blades we wire in the sheath. You break the seal, you go in the harbor. That simple."

"Not like," Jak said.

"Me, neither," Ryan said. "But it doesn't look like we got much choice."

He unslung his Steyr Scout, dropped the magazine from the well, cranked back the bolt and handed the piece over. The leader passed it to the Asian guy, who dug out a spool of wire and a pair of clippers and got to work.

In short order, most of the squad was busy wiring the companion's weapons to spec. When each man finished a piece, he handed it back to the squad leader. The bearded man squeezed a dab of some shiny gold-colored sealant where the wire's ends were twisted together. It seemed to harden almost instantly.

"Where'd you get that stuff?" Mildred asked interestedly. "I'd think it'd be set solid after all these years."

The squad leader smiled and handed back her ZKR with the trigger wired in its guard. "That's for us to know," he said, "and you never to find out."

When the considerable task was done, the leader stepped back. "That does it for the weapons you got showing," he said. "Now, how about the holdouts?"

Krysty took a deep breath. Pulling her shoulders back, making her considerable breasts strain tighter against the front of the khaki man's shirt she wore, she put hands on her well-rounded hips and did a slow roll.

"Care to search me and find out, big boy?"

Ryan's eyebrows shot up. It was all he could do to

keep from asking her if she'd flat lost her mind right here. But he remained silent. He knew Krysty didn't do much without a reason. Usually a triple-good one.

The leader actually blanched behind his black beard and eyebrows and took a step back. "N-no," he said. "That won't be necessary."

Turning to his squad he snarled, "All right, you taints! If you think the Syndics're paying us to stand around with our thumbs up our asses, I want to be there when you explain it to them!"

They turned and stomped off along the esplanade that was paved in lightweight white tufa gravel that ran around the inside of the harbor. Ryan let out a long, long breath.

"Krysty, what the hell was that?" Mildred demanded.

"Dudes like that generally don't see any point to havin' power if they can't abuse it good and regular," J.B. said laconically.

Krysty smiled with an unusually mischievous edge. "Normally," she said. "But didn't their whole attitude tell you their bosses ride even tighter herd on them than barons usually do their sec men?"

Ryan grunted. "Makes sense, since you put it that way," he said, scratching the back of his neck. The volume of sweat running down from his shaggy, curly black hair was more than mere afternoon heat in the Carib could account for. "They don't want them pissing off the paying customers, after all. Especially when the customers might come back in force and shoot the shit of the ville."

Ryan took for granted the Syndicate had some kind of pretty stout defenses against that. Even if he hadn't seen signs of it yet. Obviously the pirates had a good thing here and knew it.

"Evidently the pirates' own code tends to bind their behavior in Nueva Tortuga," Doc said, clearly thinking along the same lines.

"And nothing makes sure they keep their minds right like, say, that pair of .50 calibers the Syndicate's got set up to cross fire the harbor entrance," J.B. said, finishing Ryan's thought.

"But how could you be so sure they wouldn't want to grab the merchandise, Krysty?" Mildred asked.

Ryan saw that she didn't understand, as was so often the case since she'd awakened from her centuries-long cold sleep into a world she neither could've nor would've ever imagined. And when Mildred found something she didn't understand, she gnawed on it like a dog with a bone.

"Discipline, Millie," J.B. said. "Syndicate wants to make sure their bullyboys don't take bribes. Of any kind."

"Thus it ever is with tyrants," Doc declared. "Corruption, in their eyes, consists in their not getting their share."

Ryan squinted at the sun, which was rolling toward the ragged-topped cone of Nevis Peak, which dominated the small island.

"Let's shake the dust off, people," he said. "Standing here jawing isn't filling our bellies or getting us any closer to anyplace we want to be."

"A man might mention that the heat of the subtropical day can develop a powerful thirst, as well," Doc said.

"Where do we go?" Mildred asked.

Doc laughed again. He flung out a long, skinny arm in the same direction the Monitor squad had gone. "Why, follow the sound of music and merriment, dear lady!" he declared. "Where those are, commerce is. Whether licit or otherwise."

From that way, indeed, floated the tinkle of a not particularly well-tuned piano, a bubble of conversation, a high-pitched and slightly mad-sounding laugh.

"Not that it makes much difference to us which," Mildred said glumly.

"As long as it pays," Ryan said, "makes me no difference at all."

Krysty frowned at him. "Ryan Cawdor, you know that isn't true!"

"Truer than not, Krysty," he growled. "Now come on. We're bleeding daylight, and I got a feeling the longer we stay on this rock, the unhealthier it gets."

Chapter Five

The Blowing Mermaid, the sign read. The crudely but colorfully painted image that accompanied the words made it clear the half fish, half voluptuous nude blonde woman in question was blowing bubbles or spouting breath like a sounding whale.

"Classy," Mildred said.

"Needs must when the devil drives," Doc murmured.

"That's *so* encouraging," she said.

"Anybody got any better ideas?" Ryan's tone suggested he was addressing the group as a whole. Mildred couldn't help noticing how his lone blue eye fixed on her for just a moment—and pierced like a blue laser.

"Thought not," he said with a shrug, and pushed inside.

The smell of spilled beer, sweat and ganja smoke hit Mildred in the face like a sandbag as she stepped up to the door. Inside was dark, hot and humid. The conversation was boisterous enough that it actually overwhelmed the out-of-tune piano in the corner.

A grimy, fly-specked skylight let in yellow sun. It was enough to see by once Mildred's retinas had adjusted from the seaside dazzle outside. There were about twenty patrons in the gaudy, enough to make it seem pretty well occupied without everybody banging elbows with their neighbors.

Mildred wondered how that worked out, especially when sailors—pirates, to boot—just in after days at sea got their first taste of whatever unimaginable rotgut the tall, corpse-faced bartender with the truly remarkable gray side-whiskers was doling out. Would fear of the Syndicate's justice—and its Monitors—be enough to make everybody behave?

Mildred continued to scan the gaudy as Ryan led them to a bar that was fronted in what looked like respectable-gauge metal plate, painted some kind of drab color she couldn't make out. It looked bulletproof to Mildred's eye, which hadn't exactly been uneducated before her long sleep and revival, since she'd been raised around firearms from girlhood on. For one reason or another it seemed the gaudy's proprietors weren't willing to trust their hides entirely to Syndicate civic discipline.

She realized that shouldn't surprise her, either. While being a pirate—or any kind of coldheart bandit—could be a rational life-path in the strange and horrible world in which she found herself, it still wasn't one that bespoke good choices. Or good impulse control. She suspected it wasn't all that uncommon for patrons to haul out iron and start blasting in haste—then repent at leisure, either under the clubs or shotgun blasts of the Monitors, or while hungry, nasty fish dined on their nether regions in the harbor.

The volume of conversation dropped inevitably, and its tempo slowed to a sort of reggae-bass bubble as the

clientele scoped the new arrivals. Even with an oldie in a
frock coat, a long-haired albino kid and a tall, strikingly
handsome chiller with an eye patch, they weren't even
the most disparate looking bunch in the place. The fact
one of them—Mildred herself—was black didn't even
register. It seldom did. The wave of mutations that had
followed in the wake of the war had produced whole
new sets of folk for the masses to be prejudiced against.

"What'll it be, gentlemen, ladies?" the bartender said.
He was a big man, taller even than Ryan and wider, especially but not limited to the belly encompassed by his
stained leather apron. "McDugus Fish, at your service."

"What do you have?" Ryan asked.

"Rum and beer," the bartender said. "Also jolt."

The floor was planks, although it was covered in sawdust. The dust was yellow and smelled fresh. It actually
overpowered the other smells. Mostly.

"Have you any tea, my good man?" Doc asked. Mildred narrowed her eyes at him. It seemed such an off-the-
wall request for a pirate den as to be almost foolhardy.
While it might mean that Doc had slipped his reality
moorings again and was drifting off into the ozone, as
he frequently did, he often showed a puckish sense of
humor. Sometimes not at the best moments.

To her astonishment the bartender never batted a
heavy-lidded gray eye. "What kind?" he asked. "Green?
Earl Grey? Oolong?"

Doc raised a bushy, snow-white brow. "Such a broad
assortment!"

The bartender shrugged. "We get a lotta different cargos traded through here," he said. "So name your drink and pay for your dose. No tabs, no credit."

"Naturally," J.B. said.

While the thought of tea almost made Mildred salivate, she didn't trust the water it was made with. Given the general standard of cleanliness the Syndicate forced on its ville, Mildred figured that indicated they'd take at least similar care with their water supply. But she hadn't survived Deathlands by taking things of that nature for granted. She ordered neat rum.

Ryan and J.B. ordered beer. Doc asked for Earl Grey tea; Krysty went for green tea. Jak ordered rum, as well.

"Any jobs you know about?" Ryan asked, taking a sip from the lumpy blue-glazed pottery mug.

"Say, this ain't half-bad!" J.B. exclaimed. "Better than half-good, mebbe."

Not visibly overwhelmed at the endorsement of his house brew, the barkeep intoned, "Got plenty scuts. No jobs I know about. Might sign on to a crew. Always ships coming in short-handed. Then again, there's usually no shortage of sailors between gigs, either."

His big oblong face rumpled as he studied them. "There's always slut work," he said. "Either of the women could do. Or the kid, or you. Of course you'd have to get inspected by the Syndicate, get licensed up all proper."

If the suggestion offended Ryan, he showed no sign.

"They *license* prostitution here in NuTuga?" Mildred couldn't restrain herself from asking.

McDugus Fish reared back, rolling his eyes like an

outraged horse. "Of course!" he said. "Every aspect of every trade is carefully regulated and licensed. We can't just let people do what they want. That'd be anarchy!"

"Huh" was the best Mildred could think to say.

Mildred accepted her handleless cup of rum. Turning away from the bar, she saw Doc and Jak staring bemusedly into a dark corner. She followed their gazes. Her eyes had adjusted to the shine from the skylight and the gleam of hurricane lanterns hung over the bar, so it took them a moment to reset themselves to the gloom of the far corner of the gaudy.

Her eyebrows shot up.

"Guess the sign's not false advertising," J.B. said.

Evidently it wasn't.

A woman sat there in a wheelchair. She was bare to the waist, and a blanket covered her lap. A fishlike tail stuck out from under the blanket, by the footrests of the ancient metal chair.

She was assiduously pleasuring a fat guy who had his grimy shirt pulled up and canvas trousers down around his knees.

Mildred's first reaction was to blurt, "That *can't* be real!"

"Well, the tail is fake," McDugus Fish admitted. "Just for show. But my daughter JaNene's a real good swimmer with fins on. She was born with her legs stuck together and can't walk too good, see."

"She's your daughter?" From Krysty's tone even she, Deathlands born and raised, found this whole thing a bit hard to take.

Fish scowled defensively. "She's not a mutie or anything," he said. "It's just a birth defect, same as the albino kid, here. The Syndicate healers assured us of that!"

So JaNene was a legit mermaid. Of sorts. Of course that didn't mean she was a *close* match for the voluptuous creature on the sign. The hair hanging down in front of her shoulders was indeterminate dirty-blond and matted like seaweed, the bare tits sagging over washboard ribs were half-empty skin bags, and her eyes and cheeks were sunk in the characteristic pits of the true jolt-walker.

"You let your daughter give blowjobs for money?" Krysty said. "In the open?"

"Hey!" the bartender said. "It's all perfectly aboveboard. She's licensed and inspected and everything. And seeing as she's in the gloom, there, she isn't a distraction."

Krysty seemed inclined to push the point. Ryan took her by the arm and gently but firmly turned her toward a vacant table in another corner of the bar.

"Not our house, Krysty," he said. "We'll just sit down and wait to see what develops."

WHAT DEVELOPED WASN'T MUCH. Not very fast anyway.

"No accounting for taste," J.B. said with a bob of his head toward the corner, where JaNene Fish and her fake fish tail were busy at work. He was nursing his third beer, a dark, bitter ale. Ryan actually found it pretty good.

One of the scuts McDugus Fish referred to had swept

sawdust over a spilled beer, then swept the mess up, dumped it in an old paint can and thrown fresh sawdust from a pail in its place. Evidently there was a mill somewhere on the island. And evidently either the Syndicate or the joint's owner—who Ryan guessed was from one of the Syndicate families—or Fish himself were serious about keeping the place shipshape.

"Here, now," he heard J.B. call. "You look like a man who could use a drink."

A man had slipped in through the door with the air of a man who knew, from experience or observation, that lingering in a doorway too long just made you a good target. He didn't look the coldheart part. He was middle height, with his chest kind of sunken over a significant paunch, dressed in a faded flowery shirt open over a grimy T-shirt, khaki shorts held up by a length of nylon line, and sandals cut from old tires. His hair hung like a curtain around the sides and back of a high domed head, with a few brown strands brushed across it. His face would've been homely even if it wasn't a mass of random lumps, almost as if he'd fallen foul of a whole hive of yellow jackets.

His eyes darted left and right before dead-centering on J.B. "You talkin' to me?" he asked.

"Sure, mister," J.B. said. "Come on over. We'll buy you whatever you're drinking."

The man ran a yellowish tongue over thin lips. "I—I ain't registered, you know what I'm sayin'? I'm, uh, *clean,* and all. But I better not—"

"You got us wrong," Ryan said. He had J.B. looking

for likely prospects to pump for information with minimum cost, particularly in terms of suspicions raised, which was something they could afford little of in a place like this. "We're new in the ville. We're just looking for the angles."

"Oh. Well. That's different."

He hooked a chair from a table nearby, where a pair of villainous-looking fat women with two good eyes and about five teeth between them sat murmuring sweet nothings to each other. They were so absorbed in gazing into each other's eyes they never looked around when the chair legs went scraping away across the sawdust-covered planks.

"I'm Lumpy," the man said, seating himself between Ryan and J.B. "From the lumps, you see? Just so you know, I ain't a mutie or anything. They're parasites."

And he grinned around at everyone with a mouthful of uneven teeth in varying shades of brown, as if announcing he'd just won the trophy for having the biggest dick in NuTuga.

"Not that there's anything wrong with being a mutie," he added hastily. He was looking at Jak, who scowled.

Ryan carefully didn't look at Krysty, who *was* a mutie.

"I mean, to some there is, to some there ain't," Lumpy said. "Syndics won't have any taints here in the 'Tuga, of course. The crews love to jolly 'em up too much, you know what I mean? Bad for order. But over to Monster Island, now, muties and norms live side by side like there wasn't a thing wrong with it."

"Monster Island?" Mildred asked. "Where's that?"

Lumpy frowned for a moment. He scratched idly at a particularly prominent lump on the right side of his jaw. It seemed to Ryan that something like a hair whipped back and forth from it before zipping back inside.

A trick of the light, he told himself. He hoped so.

"Why," the disfigured man said, brightening, "took me a moment. You folks really aren't from this part of the Carib, are you? Monster Island is Puerto Rico, is all."

"That's the only reason they call it that, my good man?" Doc asked. "From the admittedly rare case of normal humans and mutants living together in harmony?"

"Well, that," Lumpy said, transferring his dirty-nailed attentions to the back of his neck. "Plus the fact the island's teeming with man-eating monsters, of course."

Chapter Six

Mildred sat back in her chair. "Oh, great," she said.

Ryan ignored her. He wasn't any happier than she was about the news that the place where they might find an easy ride back to the mainland via a mat-trans was overrun with ravenous monsters. But fretting over the fact wouldn't make it any less of one.

"Say we wanted to get back to the mainland," he said when Lumpy had ordered a rum.

The server was a black-haired, green-eyed girl wearing a leather apron over a short skirt and carrying a tray. Lumpy, anyway, didn't neglect to eye her backside appreciatively as she walked back toward the bar.

"How'd we go about that?" Ryan finished.

Lumpy sat back in his chair. He looked half-spent just from watching the girl.

"Got the jack?" he asked, still looking at her when she stood giving the order to McDugus Fish. "You can do pretty near anything, if you got the jack."

Doc laughed in wry delight. "Isn't that not ever the way of the world?" he asked.

"Say we aren't exactly flush," J.B. said. "Could we work passage?"

"You done pirate work before?" Lumpy asked. "You

all look to know your way around them blades and blasters you're loaded down with. I mean, not to pry or nothin'."

"We were hoping for more peaceful employment," Krysty said.

"Don't traders work the port?" Mildred asked. "I mean, the, uh, Mermaid even sells fresh fruit. The island doesn't look big enough to grow it all here. Unless it's all brought in as pirate swag?"

He laughed. "Oh, nuke me, no. There's traders ply here, right enough. Once they buy their export licenses off the Syndicate, they're as safe on the open sea as you and me, sittin' right here. Only they don't much like to take on crew here, if you catch my drift. Not everybody's reliable."

"Imagine that," Mildred said.

"What about other paying gigs?" Ryan asked. "Local work."

The girl brought Lumpy's rum. He grinned at her when she set it down. She ignored him as if he were an insect. She took the .22 round Ryan handed her and walked away without a word.

"Whoo," Lumpy said, "that is purely fine. Where was I? Oh. Jobs. Well, the crews bring in plenty slaves. You could sign on for Monitors, but I reckon you'd have the same objections to that you have to signing on for pirates."

He shook his head. "Can't think of much. I do some odd jobs now and then since I lost my nerve, fish some. I can fix a few things, and that's not always something you want slaves doing, know what I mean. But that's just me, and I barely scrape by. There's five of you."

"Six, actually," Mildred said. "But who's counting?"

Lumpy shot back his rum and shook all over like a wet dog. He set his empty on the table upside down with a clack. It seemed to Ryan the single shot had hit him pretty hard. Of course, he didn't know whether it was his first of the day.

"Spring for another?" Lumpy asked, looking around with eyes even less clear than they had been when he sat down.

J.B. signaled the server for another, then he leaned his leather-clad elbows on the table.

"So how about this Monster Island," he said. "How about getting passage there?"

Lumpy shrugged. "Same story as the mainland. Go for a pirate, or pay your way. Gas, brass or ass—nobody rides for free."

"So what do you think, Ryan?" J.B. asked.

"I'm thinking," he admitted.

"You considering turning pirate, Ryan?" Mildred asked.

"Would you like signing up as Monitors better?" J.B. asked.

She scowled.

"Everything lives off other things," Jak said. "Want eat, gotta kill."

"Unusual loquacity, Jak," Doc said. "And unusual eloquence. Albeit in the service of a doctrine of moral expediency."

Jak scowled furiously.

"Don't worry," J.B. told him. "I didn't get it, either."

"I did," Ryan said. "Haven't we done plenty of things to stay alive we weren't thrilled about?"

"Ah, yes," Doc said. "Steeping in shame to stay alive. I remember…the sows…."

"Stay with us, Doc," J.B. said. "The sows're long since gone for bacon."

For a moment Doc gazed around, wild-eyed, as if seeing hell-knew-what bizarre landscape peopled with alien monstrosities, instead of a surprisingly clean but still seedy gaudy house and the faces of his friends. Then the mad light left his eyes. He seemed to deflate.

"Ah, yes," he said again, with a sad smile. "Long gone."

"Should we be discussing stuff like this…you know?" Mildred asked, waggling her eyebrows ridiculously and looking sidelong at their guest.

"Don't mind him, Millie," J.B. said. "He's too sunk in rum to know what we're talking about. Or care."

Lumpy had, indeed, tossed off his second shot like water and now slumped in his chair like a half-empty sack of oatmeal. His own eyes stared without focus at the tabletop. He drooled over a hanging lower lip.

The doors burst open and four Monitors swaggered in. They were dressed and armed like the crew that had braced Ryan and his friends on the docks, and their heads were likewise shaved. Which was a little more curious this time out, since one of them was a woman, who wasn't unattractive in a blade-faced kind of way.

She seemed to glare around a lot more truculently than her three companions, as if suspecting she had more to prove than they did.

Heads didn't turn when the Syndicate sec team blew in. Conversation didn't falter, but it dropped an octave. And heads huddled down a little closer in collars, where applicable, or chins closer to collarbones where not. Ryan realized he wasn't the only man in the gaudy who was suddenly keenly aware the four were the only ones in the house with easily accessible weapons.

He smiled, ever so slightly. Not that a measly twist of wire with a dab of goo sealing it would stop him doing the necessary thing.

But then, he wasn't in any rush to throw his life away, either. He looked away from the four as they ceremoniously paid for their drinks at the bar, and back to his comrades.

"We all know finding an easy living isn't easy," he said. "Finding a hard one isn't always easy, either. We'll do what we need to to survive, bottom line."

"We always do, Ryan," J.B. said.

"We don't have to make a decision tonight," Ryan said. "But in the morning, we've got to move. So we need to know by then which way we're moving."

Krysty patted his hand. "Something'll come up, lover," she said. "It always does. One way or another."

"Krysty's right, as usual," Mildred said. "But it's the 'or other' part that worries me."

J.B. grinned at her. "What, Millie? You looking to live forever?"

"Made a good start on it already, John," she said. "Even if not quite on a par with Doc."

Without waiting for permission, Lumpy waved at the good-looking server for yet another rum. Ryan took it in; his one eye seldom missed much. He didn't object. He might have more questions to ask before they were done with Lumpy.

If the stupe doesn't drink himself under before I think of them, he thought.

Lumpy glared at the Monitors. "Bastards," he muttered. "All they do is keep a man down."

The Monitors drank, neither lingering nor rushing, then they sauntered out of the gaudy without a word to anyone. As soon as the door slammed shut, the conversation picked up. The piano player, who'd been engaged in low tinkling, struck up a brisk tune.

"Fuckin' Monitors!" Lumpy exclaimed. "Drink! Sweetcheeks, get them sweet cheeks over here! I need a drink."

Behind the bar, McDugus Fish's lugubrious face fisted in annoyance. In the corner Ryan saw a gleam of eyeball as his daughter looked to see what the fuss was. She never missed a stroke, though. A real trouper, that girl; Ryan had to give her that.

The expression on her face like a rain squall on the ocean, the black-haired, jade-eyed server approached. "I need another rum," Lumpy declared, as if suspecting she was keeping one from him.

She nodded and turned away. "And I need some of *that,* too," he said, and grabbed her left ass cheek.

She froze. All the color drained out of her face. She seemed unsure what was actually happening.

The bar went dead still. The piano player turned into a statue with her hands hovering over the keys. McDugus Fish's face went red, then white.

The door opened. The belligerent female Monitor strode back inside, followed closely by a heavily muscled black Monitor an inch or so shorter than she was. She stopped dead. A smile winched its way across her sharp features.

"So," she said, not loudly, but the gaudy had gone so still she might as well have shouted. "What do we got here?"

"Oh, shit!" Lumpy gulped. His face went puce. He let go the server's rump and tried to jump to his feet, but booze had addled his coordination as much as his sense. His legs tangled with those of the chair and they both went down in a clatter and a tangle.

He disengaged and jumped quickly. Moving like a striking mongoose, the female Monitor flowed across the floor. She was right on top of him when he reared upright.

Lumpy faced the back door, which led to the latrines out back. That meant his back was to her—and the truncheon that slammed into his skull.

Ryan heard a moist, muffled crunch. Where Lumpy had looked like a half-filled burlap sack sitting in his alcoholic torpor a few moments before, now he hit the floor like an empty sack dropped from the ceiling. He lay on his face gurgling and making vague swimming motions in the sawdust with his arms and hands.

Ryan realized that he and his companions were the only ones staring at Lumpy, or what remained of him. The rest of the patrons and McDugus Fish were all looking studiously someplace else. Except for the server, who stood looking at the twitching Lumpy with vindictive glee.

The black male Monitor enthusiastically put the boot in. Mildred winced as ribs cracked audibly.

The fallen man didn't react to repeated kicks, or a couple of experimental whacks cross the shoulders with the woman's stick. The female Monitor straightened.

"Get this trash hauled out to the curb pronto, Fish," she snapped at the barkeep. "We got strict regulations in this town."

McDugus Fish turned and bawled something at the open door behind the bar. A couple of men in aprons and, to Ryan's surprise, hairnets bustled out. They were both short and dark, one stocky, one wiry.

"They *do* have strict health regs in this ville," Mildred said, sounding bemused.

"It's like why a dog licks himself," J.B. explained. "Because they can."

She glared at him a moment, then wordlessly shook her head.

The two helpers from the back—cooks, Ryan thought—hurried up, grabbed Lumpy by the shoulders and dragged him out the door. His head hung limp, drawing a furrow in the sawdust along with his feet and hanging arms. He didn't seem to be moving or making noises any longer. Ryan wouldn't be surprised if the poor bastard had taken the last train west.

"How can we just sit here and watch?" Mildred hissed, as the Monitors walked to an unoccupied table on the far wall.

Ryan looked at her. It took him a moment to catch her drift.

"Nor our deal," he reminded her. "And I reckon we got everything that poor simp had to give."

The door opened, and two more Monitors, both males, swung in. They located their comrades, then moved purposefully to their table. They perched on the edges of their chairs, leaning forward to talk earnestly. The other two nodded.

Once again the door swung open. A fresh wave of ganja smoke rolled in on the humid gust from outdoors, and with it the noise of a half-dozen outlandishly dressed and dreadlocked roisterers.

A short, bearded black guy with dreads stuffed into a pillow-sized knit cap of red, gold, black and green stepped to one side and puffed out his banty-rooster chest.

"We be the Sea Wasp Posse," he declared. "Silver-Eye Chris be our big man. We can outdrink, outfight, and outfuck any motherfucker in NuTuga. Fear us well enough, mebbe nobody gets hurt."

If the other patrons had carefully ignored the fate of Lumpy, their gazes positively bounced off the six men who had come in. The Sea Wasps wore extravagantly flounced blouses and trousers, vests blazing with bright patches and ribbons, and weapons. Lots and lots of weapons.

Even JaNene's latest customer pulled out. He stepped away from the phony mermaid, stuffing his rapidly shrinking pecker back inside his blue denim trousers and yanking them back up by the drawstrings. The blonde turned a blank expression toward the newcomers. She rubbed her mouth absently with the back of one hand, then hanging her head, she began to cry soundlessly.

"So this is the top dog pack," J.B. said. Like the others, he didn't look directly at the garish newcomers. It wasn't fear. It was plain practicality. They were outnumbered here.

The Sea Wasps sauntered up to the bar as if they were the owners come to see how McDugus Fish was keeping the place up. For all Ryan knew, they *were*. They obviously had a hefty reputation hereabouts.

Krysty rose. Ryan looked at her. She nodded at the door to the back: call of nature. Realizing the same thing, Mildred stood to join her. Strength in numbers.

The two vanished toward the back. Krysty seemed completely at ease, but her flame-colored hair had tightened into a short, tight cap. Ryan hoped nobody would notice that her hair could and did move by itself. That would mark her as a mutie, and with this bunch, who knew what the consequences would be.

The Sea Wasps had their drinks and were leaning back against the bar insolently eyeing their fellow pirates as if deciding which one they planned to kill first. One man stood out in particular. He wasn't the tallest, although he stood about an inch or two higher than Ryan. He wasn't the burliest; that was a pale-skinned man-mountain with a beard hanging over his wide chest and kettle belly. Despite his size, he projected a big cat's readiness to spring into lethal, lightning-fast action. He had golden dreads and lightly tanned clean-shaven features that might've been handsome on somebody else. His eyes were silver, like old-time coins with all the tarnish polished off.

That silver gaze swept the crowd insolently. It passed over Ryan's table without pausing. Clearly he sized up the travelers as the lowest-threat bunch in the room.

Momentarily. Then his eyes snapped back. Two silver eyes locked up briefly with Ryan's blue one.

Unlike everyone else in the room, Ryan wasn't looking away from the Sea Wasp Posse.

The golden-dreaded man's smile widened about a half inch. He nodded just a little more. Ryan returned the gesture.

Smart enough to be dangerous, Ryan thought, availing himself of the chance to take a sip of his now-flat beer without appearing to submit. That was another reality of the world: authentic hardcases knew how to spot each other on first glance. And generally they steered well clear, unless circumstances required them to tussle. You didn't live to get case-hardened that way, as opposed to just rabid-weasel vicious, without having a well-developed sense of survival.

He allowed himself to relax fractionally. The Sea

Wasps' leader was willing to look for easier prey, if looking for prey was on his mind. The only question was how quick his pack would get the message.

They had obviously been into the weed, which Ryan knew sometimes took the edge off. But these guys *lived* edgy, and from their manner they'd been hitting the booze pretty hard, and maybe even jolt. Betting on their being made mellow by their smokes was another quick road to a shallow hole in the beach. Or just the harbor, without the necessity of being hung up, which Ryan was fairly sure was where Lumpy was destined, if he wasn't bobbing facedown already with the 'cuda nuzzling his exposed face and fingers.

The back door opened. Krysty and Mildred came in. They made for their companions' table without glancing at the Sea Wasps, who were smoking vast cone-shaped spliffs and joking among themselves. Also without obviously steering clear of them, except to Ryan's keen blue eye.

Even so, one of the Sea Wasps suddenly blocked their path. He was a wiry mocha-skinned dude, with a single-braided black goatee and tattoos of women with big bare boobs and snake bodies twining up bare, muscle-cabled arms. He had two machetes slung crosswise over his back with the hilts sticking up over his shoulders, and two Smith & Wesson autoblasters in hip holsters decorated with bright beadwork. The weapons Ryan could see were peace-bonded, which didn't much comfort him.

"So what have we got here?" the pirate asked. He had a Spanish accent. "You getting a higher-quality slut in this gaudy of yours, now, than that taint cocksucker daughter of yours, Fish-face?"

"She's not a taint," McDugus Fish said stubbornly. "It's a birth defect."

"You got smarter," the pirate said. "Figured out I got a soft spot for the redheads, huh?"

And he reached out and grabbed Krysty's left breast.

Chapter Seven

Time seemed to slow. Ryan shifted his left hand inside his long coat.

Calmly yet decisively Krysty reached up and removed the hand from her breast.

"What do you think you're doing?" she demanded, strong but not shrill.

Her eyes turned like emerald lasers to the table of Monitors sitting across the room. They were all watching.

"I thought the Syndicate had laws against assault," she said clearly.

As one, the four sec goons turned their heads away.

"Well," J.B. murmured, "remember what Oldie said about some dogs being more equal than others? Reckon this gang's the most equal of all."

"Right," Ryan said, rising from his chair. He didn't hurry as he walked toward the tableau a few paces away.

The pirate saw him coming and showed him a gap-toothed grin. "What you want here, Patch? You triple-stupe? You think you can fuck with the Sea Wasps? You think wrong, man."

And he grabbed Krysty's breast again.

"If you don't remove your hand," Ryan said, "I'll remove it for you."

The guy just grinned wider. His hand squeezed the full breast again quickly, then began to move down toward the flat plane of her stomach.

Rattlesnake-fast, Ryan's left hand whipped to the sheath on his hip, freeing eighteen inches of steel blade. Before the pirate could so much as blink it rose and slashed down.

The panga's razor-honed edge chopped the Sea Wasp's hand off just above the wrist. The hand seemed to pulse on Krysty's breast one more time and then it fell to the floor. It lay on its back in the sawdust like an overturned beetle, fingers twitching like bug legs.

The pirate stared down at the blood jetting from his stump in slack-jawed amazement. Krysty sidestepped quickly out of the way of the pulsing blood, then she and Mildred grabbed their own weapons. As Ryan had quickly and covertly undone the peace-bonding on his weapons when the Wasps came in, they were obviously undoing theirs now.

But not all of the party's armaments had been sealed in sheath or holster, of course.

The wounded man began to shriek like a horse in a burning barn. Grabbing his stump with his remaining hand, he danced in a circle, painting the patrons, the tables, the chairs, the walls, even the ceiling with arterial spray that gleamed dark in the fish-oil light.

With startling power, Doc kicked the table. It flew across the room into the faces of the other Sea Wasps.

They were too startled by this completely unexpected turn of events to react with what would surely be their normal rapid savagery.

The Monitors, a beat slower, jumped to their feet, unlimbering their scatterguns.

A dully glittering disk spun across the room. The black Monitor who'd come back from the first party grunted audibly as one of Jak's concealed throwing knives buried itself in his bare, muscle-ribbed gut. It was probably only a flesh wound. As strong as he was, Jak couldn't throw one of his relatively light holdout knives hard enough to punch through the tough abdominal wall at that range. But the man stared down at himself and shrieked in terrified surprise as if it had gutted him like a fish.

His female companion was faster and firmer. She had a sawed-off pump shotgun with a pistol grip on its shortened forearm as well as in the back. She brought the stubby weapon rapidly online, ready to spray Ryan and friends with lethal buckshot.

Instead, a loud bang went off in Ryan's right ear and a red dot appeared right above the woman's collarbone, above the neckline of her black T-shirt. More shots blasted in quick succession, forcing Ryan to squint as side-blasts from a short barrel stung his cheek.

J.B. was half standing from his chair, his right arm locked out. His right fist clenched a little black Kel-Tec P-32 blaster. It was his latest pet holdout pistol, though it didn't have much punch, being only a .32 ACP.

Which was why J.B. kept shooting, walking shots

up the Monitor's chin and cheek and putting a last one through the right side of her forehead. At twenty feet, J.B. was shooting near the absolute accuracy the tiny handblaster was capable of. But with a blaster in his hands, any blaster, J. B. Dix was both lucky *and* good.

Ryan stood, bloody panga in hand, while the Sea Wasp whose hand he'd amputated had gotten hold of himself. He tugged furiously at one of his machete hilts with his remaining hand, even though he was bleeding out fast enough through his stump that he'd go down inside another minute, unconscious or dead.

Until then, he was a threat. Krysty booted him in the balls, the impact lifting his soles a good five inches off the sawdust.

When he landed again he doubled over in agony that overrode even the pain from his arm, which shock was likely dulling already, anyway. Krysty held the short muzzle of her Smith & Wesson 640 revolver almost to the back of his head and blew what brains he had onto the sawdust in front of his boots.

At last Ryan got his SIG-Sauer out and started blasting toward the Sea Wasps as they sorted themselves out from under the table Doc had kicked into them. He didn't think he hit any of them. The bar was suddenly full of patrons who decided all at once that getting out of the Blowing Mermaid was the best survival strategy, even if it meant racing through a horizontal hail of bullets and buck. He did see Silver-Eye Chris vanish over the bar with startling alacrity.

One of the other Monitors lit off both barrels of his

sawed-off. The big pirate who'd been enjoying JaNene's ministrations was just darting past him to the door and took both charges full in his hanging gut. Screaming shrilly he went down, trying to stuff purple-pink coils of intestine back into his ruptured belly.

J.B. fired again, but Ryan wasn't sure at what. They'd stepped away from each other.

Doc streaked past, his coattails flapping like stork wings. In a flash, Ryan saw he had his sword in one hand and the ebony sheath in the other. The Monitor with Jak's throwing knife stuck in his belly had apparently realized the thing hadn't punctured anything vital. Ignoring it, he swung his own pump gun to bear.

With a fine fencing lunge, Doc ran him through the right shoulder. He cried out again, dropping the scattergun.

The blaster was slung around his neck on a waist sling. Rather than falling free, it dangled. Even though neither wound seemed fatal, the Monitor decided two new holes in his hide was enough for one day's work. Letting the blaster hang, he turned and joined the crush of customers trying to fight their way through the open door.

Shouts from outside suggested others were trying to fight their way *in*. Ryan dashed toward an overturned table and took cover behind it, to see J.B. grinning at him from behind another.

Shots were coming from behind the bar. Ryan risked a look out to see a couple of heads seeming to stand like apples on the upper surface, with handblasters stuck out in front of them. As he looked a head jerked. A whole divot of long black dreads was knocked off the back.

The head vanished. The hand and the silver Beretta handblaster it held slithered back out of sight. Ryan glanced over to see Mildred, crouched behind a jumble of chairs and a table, bringing her .38 Czech target revolver back online.

Then he saw two forms struggling off to the side. Krysty was still in the open. The biggest of the Sea Wasps was grappling with her. He was a great black bear of a man with a grimace full of gold teeth, a black beard and a vast mass of dreadlocks swinging from his cannonball head. He held a big butcher knife point-downward in a ham-sized fist. Krysty held the knife off with one hand while the other held his hand away from her throat.

"Krysty, get down!" Mildred shouted. Ryan raised his SIG, looking for a clear shot, but the pair was battling too wildly for him to risk it.

Of course, it wouldn't normally be possible for a woman to resist a near giant like that, hand to hand. Even a woman as tall and well muscled as Krysty.

As Ryan watched over the three-dot sights of his handblaster, a change seemed to come over her. He couldn't have put his finger on what it was, exactly. She seemed larger, somehow. He knew then that she had called on the power of the Earth Mother, Gaia.

Krysty picked up the big bearded man and threw him across the bar. Bottles with faded labels shattered.

He disappeared in a cascade of glass shards, brown liquid and the broken halves of the heavy hardwood shelf.

Usually Krysty had a bit more staying power, but she collapsed onto the floor. This time, channeling the power of Gaia drained her like a cut artery.

By reflex Ryan started up to help the woman. Then it hit him: if she's down, she's out of the line of fire.

Not safe. Nobody was safe in a blasterfight, especially at such close quarters. But no enemy was likely to waste a shot on her while her friends were still shooting. And while one or two of the Sea Wasps behind the bar had gone down with the huge man, at least three were still popping up to loose a round or two before ducking back behind the armor-plated bar. Including their unmistakable silver-eyed leader.

Taking quick aim, Ryan popped the two lanterns hung behind either end of the bar. One promptly went out. The other stayed lit long enough to ignite the gush of fish oil from the punctured metal reservoir.

Blue flames whoomped into life behind the length of the bar. The alk in the bottles the big man had broken was potent. To add fuel, literally, to the flames Ryan shot fast holes in the two lanterns suspended directly above the bar. They produced rains of fire as their spilling fuel took light.

Screams pealed from behind the bar. The giant rose howling. Flames from his burning dreads haloed his agony-racked face as he beat at his blazing back with blistering hands.

Two shots cracked from behind the bar. The big man

quit screaming. He sagged back against the wall, then slid slowly out of sight, leaving a smear of flaming alcohol.

Somebody—Silver-Eye Chris, Ryan had little doubt—had chilled him, not to put him out of his misery, but because he was endangering his comrades with his flailing and flaming.

The Sea Wasp leader darted out from behind the bar. Twin semiauto handblasters blazed from his fists as he hunched over and ran to the exit that led to the outhouse. Three more of his posse followed in quick succession, one smoking and one trailing flames from his military-style jacket's back and left sleeve.

The gaudy reeked of spilled alcohol, fish, voided bowels, the eye-watering smoke of burning hair and the stench of burning flesh. Cautiously Ryan started to rise from the dubious shelter of his table to go to Krysty's aid.

Two things happened. The logjam of patrons fleeing out the front door cleared, admitting a rush of Monitors and dreadlocked pirates he guessed were Sea Wasps waving blasters and blades, with not a "peace-bond" in sight. Ryan turned, snarling, bringing the SIG to bear on the new threat.

And up from behind the bar, roaring and silhouetted in flames, rose McDugus Fish. He had a short-barreled machine pistol clutched in beefy fists, and he sprayed the wrecked room with 9 mm messengers of death.

Jak's Python bellowed, its flash huge and report ear-shattering in the close space. A black Sea Wasp with a bundle of orange dreads went down in the front entrance, blood spraying from his thigh.

From the corner of his eye, Ryan caught sight of Doc. Sword in one hand and the dead Monitor woman's pump shotgun in the other, he vaulted an overturned chair with his long coat billowing behind him like a cape. He raced straight at the bar, where McDugus Fish had just slapped a fresh magazine into his stubby autoblaster.

The huge barkeep tried to bring the blaster to bear on Doc. With a mighty leap the old man sprang to the bar top and kicked McDugus Fish in the face. The bartender fell back out of sight, triggering a burst that brought a cascade of dust and wood splinters falling from the ceiling. His head cracked one of the stout plank shelves in two, then he slumped out of sight.

Doc turned and loosed his own brain-imploding blast into the ceiling from the scattergun.

"All right, you scurvy devils," Doc shouted. "Who wants to order a last hot meal of *lead?*"

At the storm of gunfire, the inrushing crowd stopped dead, then flowed right back out.

Ryan, Jak and J.B. were instantly in motion, hurling tables and chairs into the doorway in a makeshift barrier. Mildred fired shots through the windows to discourage people from poking their faces in.

In the corner, abandoned by her customers, JaNene Fish sat with palms pressed to gaunt cheeks, screaming.

Smoke filled the doomed gaudy to the rafters. His eye stinging, Ryan moved quickly to Krysty's side. Her limbs moved feebly, without apparent purpose. But at his touch she sat up quickly and smiled at him. "I'm all right, lover," she said, getting to her feet.

She wobbled, giving her words the lie. He caught her arm.

"We got to go, people!" Ryan shouted. "Out the back. Jak, clear the way."

"Okay!" Jak exclaimed. His pack already shouldered, he ran to the back door. He pushed it open a hair, took a three-second look then slipped out.

Ryan grimaced as he heard shots, including the glass-edged boom of Jak's Python. Somebody screamed. It wasn't Jak.

The one-eyed man hurriedly helped J.B. and Mildred on with their packs.

As the companions headed toward the back, blasters flashed at the front door, the bullets cracking past Ryan's ears.

Once through the back door, he quickly sidestepped to avoid silhouetting himself against the increasingly bright flame light. They were in an alley between neat, small buildings, built of planks painted white.

The alley didn't even smell that bad, considering the purpose the gaudy customers used it for. The outhouse pit was well limed.

Blasters flamed across the street to Ryan's left. Holstering his handblaster, he unslung the Steyr Scout long-blaster he had hastily slung beside his backpack. Without bothering to loop his left arm in the shooting sling, he threw the weapon to his shoulder. Through the sight he got a quick view of unmistakable dreads behind some kind of out-thrust handblaster.

He fired. A dark cloud puffed like smoke behind the target's head and the shooter went down. Ryan saw other dark figures fleeing, apparently discouraged by their friend's fate as well as the longblaster's boom and flash.

Lowering the Scout, Ryan looked around. Alarm spiked through him. "Where's Krysty?" he demanded.

"Went back in," Mildred said, holding her wheel-gun out one-handed, looking for targets. For the moment none showed themselves, although Ryan could hear shouts from around the front of the building.

Biting down an impulse to ask Mildred why she hadn't stopped her, Ryan turned to head inside, himself, despite the gray smoke that rolled out the top of the door frame.

A hand clamped his arm hard. He turned, snarling. J.B. had him by the biceps. The armorer was one of mebbe two people alive who'd dare get in the way of the one-eyed man.

"Wait," J.B. said calmly. "She knows what she's doing. Always does."

And then Krysty boiled out in a cloud of smoke, shoving JaNene Fish's wheelchair in front of her.

She pushed the screaming girl well clear of her father's burning gaudy, then turned to face Ryan.

"I couldn't leave her to burn," she said defiantly.

Sure you could, he thought.

"She never did us harm," he acknowledged.

"What about her dad?" Mildred asked.

Krysty shrugged. "Reckon he can see to himself," she said.

Mildred's dark face paled. She started to push inside. Ryan remembered her own father had been burned to death by coldheart crazies called the Ku Klux Klan when she was little. She had a thing about that.

Krysty put herself in the other woman's way. "He was crawling over a bunch of furniture out the front door when I hauled the girl out," she said.

Mildred nodded. "Wonder where Silver-Eye went."

"Somewhere else, in a triple-hurry, after Jak put a big old hole through the dude standing next to him," J.B. said. He nodded at a pair of boots jutting into the alley from behind an outbuilding a few yards away.

A dark figure whipped around the near corner of the gaudy. Heavy braids flew wildly as he turned to attack.

The flash from a stub shotgun barrel underlit a startled expression on the wide dark face as Doc, standing with his back to the wall, pushed the weapon almost into the Sea Wasp's lean belly before firing.

The man doubled over as the charge of buck punched his entrails to jelly, then fell mewling and clutching himself in agony.

"Avast, ye varlets!" Doc shouted, brandishing his sword in his left hand. He had the sheath thrust through his belt. "Come and take your medicine!"

"Come on, Doc," Ryan called. "Time to power out of here."

"Where to, lover?" Krysty asked.

"Docks," Ryan said. "We need a ride off the island. In kind of a hurry."

"Don't reckon anybody'll be eager to give us one, Ryan," said J.B., pointing his shotgun cautiously in the direction from which the gut-shot pirate had come.

"I didn't plan on asking," Ryan said, feeling a grin peel back his lips.

They turned to go the other way.

"Thank you," the phony mermaid called feebly from her chair across the alley.

"No problem," J.B. replied.

"If you want, you know, a freebie—"

A pair of pirates bounded around the corner. Quicker on the uptake than their moaning buddy, they both dodged back a half second before a blast from J.B.'s M-4000 shotgun blew a shark bite out of the corner of the gaudy in a shower of big wood splinters.

"Thanks for the offer," J.B. said with a courteous tip of his hat, "but we're going to have to pass."

Ryan and J.B. turned and ran to catch up with their companions.

Chapter Eight

"By the three Kennedys!" Doc exclaimed. "Stymied! So near and yet so far."

Krysty sighed. Even she, with her Deathlands-honed endurance, felt winded after their race through the darkened streets. They hid in a narrow alley between waterfront warehouses, examining the Sea Wasp Posse's flagship, the *Wailer*. The clean-lined, gleaming-white ninety-footer was tied up to a stone jetty. A wooden gangplank fixed to the rail bobbed gently on the harbor swell.

It also had a crew fully alerted by the ruckus in the ville. As evidenced not just by the angry-seeming sweep of its searchlight, but by the pair of alert-looking pirates who stood at the head of the gangplank, one armed with a remade AK, one with an MP-5. A bearded man with wildly bushy dreads crouched behind the welded splinter plate of a battered Browning .30-caliber machine gun, sweeping its perforated barrel back and forth restlessly like an insect's antennae.

Only a skeleton watch had been left aboard the motor yacht while the captain and crew enjoyed shore leave. But it was more than enough to cut the fugitives to bloody shreds if they tried to force their way aboard.

And they were definitely being hunted. Krysty could hear shouts and curses a few blocks away. The pursuers had lost their trail. Furious pirates and sec men combed the ville street by street.

"Here's the plan…." Ryan said.

JAK SWAM THROUGH SHADOWED water with strong, inaudible strokes, keeping his arms and legs fully beneath the rocking surface. The vibration of the big yacht's diesel engine stirred his guts.

The Gulf Coast bayous where Jak had grown up hadn't invited swimmers. They were full of aggressive gators with a marked appetite for human flesh, not to mention monsters even more scary and less natural.

But Jak had grown up not just a hunter but a bandit, fighting against cruel barons. He had earned the name White Wolf for both his appearance and his savage cunning.

Jak didn't know if people swam in NuTuga harbor, but by the smell he doubted it. The Syndics could write all the laws they wanted; a harbor just naturally attracted junk and spilled fuel and all kinds of nastiness. Not that Jak cared. It wasn't as if the bayous smelled like hyacinth blossoms, either.

The key thing was that the jacked-up rump crew on board the *Wailer* was focused entirely on repelling boarders coming at them from shore. It seemed triple-stupe to him. But he wasn't one to question an advantage.

He had slipped into the water quickly and without a

splash in the shadow of a stone jetty forty yards behind the yacht's stern. First, he swam straight out and found the nylon aft anchor cable. It was slippery, slimed with algae. Even he could tell Silver-Eyed Chris was as finicky about his ships as the Syndic families were about their pirate haven. But, as with the harbor itself, it was extremely difficult to keep the sea's vigorous nature from asserting itself.

As slick as it was, the thick rope gave him hand- and footholds. He broke water without so much as a whisper of sound and slithered straight up.

He was barefoot, dressed only in sodden jeans and a vest that held his throwing knives. His current favorite blade, a Cold Steel Natchez Bowie with an almost-foot-long blade, was clamped in his teeth.

Along with his boots, he'd also skinned off the loose T-shirt he wore beneath the vest. When the Monitors had searched him for weapons, he'd simply swept the vest halves back, along with the jacket, while they peace-bonded his Python and the bowie in their counter-balancing holsters on his hips. They'd never seen the leaf-bladed throwers.

Peace-bonding. What a triple-stupe idea. He had naturally busted the sealant caps and untwisted the wires the instant they were out of the Monitor patrol's sight and none of his companions was looking. Ryan would've gotten hot beyond nuke-red, of course. But Jak reckoned it was easier to get forgiveness than permission.

Cautiously, Jak lifted his dripping head to peek at the afterdeck. A lone sentry stood fixated on events ashore, either on the billows of yellow-lit smoke from the random blazes Jak had helped set in trash bins or storage shacks, or keeping watch for intruders rash enough to approach the yacht despite the spotlight's actinic sweep and the powerful machine gun mounted in the bow. He was skinny even by Jak's standards, emaciated almost, with a huge mass of dreads stuffed into a knit cap. He carried a hunting-style bolt-action longblaster slung butt-down, as if he didn't plan on shooting it in a hurry.

He was also remarkably tall, at least six and a half feet. It made no difference to Jak. He slithered over the rail, making no more noise than the sentry's shadow falling on the smooth-stoned deck planks. He took the big knife from his teeth, then gathering himself, he sprang.

Jak slammed against the man's back, the protruding shoulder blades gouging him in the chest, the rifle butt of the longblaster cracking hard against the outside of his right knee. Ignoring the jab of pain, Jak pulled the man's head back and stabbed the big bowie knife through the right side of the man's throat, just forward enough to clear the spine. Then he punched outward with ferocious force.

The man's body's convulsed. A great sheet of blood shot out of the ruptured throat, arterial spray from the severed carotid jutting into the air like ink from a frightened squid. Jak heard a great gurgle as the man tried to scream in terror and agony.

But no cry came out. The blade had violated the airway as well as ripping through the cartilage of the

Adam's apple. Instead, the sound turned to a hideous bubbling wheeze as blood sloshed into lungs and belly.

Jak continued to cling. Spasms racked the man's body as if he were getting repeatedly kicked by a horse. They didn't last long.

The sentry dropped abruptly, as if his bones had dissolved within his gangly body. Prepared, Jak got his feet under him and braced when they hit the deck. The man's deadweight was considerable. He let the man down easy, still making no sound louder than the blood splatting on the deck.

The Sea Wasp would die of blood loss to the brain long before he could drown in his own gore. Jak's throat slash turned the target off almost as quickly as beheading him would've done. Like any true hunter, Jak made it a point of pride to grant his prey the quickest, cleanest death possible.

He rose to a crouch, shaking blood from the back of his left hand. Slipping a leaf-bladed throwing knife from his lightweight vest, he turned toward the square back of the yacht's cabin. Faint light showed amber through the polarized glass. Engine rumbles vibrated up through his bare soles. Muted conversation and mellow chuckles sounded from inside the structure.

He wasn't particularly surprised by the strong odor of ganja smoke from the pilothouse. Silver-Eye ran a tight ship, but his pirates were only human. If his sentries were terrorized into staying straight, that was probably as much as the stone-hearted boss could ask.

Jak slipped forward, cat-footing on bare feet.

A door opened in the starboard side of the low, rakishly streamlined cabin. A head with thick dreads poked out in a cloud of marijuana smoke. He looked aft and saw the white ghost not fifteen feet away. He opened his mouth to scream.

Jak's right hand whipped forward. The throwing knife glittered in a dull arc to socket itself in the prominent Adam's apple. The open mouth emitted a strangled gurgle that died in a rush of blood. The pirate fell.

A horn commenced to wail from the pilothouse. Yellow light silhouetted the cabin as the Browning in the bow opened up in a thunderous stutter.

THOUGH THE .30-CALIBER BURST was clearly fired randomly, and raked the waterfront a good forty yards to the west, J.B. ducked instinctively behind the pile of stout casks at the corner of a warehouse.

Behind him Mildred uttered a soft moan. "I hope Jak's all right."

He grinned but said nothing. Of course the kid was all right; he had more lives than a cat and was harder to hit than a swallow chasing flies through twilight. Saying that was just her way of letting go of tension.

Holding his fedora in his left hand, J.B. poked his head above one of the barrels that smelled strongly of whiskey, of all things. He saw the machine gun swinging his way. The pirate crouching behind the splinter shield, with only his legs visible behind the weapon's columnar mounting, was blazing through a belt of linked ammo in a single long burst that would burn the barrel out directly if he didn't ease off the trigger.

J.B. hoped he wouldn't do that. And not just because, as an armorer born as well as trained, he had a marrow-deep love of weapons.

The machine gun's strobing muzzle flame was brilliant yellow and big as a wag, stretching almost all the way to the stone dock. The burly weapon's noise and blast were so ferocious that J.B. had to squint his eyes against their stinging impact.

His lips skinned back from his teeth as the perforated barrel swept closer. He wanted to stay poised to make his move, but the jacketed .30-caliber bullets would rip right through the wooden walls of the warehouse to get him and Mildred, and shatter the barrel barricade like a giant hammer.

He heard booming impacts as bullets began to rake the warehouse facade. Then the eruption of noise and fire cut off.

Now J.B. heard the crack of Ryan's Scout Tactical longblaster echo between the waterfront buildings through the ringing in his ears. It hadn't been a long shot—perhaps a hundred, hundred and twenty feet, max—but in the dark, through a dazzling cloud of muzzle flash, Ryan had managed to hit the tiny sliver of brainpan exposed by the slit in the armor plate that protected the gunner.

But that was Ryan all over. Steady.

"Showtime," J.B. said to Mildred, without looking over his shoulder. Cramming the hat back on his head, he straightened and stepped around the pile of casks. His left hand caught the short foregrip of his Uzi as he brought it to his hip.

The two guards at the ship's gangplank had their weapons up and were pointing them toward where Ryan's longblaster had flashed. They didn't fire. They were probably too disoriented by the abrupt explosion of events, and by the violent hammering of noise and blast from the machine gun, as well as its abrupt cessation.

They got no more chances. J.B. cut them down with two quick bursts of 9 mm rounds.

A man started to emerge from the cabin by the hatch. Firing past J.B.'s right shoulder, Mildred drilled the pirate through the forehead. He sprawled atop his buddy, who was still thrashing and kicking as he strangled on his own blood.

Krysty and Doc bolted from the street to J.B.'s right, half a block west. Like a big night heron, his coat flapping like wings and long skinny legs pumping, Doc led the way up the gangplank. He could move like a young man when motivated. Krysty was hard on his heels. J.B. and Mildred covered them as they hit either side of the open hatchway. They dropped their packs to the deck and got ready to roll.

A flash and crack went off on the other side of the long, low cabin. Another pirate had thought to go out that way. Fortunately, Jak had positioned himself to nail the man with his Magnum handblaster.

For a moment Doc stood beside the cabin, his silver hair wild, a mad light blazing in his eyes. He held his huge LeMat wheelgun in his right hand and the sawed-off pump gun in his left. He swung inside the hatch, disappearing to the right. Fire flashed and handblasters boomed as Krysty wheeled in behind him and stepped to the left.

J.B. raced up the gangplank, traveling its length in heartbeats.

He covered left as he ran forward past the end of the cabin, but nobody crouched in wait for him. He let the Uzi drop on its sling and waved for Mildred to follow him from cover.

As J.B. shed both his pack and Ryan's, he saw her start toward the ship holding her handblaster muzzle-up. Mildred wasn't fast, try as she might. She was also carrying Jak's pack along with her own. At least she didn't have far to go. As she started across the gangplank, J.B. kicked aside the dead pirate sprawled behind the Browning and took his place.

A few seconds passed, then Ryan appeared, running flat out, his longblaster slantwise across his chest. As he headed west from the street, a mob of pursuers burst onto the waterfront behind him.

Roaring in triumph, they leveled blasters at Ryan's fleeing back.

Chapter Nine

The Browning's receiver hadn't cooled much, J.B. realized, but it would have to do. He swung the blaster around and cut loose into the pack of coldhearts. The bullets smashed them like bottles on a rail fence, but instead of glass fragments they spattered blood and random chunks of bone and flesh. A couple of pirates may have dodged in time to avoid having more holes put in their hides. It didn't matter to J.B.; he was keeping his friends and himself safe, not chilling for its own sake.

Ryan pounded up onto the yacht. J.B. moved the machine gun to the left. He blasted the opening of the alley where he'd hidden with Mildred a few moments before. Then, as Ryan raced into the cabin, vaulting the pair of pirate chills, he turned his attention to the street Krysty and Doc had emerged from.

Even through the powerful vibration the blaster imparted to the deck through the mounting, J.B. felt the engine rev up. Mildred had gotten below and powered it up by hand. Krysty ran past to cast off the line tethering the bow to shore and winch up the forward anchor, or cut it loose.

J.B. was in his element. It was a rare treat to get to fire a big old blaster like this, full rock-and-roll, with a big box of somebody else's ammo to burn through. He swung the barrel back to scatter another group running up the street toward the gangplank.

The armorer saw more shadows up the street and ripped off a couple of bursts at them for good measure. He saw Krysty drop the disconnected gangplank into the harbor and felt the diesel's throb swell in volume up through his boots and shinbones and the *Wailer* pulled away from the dock.

Glancing down, he saw that he had plenty of ammo in the can. This particular belt was near out, though. As if in response to his thought, Jak materialized and handed up the end of a fresh ammo belt just as the old one ran dry. As the spent links clattered musically on the deck, J.B. opened the big weapon's feed tray and popped it in.

He blasted up the waterfront as they pulled away. He gave special attention to the stone blockhouse of the Monitor station with its black-on-white flag flapping overhead. He mostly created a shower of black lava dust, although he thought a few rounds went in the shooting slits. A stray shot or two chopped the flagpole and brought down the skull and crossbones. Bonus.

Keeping his focus soft so that any sign of major movement onshore would catch his eye, J.B. turned his attention to the smaller, stumpier yacht they were passing. He blasted it low in the stern, hoping to foul up the engine, if it had one, or at least the steering. Then, as the next ship came alongside, he did the same to it.

J.B. became aware of people nearby. He let off the trigger for a moment to allow the barrel to cool. It wasn't glowing yet, but the heat shimmer over it was plainly visible, distorting the lights of the ville.

Doc had come to stand behind him. J.B. realized that besides the pilothouse, where Ryan was presumably steering the ship toward the harbor mouth, *behind* the Browning was the best place to get away from its terrible racket and side-blast.

"You are not making any friends, shooting those other ships, John Barrymore!" Doc yelled, leaning close. Good call. His ear was ringing loud enough to beat a band, even though the blaster wasn't currently going off.

He laughed. "We aren't likely to be visiting here again, anytime soon. Best to cut down on pursuit, I reckon."

The harbor shore curved out west, to the sea. Instead of running straight, Ryan followed the land, staying just outside ships moored to the docks, veering only enough to clear other vessels standing farther out. Krysty appeared as J.B. was blasting more anchored ships.

He let go the trigger again. The receiver made popping noises audible even above the ringing in his ears as it cooled.

"Ryan's taking her close by the north edge of the harbor," Krysty shouted. "He says he's spotted a machine-gun emplacement there. He wants you to take care of it and discourage anybody from manning it."

J.B. winced. A heavy blaster like this one didn't make an ace in the line target. Sure, a bullet through the vitals wouldn't do a person any good, but the .30-cal, for all its strengths, wasn't a precision instrument. A good receiver hit would jam a machine gun, and there was a dreamer's chance of fouling the mount with a hit, so the piece wouldn't traverse. But it was all a matter of strike or shit-out-of-luck; there was little skill in it.

Then he shrugged. Ryan knew that, sure as he did. The one-eyed man would never be the weaponsmith J.B. was, but he did know his way around a blaster.

Krysty clapped his arm and pointed northwest. On an artificial extension of the harbor edge, built out of broken lava rock, was a revetment of sandbags with a big blaster, a .50-caliber Browning.

A blockhouse was set just inland of the blaster on the artificial spit. As J.B. swung the barrel of his machine gun that way, he saw figures break out and sprint across the brief intervening space.

Though his own barrel had *just* cooled from a low, unhappy cherry glow, he dusted them with three quick bursts.

"Give me a hand shooting, people," he shouted. "If I melt this bitch down, we could be in a world of hurt!"

His companions didn't need more encouragement than that. Another figure darted from the blockhouse. Krysty cut loose with an AK she'd picked up from a dead pirate, and Jak banged out shots from a blaster he'd picked up. Doc lit off .44-caliber shots from his big replica handblaster, though the range was a good two hundred yards, and even Mildred would have had a hard time hitting a man-sized target at that range.

The man went down, whether hit or scared J.B. didn't know. It didn't matter all that much. Then, an unpleas-

ant thought occurred to J.B. He walked around the pintle mount, traversing his gun 180 degrees, toward the
similar emplacement he feared was located a mile south.
But his Browning was designed for long distances, spat-
tering an area with lead instead of hitting targets with
nail-driving accuracy.

Unfortunately, the distant emplacement was identical
to the one he and his friends had just suppressed, with
a Browning that shot farther and hit harder than his.

Even as he was eyeballing the proper elevation to
fire at the distant gun emplacement, he saw a big yellow ball of flame blossom toward him. The burst missed
high. As J.B. brought his own weapon to point at the
flickering ball of light, the half-inch slugs passed overhead with a rushing noise like wind in the rafters of a
tumbledown shack. A moment later the muzzle thunder
rumbled to his ears.

His companions looked toward the far machine gun,
which flamed again. This time the shots fell short by a
good hundred yards, though they sent up white geysers
of spray as high as the *Wailer*'s tall mast.

"I take it they stand a substantially better chance of
damaging us than we have of silencing them," Doc said.

"You might say that," J.B. replied. "'Specially since
they just bracketed us. They ought to have the range
now."

J.B. felt the diesel thrum deepen and grow stronger.
The ship began to pick up speed, turning hard to port
just as the distant .50-caliber weapon cut loose again.
The shots roared low overhead.

J.B. nodded, waiting for the gun to cool. Ace timing, Ryan, he thought. Had Ryan not turned the craft sharply just when he did, the burst would've caught them.

From aft came a strange, short rush of noise. Suddenly a light flared, about a hundred feet south of the ship's port side. With a buzzing roar it streaked toward the distant enemy.

The .50-caliber machine gun continued to blast at them. A hit on the deck between the mount and the prow knocked up a three-foot splinter of plank. J.B. grimaced, waiting for the inevitable....

A brighter flash suddenly overrode the big machine gun's muzzle flare, which immediately went out in the double flash of a tandem warhead.

Through residual ringing in his ears, J.B. heard a shouted "Yes!" from astern.

He grinned. It was unmistakably Mildred's voice. He stayed alert, waiting for the other machine gun to open up again.

"Did you see that?" Mildred approached him from between the portside railing and the cabin's streamlined flank. "Did you see that? *Nailed* those mothers."

"What in Gaia's name are you carrying, Mildred?" Krysty asked mildly.

Mildred swung a thick, stubby tube with a ring for its back end that almost doubled its width off her shoulder. J.B.'s brows shot up. He recognized it, sure enough.

"This?" She slapped the side of the tube, grinning. "Only an FGM-148 antitank missile, otherwise known as a Javelin. They were the hot new thing with the U.S. military when I went under the knife."

"Pirates must use them to convince ships to stop when the machine gun doesn't work," J.B. said, nodding approval. "Somebody must have looted a stash."

"How did you ever learn to shoot one of those?" Krysty asked.

Mildred laughed. "J.B. isn't the only one who knows weapons!" She grinned. "Also it has a little cartoon on the side with instructions."

"So may I take it, ladies," Doc said, as if nothing untoward had been happening, "that yonder villains are no longer liable to afflict us?"

"Yonder villains got their asses blown up," Mildred replied.

"Ace," Jak said, padding up to them.

"Good job!"

Heads turned. Ryan looked out a port in the front of the cabin where the bridge was.

"Somebody better go check for damage double-quick," he shouted. "Bastards ripped us pretty good a couple of times."

Jak nodded, frowning. "Smell fuel. Stinks."

"Fireblast!" Ryan said. "Somebody jump on that. If we're going to have to swim to Puerto Rico, I want to know about it now!"

Chapter Ten

"They're still behind us, Ryan," Mildred called from the stern where she was keeping lookout in the afternoon sun.

Ryan grunted. He hadn't expected the pirates—or the Monitors—to give up pursuit.

Ahead the island of Puerto Rico rose from blue ocean like a fuzzy green iceberg.

"At least we're almost to Nuestra Señora," Krysty said from the open hatchway.

"Good thing, too," he said, "because we're running on fumes as it is."

The big machine gun had holed them a dozen times before they'd been able to use the Javelin to put it out of commission. But, big as .50-caliber slugs were, it took a lot of them to damage a yacht. The few holes the bullets had punched below the waterline had been easy to plug.

But they could also hit something vital that was smaller than the entire hull, and one had punctured the portside fuel tank. They had just enough in the starboard tank to make the run from NuTuga to their destination.

"Are they gaining on us, Krysty?" he asked.

"No, lover."

"That's something, anyway."

"If the charts that our unwilling hosts so thoughtfully provided are correct," said Doc from the map table near the wheel, "we should come in sight of the ville for which we are headed as soon as we round this promontory."

"Thanks," Ryan said.

He guessed the charts were accurate. Whatever else you could say about the Sea Wasp Posse, they apparently knew their business and took it seriously. They were successful, after all.

It turned out they made and maintained careful charts of the whole West Indies. That included careful annotations as to both targets and dangers. Like a lot of Puerto Rican ports, the ville of Nuestra Señora offered both. It was prosperous, as such places went, though a lot less grand than NuTuga. But the people were also relatively well armed and vigorous about defending the place.

As tough as the Sea Wasps were, they were also smart. They knew to look elsewhere for easier prey.

Which made Nuestra Señora an ideal port of call for Ryan and company, in their current circumstances. Provided the locals could be persuaded to regard *them* as anything but coldhearts, of course.

"Take the helm, Doc," Ryan said. "I want to go check on our friends back there."

"Certainly, my dear Ryan."

Doc moved behind the console of instruments and blinking lights, only some of which worked. He had his coat off and his shirtsleeves rolled up, exposing his bony white wrists. The old man seemed alert and focused, moving more like a man younger than Ryan—his real age, as opposed to his apparent one.

"A stern chase is a long chase, my naval acquaintances told me back in my day," he said as Ryan started out of the cabin.

"Yeah. Reckon that's why we're still breathing."

He went out blinking into the bright morning light. The sun had risen a couple of hours before. They had run the engine as fast as they dared all night. They couldn't redline it; if it failed before it had done its job they were stone chilled. Which restricted them to maybe twenty miles per hour.

From the cabin door Ryan glanced at Jak, alone in the prow, his long white hair streaming off to the side like a banner. Ryan grinned. He thought the kid looked like the hero from an ancient sword-and-sorcery paperback he'd read as a boy in Front Royal.

The one-eyed man turned aft and walked toward the squared-off stern, where J.B. and Krysty stood by the railing gazing back along their wake. Jak declined to join them, claiming he was only interested in looking ahead. Ryan could see his point. Watching the pursuit creep slowly up on them wouldn't load any blasters for them. Or make them feel better about life.

"How's it going?" Ryan asked his companions.

Krysty turned, flashed him a big smile and gave him a quick kiss.

J.B. stood peering through Ryan's Navy longeyes at the lone ship steaming in pursuit. It was another yacht like the one they rode, though mebbe a few feet shorter.

"Still gaining?" Ryan asked.

"Yeah," J.B. said. "Slow but sure." The vessel's white prow, with its white mustache of foam, was about a mile and a half astern.

"If this ville we're headed for's where their charts say, we should get there with room to spare," J.B. said. "'Course, if it *isn't,* we're liable to run out of fuel, anyway."

"Still just the one?" Ryan slipped his arm around Krysty. She snuggled in next to him.

"No sign of the other two." A trio of vessels had managed to power forth from NuTuga harbor to chase the stolen yacht.

"Don't reckon they could catch up, anyway," Ryan said. "If they could, they would have caught us already. Not sure that the first one to give up is even still afloat."

J.B. chuckled. No one aboard the *Wailer* had any way of knowing what exactly had happened. But somewhere in the wee hours of the morning, flames had suddenly flared up on one of the three enemy ships, a much smaller schooner. It had fallen broadside to them; the binocs showed frantic activity silhouetted by yellow flames leaping ever higher as the crew tried to fight the blaze. It could've been anything, from a catastrophic engine overheat to some triple-stupe smoking a spliff while cleaning engine parts with gasoline.

Neither of the other pursuers had paused to help their buddies. Well, Ryan thought, they don't call 'em cold-hearts for nothin'. Sometime between then and dawn the other ship had dropped back and been lost to sight, again for reasons unknown.

Which left the lead vessel. Ryan took the longeyes from his friend, adjusted their spacing and focus, then grunted. They'd way overcrewed the sleek motor sailer, which was common pirate practice. Judging by some black outfits on the crew lounging around the railing, they did have some Monitors among them. There were at least twenty of the bastards aboard. Standing in the bow—where, as far as anyone could tell, he had stood all night—was Silver-Eye Chris himself, looking like grim death.

Even through the powerful glass, the pirate chief's face was just a pale blur. Ryan didn't need to see his expression to know it.

"Reckon that bastard would keep after us if his damn ship was afire stem to stern," J.B. said, intuiting the object of Ryan's attention. "Even if his dreads were burning like so many candles."

"He has motivation," Krysty agreed.

"Yeah, you're right," Ryan said. "Any idea yet what that thing is under the tarp behind him?"

"It's either a heavy weapon or a mount for one," J.B. replied. "It has to be, or pretty near, on a pirate ship like that. Otherwise they'd've unbolted whatever it is, and sold it on the beach or chucked it overboard."

"If it's a heavy weapons mount, wouldn't they have mounted the weapon already?" Krysty asked.

"Mebbe not," Ryan said. "If it was a machine gun,

say. Like the one we had. Or the bigger bastard firing at us last night."

They had unbolted the Browning and its mount from the deck and pitched them into the sea. As J.B. feared, he'd burned out the barrel during the final exchange with the distant shore gun. A flashlight inspection of the bore revealed he'd shot out the rifling and had fired at least a few rounds as if it were a shotgun or a crude black powder musket. Without grooves to impart a spin, the bullets tumbled pretty much right out of the muzzle and splashed down any which way in the water, probably no farther than fifty yards away.

There had been no spare barrel in stowage. Nor was there a reload rocket for Mildred's new launcher. Somehow Ryan couldn't bring himself to grouse about the luck; they'd had more than they deserved, maybe, to get away as clean as they did.

J.B. thumbed up the brim of his fedora to scratch his forehead. Sweat was running down his face.

"If you held my feet to the fire," he said, "I'd guess it's a mortar of some kind. Eighty-one millimeters, most likely. That's what the old U.S. military used."

Ryan frowned. An 81 mm mortar would be bad enough. But things could get plenty worse.

"Could it be a four-deuce?"

J.B. grunted. "I can't rightly say yea or nay," he said. "But I doubt they could reinforce the deck enough that a four-point-two-inch mortar wouldn't punch right on through with the recoil."

A 4.2-inch mortar was serious ordnance. It shot a long

way and a solid hit would basically blast the *Wailer* to flaming splinters, along with its passengers. Ryan had encountered one or two in his day.

"Why aren't they shooting it at us, if that's what it is?" Krysty asked, shading her eyes with her hand to look at the enemy yacht.

"Just wasting ammo," J.B. said. "Moving target, shooting from a moving platform, both moving all kinds of ways at once. Plus it lobs shells on a real slow, looping trajectory." He shook his head. "Naval gunnery like that takes a lot of practice even with straight-shooting cannons."

"Well, they *are* pirates," Krysty said.

"However many shells they got for that thing," Ryan said, "they don't have enough to practice those kinds of shots."

"Well," she said with a smile and shrug, "maybe our friend back there's unwilling to risk damaging his stolen property."

Ryan lowered the longeyes and exchanged a glance with J.B. "Don't reckon old Silver-Eye back there would hesitate a second to set this boat afire with his own grubby hands, long as he thought there was at least a fifty-fifty shot we'd burn with it."

"Where's Mildred?" Ryan asked.

"Down with the engine," Krysty said. "Of course. She treats it like her baby."

J.B. grunted, although he smiled ruefully. He was certainly a better engine mechanic than the physician, although she was a pretty fair tinkerer. But somehow it'd

become important to her to take the *Wailer*'s diesel under
her wing. Ryan couldn't see as it made much never mind
either way. The engine was running smoothly enough,
and if it crapped on them they weren't likely to have
time to take it apart and fix it anyway.

A painfully loud honking blared from the cabin behind them. It was the yacht's horn, which had given
the alarm last night—too late to do its skeleton crew
any good. Ryan turned, annoyed with himself for being
startled by the noise, and saw Doc leaning out the cabin
waving excitedly toward them.

"What is it?" he called.

"Come see for yourself, my dear Ryan!" Doc called,
and ducked back inside to take the wheel again.

Ryan looked at his companions. They shrugged in
unison and walked briskly forward.

Even before they cleared the low cabin, Ryan could
see they had come around a big steep headland of volcanic rock so densely overgrown it showed only flashes
of black rock and soil. If the pirate maps were right, the
ville of Nuestra Señora should be in plain sight now.

It was. Ryan stopped dead, a pace in front of the
cabin.

Nuestra Señora was a decent-sized settlement, if nothing compared to NuTuga. It boasted at least a hundred
buildings, from structures with solid-looking white-
washed walls to mere huts with palm-thatch roofs and
flexible screens for sides that would be rolled up when
the weather was fair. It was a common construction style
on the Gulf or West Indies coasts, where stone or con-

crete or even brick weren't always accessible, and a hurricane was going to blow down anything less stoutly constructed once or twice a year, anyway.

But it was hard to tell many details about the ville, because much of it was on fire.

"Eyes skinned," Ryan rapped.

He saw more smoke than actual flame, suggesting the blaze had burned for some time.

"Whoever did this could still be hanging around."

"So much," Doc intoned from inside the cabin, "for the good citizens of Nuestra Señora aiding us in standing off the cutthroats."

"In other news," J.B. said from right behind, "the Wasps are unwrapping that weapon on their foredeck."

Ryan glanced back. He considered unslinging his Steyr Scout to try to discourage Silver-Eye and his people from using whatever horror it was they were unlimbering.

But range, wind and relative motion would have made it a waste to take the shot. He wasn't that good. *Nobody* was that good.

A good bullet-sprayer like the *Wailer*'s pintle-mounted .30-caliber machine gun would've worked just fine. Spilled blood won't go back in the body, Ryan reminded himself with a quick frown, no matter how hard you push.

He ducked into the cabin. "I'm taking the wheel, Doc," he said.

Doc stepped nimbly aside.

Ryan steered toward the Nuestra Señora docks. They

at least looked intact. It would take real effort and probably a fair amount of gasoline to torch the waterlogged planks. A few small craft, hung with nets, bobbed at anchor in the little bay. Their paint was faded and flaked away, but they showed signs of being kept in the best repair that ville people with few resources could manage.

The vessel shuddered as he drove the throttle forward. The engine needle shot past the redline and pinned. He heard as well as felt the diesel begin to knock precariously.

A moment later, Mildred rushed into the cabin from belowdecks, her eyes wild and cheek smudged with grease.

"Ryan, what's going on?" she demanded. "Are you trying to blow up my engine?"

"If you'll take a look around, Mildred," Ryan said mildly, "you'll note it isn't rightly *your* engine, or even *our* engine. It's *their* engine."

He jerked a thumb back over his shoulder. From the corner of his eye, he caught her goggling at the nearness of the pursuing boat and the flurrying activity on the foredeck. Not to mention what they'd more than likely uncovered by now.

"J.B.," he called out, dodging them behind a battered boat with high-raked bow and stern almost like an Asian junk. "Stop your skylarking and get below. You've got preparations to make."

"Got you."

He could almost hear the grin in the armorer's words.

"Ryan," Mildred said, "we are about to dock at a ville which is on fire."

"Hard as you might find it to believe, Mildred," he said, "I noticed that."

"And, Ryan? I think they're getting ready to shoot at us with a—"

A whistling scream raced across the sky.

Chapter Eleven

Ahead and off the *Wailer*'s starboard bow, a fishing ketch flew apart in a yellow flash and a whirlwind of splinters.

"Mortar, yes," Ryan said. "Reckoned that, too. Brace for impact, and pass the word to the rest!"

The dock was stoutly built of wood atop massive pilings. A bunch of great big old tires served as bumpers, tied to the wharf with windings of hairy rope.

They were going to come in fast, even though he had the engine whining in full Reverse now. He'd just as soon have gone in balls-out and rammed the dock. It wasn't *his* yacht, and it looked as if the locals weren't in much position to complain if he busted their waterfront all to shit. But there was a chance that, if he hit hard, all he'd do was knock a huge hole in the bow and bounce the ship off the dock. It would sink like a stone and quite possibly drown one or all of them within spitting distance of land.

Clinging to the steel bar inset on the console, apparently for purchase in high seas, Ryan spun the wheel hard to port. The fact that the propeller was turning backward didn't change the flow of water past the rudder. The yacht swung counterclockwise, the starboard side slamming into the huge tires with a squeal and a crash.

The jolt felt as if it would knock Ryan's eye out of its socket. Jak, standing unperturbed in the prow, heaved a coil of sturdy nylon line onto the warped planks of the dock. Then, as the ship rebounded, he leaped the widening gap like a puma, landed lithely on the dock and began to tie the vessel up.

Ryan cut the engine and abandoned the wheel. Doc was picking himself up off the deck, making a show of brushing off his trousers.

"Do not worry about me, my lad!" he sang out brightly. "I am as fit as a fiddle."

Ryan thought Doc seemed a tad too cheerful. Sometimes the man acted most wired up right before he was about to lose himself in the fogbanks of his mind. But Ryan couldn't waste much time wondering about that; it would happen or it wouldn't.

Instead, he stuck his head out the starboard hatch into a breeze where the intrinsic reek of rotting sea life was overridden by the stinks of wood smoke, diesel oil and roasting human flesh.

He looked aft. Krysty stood on the dock, encouraging a dubious-looking Mildred to leap the treacherous gap between ship and shore. Behind them, the shake roof of a plank building had fallen in, leaving only a smoldering skeleton of rafters.

As they'd approached the ville, Ryan had told his friends to pile their backpacks in the bridge behind him.

That way they'd be easy to grab if they had to clear out the yacht quickly.

Shouldering his own pack and slinging his rifle, he caught up Krysty's and Mildred's packs, as well.

"Fit to carry the rest?" he called to Doc.

"Indeed."

"Take them forward and toss them to Jak. Follow right after."

Ryan went straight out the door, heading toward Mildred, who was still dithering about the yard-wide jump over water that was grubby with ash and greasy with runoff. Following another roar close to portside, the *Wailer* rocked violently, slamming Ryan into the starboard rail.

The impact would have broken his ribs but Krysty's backpack served as a buffer. Ignoring a huge sluice of warm stinking water that splashed down on him, he ran the rest of the way to the stern.

With a heave of his arm he flung Krysty her pack. Reacting with her usual quickness, she fielded it as easily as if it had been a pillow. Likewise Mildred's pack, which followed as soon as she'd swung her own onto the dock.

"What about—" she started to ask, holding the big pack in her hands.

Mildred slowly sat up from where she lay next to Krysty. The mortar blast had knocked the ship against the tire buffers and flipped her right over the rail onto the dock. Then the water had rushed back, sucking the vessel out to the full length of its mooring lines.

Ryan never hesitated. He backed up a few steps, took a run at the rail and jumped.

His boots hit the rope windings on top of a tire. He'd landed just a hair short. His soles hit the outside, so that his momentum went mostly into the rope and the tire rather than impelling him forward to safety.

For a moment Ryan hung in the balance with his heavy pack inexorably pulling him back into the water, where he'd be crushed by the boat, now drifting back toward the dock.

Krysty grabbed Ryan by the sling of his Scout and hoisted him off the bumper. Swinging around, she deposited him and his pack on the planking, which boomed hollowly beneath his boots.

A mortar round cracked off somewhere inland. They all ducked.

"Grab the packs and let's get to cover," Ryan said.

He spun back to face the ship and harbor, unslinging his longblaster. Another mortar bomb whistled well overhead to burst inside the ville to his right.

As he fed his left arm through the shooting loop of his sling, he glanced toward the *Wailer*'s prow. He was in time to see Doc midflight, his arms and legs windmilling, coattails flapping behind him like stork wings. He landed on the dock beside Jak and went down to one fist to catch himself. Then, as if he were no older than the albino youth, he straightened.

Ryan craned to look past the *Wailer*. Another mortar round burst in the harbor. The boat rocked fore and aft.

J.B. rushed out the starboard hatch, clamping his

fedora to his head with one hand. Hardly breaking stride, he jumped onto the rail and then took an ungainly flying step toward the dock as the gap widened again.

He hit and rolled, then came up grinning. His hat never left his head.

"One would not think it to look at him," Doc said, "but John Barrymore is quite agile."

Ryan smiled briefly. "We need to move with a purpose," he said, hearing shots and shouts as the pirate yacht entered the harbor. "We'll take up position somewhere in the ville, well back from the waterfront but with decent lines of sight."

They grabbed their backpacks and headed into the ville. It seemed as if half the buildings were burned out, while the other half still burned.

Nor was that the worst of it. Up close, Ryan's eye confirmed what his nose already told him. The huts hadn't been empty when the ville was torched. Bodies lay sprawled in the streets in pools of blood that congealed beneath buzzing clouds of flies. Some had been shot, others hacked or stabbed. Some had their heads staved in. Bodies lay half in doorways and hanging out of windows.

One young girl, who couldn't have been more than fourteen, lay on her back between two half-burned huts. The rags of her clothing lay open around her, soaking up her blood. Her eyes stared blankly at the cloudless Caribbean sky. She had clearly been assaulted then killed.

"Let's go!" he called. Krysty and Mildred emerged from hiding in a half-plank hut that had burned so thoroughly you wouldn't think two people could hide in there. Ryan sketched out his plan.

"Why?" Krysty asked. "Why not just disappear into the woods and get away clean? I mean, yeah, they're shooting the mortar and all. But they're as likely to hit us here by accident with a short round as drop one right where we happen to be leaving town."

"We don't know yet how hard and fast the pirates'll come," he said. "May have some trackers with them, too."

Jak snorted loudly at that. He had nothing but disdain for the tracking skills of the sort of person who'd be in the pirates' employ. Probably wrongly: there were no doubt bayou rats among them, or at least some Nu-Tuga crews, who had the same background and the same skills as Jak.

"If we need to discourage them from chasing us," Ryan said, "I'd rather do it here. Even you have to admit, Jak, hunting men in a ville's way worse than out in the brush."

Sullenly, Jak nodded.

"It took a sizable force to do this much damage, chill this many folk," J.B. said. "We don't want to run into them while escaping the Wasps."

"What if they come back to investigate while we're discouraging the pirates?" Mildred asked.

"You'd have to be double-stupe to want to wander toward the sounds of a firefight, Millie," J.B. said, trying to mop sweat from his forehead—his handkerchief was already so damp from body sweat and humidity, he was only redistributing it.

Ryan grinned. "What could be better for us? We get them confronting each other and slip away while they're sorting things out. All right, people. Let's hunker down. Now."

In moments he was crouching next to J.B. behind a wooden cart that had overturned, spilling a load of coconuts into a street covered with dirty-white tufa gravel. About thirty yards to their right, Krysty, Mildred and Doc were hiding in a fallen-down shack closer to the ville's central plaza. Jak was somewhere, possibly prowling. Ryan was content to let the kid go his own way, knowing he'd be skinning his eyes, and all his other senses, to keep his friends safe.

The mortar chugged as the pirate sloop motored to the dock like a sleek white shark.

"They're going through those rounds like there's no tomorrow," J.B. said, shaking his head. He hated waste. Especially where good ordnance was concerned.

Ryan frowned. Silver-Eye Chris continued to stand, tall and fierce, in the prow, heedless of the mortar going off right behind him. It had to be as uncomfortable as hell.

J.B. chuckled. "He looks pissed."

"Yeah," Ryan said. The pirate boss had a red scarf tied around his dreads bandana-style, and a longblaster with a folding stock slung over one shoulder.

The pirate sloop came about, sliding alongside the moored *Wailer*. Lines were thrown. As nimble as howler monkeys, pirates leaped the gap to make the vessels fast. Some hauled on other lines to pull the vessels beam to beam while others, bristling with weapons, crowded into the cabin and presumably down the hatches. The *Wailer*'s superstructure hid Silver-Eye from view. Ryan had no idea whether he crossed to his erstwhile flagship or was waiting for his crew to clear it.

Ryan noticed several men in Monitor black at the enemy ship's rail. They seemed content to watch the pirates work. One of them looked to be the bearded dude who'd led the squad that braced Ryan's group on arrival at NuTuga.

It was all happening not two hundred yards away. Ryan didn't really need his longeyes. Plus he didn't want to risk giving away their position by having the lens reflect the glint of sunlight.

J.B. tsked and shook his head. "You know," he said, "it's a pure shame, in a way."

"What is?" Ryan asked. He didn't take his eye off the scene on the conjoined ships. He had to admit Silver-Eye Chris's crew were good at what they did.

"They may not've had more reloads for Millie's Javelin launcher," the armorer said, "but they did have a full crate of good old C-4, in convenient one-kilo blocks."

Ryan cocked the brow of his good eye at him. "You mean—"

He snapped his gaze back toward the waterfront just in time to see the whole deck of the *Wailer* bulge upward, the cabin rising into the air. For what could only have been a slice of a second, it appeared to Ryan as if the structure was going to hold miraculously together. Then the top blew open to belch a swelling yellow fireball into the sky.

Ryan saw at least two bodies cartwheeling up and away from the blast, and one round, dark, twirling object, which Ryan identified as a detached head as it vanished off to his right. And then only by the thick dreads flying like streamers behind it.

A wave of sound rolled across them, riding a blast of hot air.

From stem to stern the *Wailer* gushed fire like the fresh-opened vent from a volcano.

J.B., who often seemed to have more feelings for machines than men, was shaking his head again. "Damn shame," he said.

A white flash abruptly overrode even the inferno erupting from the wreck. For a moment the flames lay down, revealing a fireball that enveloped the whole front end of the pursuers' ship. Then a second explosion shattered the other ship. In an instant it was sinking, its bow blown off. The blast's noise was like a moving sheet of steel hitting Ryan in the face, and the sound cut at his ears.

"Huh," Ryan grunted.

"Ho-lee *shit!*" Mildred exclaimed from her hiding place.

"I didn't expect *that* to happen," J.B. said. "Looks like a mortar round they were about to drop down the tube went off. Set off the rest of their ammo stowage. Explosives must have gotten unstable with age."

"You think?" Ryan asked dryly.

He turned to his friend. "Nice boobie, by the way."

J.B. grinned and ducked his head. "Like I say, it was a damn shame to waste all that lovely moldable plastic explosive." He glanced back at the two stricken, blazing wrecks. "But I reckon it went to a good cause."

"I reckon."

"Besides," the armorer went on, slapping a pocket of his jacket, "I did slip some C-4 and some detonators in here for good measure."

Ryan laughed and slapped his friend on the shoulder. "Let's go."

He rose halfway and ran in a crouch to where the women and Doc lay staring in amazement at the devastation. Buildings were blazing all over again from the flaming wreckage and fuel that had showered them.

"Our good armorer has produced quite an exemplary holocaust with his wiles," Doc said when the two men slipped into the rubble behind him.

"Come on," Ryan told them. "Let's check the ville before we head out."

"You're kidding," Mildred said. "In case you missed it, Ryan, the place has been sacked!"

"Looks to me like this was about teaching somebody a lesson instead of stealing shit," Ryan said. "It's not like we can afford to pass up a good chance at scavvy."

"What about the pirates?" Krysty asked.

"Reckon any who survived are going to have other things on their minds than chasing after us," Ryan said.

"They're probably all bleeding out of the ears from busted drums."

"Are you sure it's safe?" Mildred asked.

"Never safe."

Everybody jumped and turned. Jak crouched a few feet away. He grinned at them in triumph for taking his cunning, wary companions by surprise.

"Want safe," the youth said, "wait dead."

IT WAS MIDAFTERNOON when they left the ville, heading into thick brush that sprang up surprisingly close to the ville's inland edge. Cultivated fields lay to the west. Some of them smoldered, too.

The frog that plopped onto the path in front of them was as big as a human head with legs.

"Muties!" Jak spat, shying away as if the thing had poisoned fangs. "Dangerous!"

The grass to either side of the path leading away from Nuestra Señora rustled, revealing more of the outsized frogs. Their chirped *co-kee* came from all around. The rest of the party reacted less theatrically than Jak had, but they still steered wide of the enormous hoppers.

Ryan scowled. "Do we even know that they're dangerous?"

This struck him as a double distraction from their actual business, which was getting into the forest and losing themselves before the pirates and Monitors—or, more precisely, their vengeful survivors—caught up with them.

J.B. screwed up his face. "I'd have to say that just

about anything weird we've ever encountered in the Deathlands was dangerous, Ryan."

"Good point," Ryan said. "All right. Watch the fire-blasted frogs, then. As if we don't have enough to look out for already."

Whoever had hit the ville had hit it with a vengeance. As Ryan perceived, they'd seemed more interested in killing people and breaking things than looting the place. As if they wanted to make an example.

"It took a big force to raze the ville," Ryan said again as they marched up a trail that led through lush growth into the steep, thickly forested hills that backed the ville.

"An army, one might say," Doc said. "Although raiders rather than conquerors. But I suspect that plays a role in their future plans."

"So what does that mean for us, Ryan?" Mildred asked.

"It means," said a voice from just ahead, "that you don't need to worry about that shit. Your road ends here, motherfuckers!"

Chapter Twelve

Silver-Eye Chris stepped onto the path, his assault rifle leveled at Ryan from the waist. A pair of henchmen stood up out of the bush, left and right of the trail, pointing longblasters.

The companions had walked open-eyed into a trap.

The pirate might have gotten the drop on them, but he definitely looked the worse for wear.

The whole right side of his face was charred black. Raw, angry flesh peeked through where it had cracked. His eyebrow was gone on that side, as were most of the dreads. His left sleeve was missing, and his arm was almost as blackened as his face.

But both silver eyes still stared wildly from the charred ruins. And his left hand, now little more than a bloody half-roasted claw, held the AK's wooden fore-grip steady enough.

One of his wingmen was a wiry black Sea Wasp with heavy beads in his dreads, who looked uninjured. He had a machete with a spiked knuckle-duster bow stuck through his belt and carried a Mini-14 semiauto longblaster. The other was a Monitor. His regulation bald head was gashed from side to side; his face was smeared with browning blood where he'd made a halfhearted attempt to wipe it off. It pooled under his eyes, at the folds of his evil grin, and caked in his blond beard. He had a bandage around his left thigh that was soaked through with blood. He aimed a pump shotgun that had the full nylon tactical buttstock but had its barrel sawed off flush with the end of the tubular magazine.

Pain and rage had to have made the pirate lord go mad, Ryan thought, standing frozen behind Jak with his Scout longblaster held diagonally in patrol position in front of his body. *Otherwise he and his pals would've let their blasters do their talking for them from cover, and we would already be chilled.*

Not that they weren't likely to be dead soon, anyway. The wind, which had been blowing in from the ocean and carrying both the sight and smell of the burning ville's smoke inland, away from the *Wailer* on its approach, had either changed or was blowing from a different quarter in the forested foothills behind Nuestra Señora. Otherwise Jak's keen nose would have detected the presence of the ambush before they all walked into its kill zone with eyes wide-open.

"If you weren't all triple-stupe," Silver-Eye Chris rasped, "you'd make a play for us and end it right now. Of course we'd just blast your legs out from under you, but at least you'd go down trying. We're gonna have us some fun with you fuckers. You hear me? Some nuke-shittin' fun!"

His Monitor companion scowled and kicked at an overlarge frog that had hopped up against his injured leg and almost seemed to be sniffing the blood-crusted ankle of his boot. With a dismal croak it jumped a couple of feet to land right beside Silver-Eye Chris.

"Start layin' 'em down, boys and girls," the pirate said with a mad gleam in his eye. "Nice and easy, that's— Ow, fuck!"

The last was directed straight downward, where the displaced giant frog had suddenly clamped its jaws on Silver-Eye Chris's leg above his boot. From the shrill edge in his voice it wasn't just surprise that an innocuous creature like that would have the balls to bite a man.

The man suddenly threw back his charred dreads and shrieked in a glass-breaking pitch.

His friend couldn't help turning toward him in shocked surprise. Then the Sea Wasp staggered and clapped a hand to his neck, where one of Jak's throwing knives had suddenly sprouted from his Adam's apple.

Catching himself in midturn the Monitor started to swivel back. Before he could do so, Ryan whipped his Steyr around and shot him through the chest.

Jak was going for his Python. The man he'd nailed with the thrown blade wasn't mortally hit; he was pumping out wild shots from his 5.56 mm longblaster.

As Ryan speed-jacked the bolt on his longblaster, J.B. shot the Sea Wasp in the gut with his M-4000 shotgun. The man gasped and doubled over as the shot punched into him.

Silver-Eye Chris paid no attention to the unhappy fates of his two henchmen. He was screaming like a man on fire.

The frog clung to his leg, while others hopped purposefully toward the pirate captain. Astonished, Ryan saw a flash of fangs like curved yellow needles as a second creature opened its jaws and crouched to spring.

Like corrupted vines growing at hyperspeed, the veins on the backs of Silver-Eye's hands were turning black and swelling out of his skin. The dark death tentacles shot up his neck and enveloped his face. His screaming died to a strangling gurgle as his throat swelled shut.

Paying no attention to the pirate boss's terrible fate, Jak pointed his huge silver handblaster and fired into the crown of the gut-shot Sea Wasp's head. Ryan saw his eyes blow out of the sockets to the extents of his optic nerves before he went down face-first in the brush.

Keeping the longblaster cautiously leveled, Ryan stared in horrid fascination as the flesh of Silver-Eyed Chris's hands and body turned blue around the black veins and swelled grotesquely. Suddenly, his face exploded as if it were a huge discolored zit pinched between giant fingers. Yelping, Ryan jumped back to avoid the shower of reeking black corruption.

"Holy crap!" Mildred said from behind him.

"It would appear that young Jak's assessment is vindicated," Doc announced in tones of scholarly interest. "These frogs are indeed dangerous mutants. They appear to possess fangs, as a highly efficient delivery system for a remarkably fast-acting hemolytic venom."

"Talk sense, Doc!" Jak hissed, as he backed away from the frogs, holding down on them with his silver Python. He apparently couldn't decide whether to waste bullets on them or not. Which, to Ryan's mind, showed sound judgment, since the frogs were now converging on the pirate's half-headed body, thrashing amid the brush. They showed no interest at all in the people still on their pins.

"He means," Krysty called, "that we should stay away from these little guys."

"Amen," J.B. said fervently.

THE COMPANIONS, EXCEPT JAK, who was on sentry duty, sat around a small, smokeless fire of dead brush in a pocket on a brushy hillside. Tumbled volcanic rock and granite boulders screened them and the small, flickering fire from view above and below, while permitting easy access to lookout points over the hills down to the ocean.

As Ryan said, whoever had attacked Nuestra Señora had been more interested in wiping it out than looting it, which was a rarity in itself, in this day and age. Of course, there were ample signs of plundering. A commander who tried to prevent that altogether would wind up accidentally shot by his own sec men. Nobody had it that soft, no matter how relatively well-off they were. But they hadn't been very thorough or systematic about stealing. They had clearly grabbed whatever most struck them as they went about their highly methodical business of butchering the inhabitants.

They were eating a red snapper J.B. had found in the fallen-in ruins of a hut. Already scaled, with the head chopped off, it was still a good ten pounds. The householders had obviously been interrupted in preparing a meal. Jak had turned up a pot of cooked beans in another hut nearby.

"One wonders at such total devastation," Doc said. He had eaten lightly and now sat hugging the long skinny legs drawn up before him and gazing into the little fire. "Why would they so assiduously slaughter all the inhabitants?"

"Doubt they did," J.B. said. "Took some off as slaves, most likely."

Mildred shuddered. "Why? I mean, why bother? Obviously stealing stuff wasn't their priority. You can't tell me this was just a slave raid, either. Whoever did this was a major force by today's standards. And it's like what they really cared about was wiping Nuestra Señora off the face of the earth. Why would anybody do that?"

"Politics," Ryan said.

"Somebody wanted to make a point, good and hard."

"Well, the Nuestra Señorans sure got the point," Mildred said.

He shook his head. "No. This was, like, incidental. Yeah, pretty clearly they did something to piss somebody off. But the point to something like this is to show other people—*live* people—what happens when you do piss them off."

J.B. shrugged. "You got that right, Ryan," he said. "The dead don't learn too many lessons."

"'The undiscover'd country, from whose bourn no traveller returns,'" Doc intoned.

And just as Mildred was reflecting that she was undoubtedly the only other member of the group who recognized the quote, Ryan blindsided her.

"Hamlet," he grunted. "Yeah. He sure showed how the man who outsmarts himself is the biggest stupe of all. His simp friend turned out to be the smart one after all—the guy who took over there at the end, when everybody chilled everybody else."

"Fortinbras," Doc said.

"Yeah, him."

"Clearly, my dear Ryan," Doc added, "no one with any wit left to them would confuse you for either individual. You show deficiencies neither in thought nor in action."

Certainly conscience doesn't make any coward of him, Mildred thought. In most ways neither Ryan nor his contemporaries, except Krysty to some extent, showed much sign of what she'd been raised to regard as a conscience at all. Yet on the whole she had to say they were good people. Damn good ones.

And Ryan Cawdor, for all that he was hard, and even ruthless, might be the best man she'd ever known, other than her father. She reflected on how "moral" her own time had been—with all its self-righteousness and moralizing and insistence on its monopoly of conscience. Yet, cowardice really did seem to characterize it, in a moral sense—and in the end, all their self-professed rectitude and concern for their fellow men hadn't stopped the people of her time from wiping themselves out almost completely....

She was considering the notion that she'd disappear

up her own butthole if she kept following those lines of thought, when a sudden commotion broke out from the rocks right overhead.

Doc kicked the fire over. Krysty jumped up and quickly kicked dirt over the coals, smothering them. Everybody fanned out, crouching, blasters in their hands, covering all directions.

"Don't chill him!" Ryan rapped out. "Bring him here, Jak." He'd had his back to the upslope side. Now he rose smoothly and turned, taking up his Scout and aiming it upward.

"Ow!" an adolescent male voice cried out of sight above. "*¡Mierda!* Take it easy, *coño,* I'm coming!"

A kid appeared at the top of the black boulder clump. He was a few inches taller than Jak and wearing ratty cargo shorts and a green army tunic. Disheveled black bangs hung in a soot-smudged face. A big bruise, gone past purple to a dull rainbow, yellow and green and mottled blue, covered the left side of his face. He had some kind of longblaster strapped to his back, alongside a backpack, and had a big double-action revolver stuck in a battered leather-flapped cross-draw holster on the front of a web belt.

"You a spy?" Ryan asked.

"We should be careful, Ryan," Mildred said. "Maybe he's with whoever did that to the ville."

"You lie, *puta!*" the youth shrieked in a spray of spittle. He thrashed until Jak's big bowie drew blood.

"Easy," Ryan said. "It took an army to waste the ville

like that. If you're not with an army, you're damned well-heeled. You better have a good story, boy."

"Let me go," the youth said sullenly, "and I'll tell you."

Ryan grinned. So did J.B. and Doc.

"Not likely, junior," J.B. said, taking off his steel-rimmed specs and scrubbing them with a handkerchief.

Ryan gestured. Looking as if he really wanted just to lay the kid's throat open with a swift, savage cut, Jak pushed his prisoner down and around to the depression where the campfire burned low. He had the kid's right arm twisted up to his shoulder blades in a hammerlock.

Mildred helped J.B. relieve the prisoner of his pack and weapons, which they handed to Doc and Krysty. Instead of watching them, Ryan stood looking everywhere but at the scene, his longblaster cradled in his arms and his ice-blue eye alert. Jak and J.B. trussed the kid's hands behind him. Then, sitting him down gently but forcefully by the fire, they tied his ankles together with nylon line from their packs.

Krysty had laid the pack down on the other side of the fire. Doc set the weapons out next to it.

"All right," Ryan said, turning back. He leaned the rifle against his pack. "Jak, good job. You can go back on patrol now."

Jak's red eyes flared. His dislike for the captive was almost palpable.

"What have we got here?" Ryan asked the others as Jak vanished back into the dark.

"Dark night!"

J.B. was turning over the prisoner's longblaster. He had an expression of almost childlike wonder on his face.

"Kid better have a triple-good yarn, to account for why he's toting a longblaster like this one," the armorer said in reverent tones. "Ryan, do you have any idea what this is?"

Chapter Thirteen

Ryan frowned. He didn't care for games, even when his best friend played them.

"No, I don't, J.B.," he said. "But I suppose I couldn't stop you telling me without chilling you on the spot."

Unfazed, J.B. laughed. "You got that right. This long-blaster is called a DeLisle carbine."

The name tickled the back of Ryan's brain, which only made him more peevish. "Meaning what? Will you stop walking all around the muzzle and get to the damn trigger?"

J.B. tossed the piece to him. Ryan caught it handily. The weapon was shorter than his Scout, but surprisingly heavy.

"Why's the barrel so thick?" he asked, examining it.

"That's an integral suppressor," J.B. said. "True silencer, actually. That puppy shoots regular .45 ACP handblaster balls, just the same as that Para-Ordnance P45-14 the kid has—another surprisingly sweet piece to pack if he isn't a coldheart, I have to say. Because the bullet comes out less than the speed of sound, there's no crack from it. And because the bolt-action locks up tight—it's built on an old Brit Lee-Enfield .303—not much more than a whisper of sounds gets out, at all."

"I remember reading something about these," Mildred said. "Didn't the British use them for commando missions in World War II?"

"This blaster's a hundred-fifty years old?"

J.B. shook his head. "Nope. Pretty new, by the state of the metal and the furniture."

"Surely nobody on the island is manufacturing longblasters," Krysty said.

"Not manufacturing," J.B. said. "Smith job. Modifying. Like I said, somebody took an old-days Enfield action, or mebbe an Ishapore like that Oldie of the Sea guy had. Cartridges were the same width as a .45, so mostly what it amounted to was putting on a new barrel, with some holes drilled in it to let the gas bleed into the silencer. And jimmying the receiver to take magazines in the right caliber—probably just handblaster mags. Mebbe both standard for 1911s and the double stacks like the Para-Ordnance shoots. Am I right?"

The captive nodded sullenly.

Ryan handed the weapon back to the armorer, then he turned the full blue fire of his glare on the prisoner.

"All right," he said. "Who were you spying for, if it wasn't the coldhearts who torched the ville?"

The black fury that flamed in the youth's dark brown eyes sure looked real to Ryan. He felt the return glare like a punch. The kid had balls, but he also had the sense not to flare off too much, considering the situation he was in.

"I'm not spying for anybody! I just wanted food."

"Don't play games with me, boy," Ryan said. "You're

mighty young to end the night staring up at the stars. But not so young I won't put you that way if I don't hear your story now, and hear it straight!"

Mildred and Doc were going through the pack. "For a fact," Doc said, "our young guest is not carrying any food beyond some dried fish. And that is mostly crumbs, it would appear."

Krysty knelt facing the captive. She wasn't so close he could reach her with a sudden lunge. Not that he was liable to do much with his hands tied behind his back. But Krysty hadn't stayed alive by taking any more unnecessary chances than the rest of them had.

"So you aren't with the people who attacked Nuestra Señora," she said.

He shook his head wildly, and Ryan was startled to see tears drawing bright lines of reflected firelight down his dark olive cheeks. "No! Those putos killed my family, my friends! They took my sister!"

Krysty looked at Ryan in surprise. "Who attacked the ville, then?" he asked.

"It was El Guapo," the boy said. "And his fucking mutie monster henchman Tiburón. I hate them! I want to see them die twisting in their own guts!"

"Whoa! Slow down, boy," Ryan said. "Those two didn't do all that by themselves. It took an army."

"The Handsome One has an army," the boy said. "Two hundred coldhearts, mebbe more. He intends to conquer the whole island. That's why he destroyed Nuestra Señora. We wouldn't bow down to the bastard!"

"You intend to take on an entire army by yourself?"

Doc asked. He shook his head and tut-tutted. "Brave, to be sure. But scarcely practical."

"I don't care," the captive said. He was wagging his head from side to side in frustration. "How can I make you understand?"

"Tell us what happened," Krysty suggested gently.

"How do I start? There is so much."

J.B. hunkered down, across the fire from the prisoner. "You could always start at the beginning," he said. "That works."

"What's your name, kid?" Ryan asked. "You can take it from there. We got all night."

"My name is Ricardo Morales Goza," the boy began. "My parents call—called me Ricky. I was sixteen years old last month."

"Go-sa," J.B. repeated. "Kinda funny name."

"That's Spanish," Ryan said. "Your family name's Morales, right?"

Ricky nodded.

"Just like they do in Mex Land, see. All right, get on with the telling, kid."

His father was José Morales, he told them, his mother María Elena. His father was a leading merchant and trader in the ville of Nuestra Señora, while his mother ran their store in town with the help of his older sister Yamile.

Ricky grew up active and happy, with an active mind. He was always prying into things. Sometimes it got him into trouble with adults, sometimes with other kids of the ville. His sister, who was very beautiful but also could be tough at need, had helped pull his butt out of countless scrapes and never told their parents about them. They would have disapproved, for they were raising the boy to live right, by their lights.

But even Yamile, much as she adored Ricky—and he adored her—couldn't be around all the time. He was undersized as a child, had only gotten a growth spurt a year or two before. He learned to take care of himself. He became a scrapper.

He became even more adept at evading people who were pissed at him—especially the older kids who liked to bully him. Then, he began to lure them into surprises—a plank positioned to whip up and smack an unsuspecting pursuer in the face, a bucket of slops that tipped off a fence when an enemy ducked through the inviting hole that Ricky had slipped through a heartbeat before.

Seemed people were often pissed at him. As a kid on the small side, he learned attitude early on. When he started to grow out of his clothes at an increasingly rapid rate, he didn't outgrow the attitude. He still had a smart mouth on him. And perhaps not the best judgment about when and with whom to run it.

The ville folk could fight and fight hard at need. Ricky remembered a couple of times when strange ships came from the sea, filled with strange, angry men. There had been shooting then, and screaming and ships burning. Each time, the surviving pirates went away as fast as they could. And each time life quickly returned to a pleasant, peaceful routine.

Eventually Ricky's propensity for trouble caught up with him. José and María Elena despaired. They were trying to raise a good boy. They had taught him to read and reckon, and to know right from wrong. Why did he treat them that way?

His uncle, María Elena's brother Benito, intervened. An oddly built man, with a round balding head, a squat body, bowed legs and long arms, Benito was the town mechanic and smith. María Elena loved her brother, and her husband liked him and had a fair regard for him as an honest dealer. But they, like many people in the town, seemed to find Tío Benito less than completely respectable. Some of it was that he liked to drink a bit more rum or palm wine than was sometimes good for him. But largely because he was so obsessed about doing things with his hands, always making or repairing machines of all kinds. Though he held with reading, and reckoning, too, he didn't hold much with people who thought and talked all the time instead of doing.

And the things he did seemed to smack of the preoccupation with science and technology that characterized the old days, the predark days: the very things that burned the world, and brought on the Long Winter and the terrible years that followed.

But Benito was necessary and valued. And although he could be cranky he was generally well liked.

Benito volunteered to teach the errant Ricky. He'd noticed the boy's handiness. He reckoned he could find ways to put all that energy to use that didn't involve him getting into trouble and bringing shame upon his oh-so-respectable family.

Ricky's parents hesitated. That wasn't the life they intended for their only son.

They argued late into the night. It seemed to Ricky, lying in a side room on a pallet next to his softly snoring older sister and not even trying not to overhear, that they swapped sides with a certain regularity.

But he had a knack for the sort of thing his Tío Benito did. They couldn't deny that. He had no inclination to follow his mother and father as shopkeepers, though he did enjoy the yearly trade expeditions his father had taken him on every year since he was ten. But he was more interested in talking to new people and hearing their stories, in listening to the hired sec men tell tales of their rougher, readier lives, than he was in actually doing any kind of business.

It wasn't as if they didn't have a child ready and willing to take over the shop when it came time. Yamile seemed to thrive on the very things that stultified her brother. She loved the buying and selling and calculating. She was sharp, and learned fast and eagerly. She could trade tough when she needed to. Her sweet smile and blossoming beauty tended to lull even those who knew the family into underestimating her, either her keenness or her toughness. Which never worked out well for them.

She never cheated anyone. Their parents raised them better than that. But driving a hard bargain was a virtue, not a sin. And they taught her to give value for value, always. Anything else was the code of the coldheart, and to be shunned.

So it was decided. Ricky would still study and do certain chores at home and in the shop. But he would become his uncle's apprentice.

He took to it like a monkey to climbing. He loved machines, too, the way they worked, the marvelous way, almost a miracle, that disparate parts came together to function, to do things. Not just mechanical pieces, either. His uncle had a windmill, which sometimes ran noisily and annoyed the neighbors. But it fed a generator and recharged various batteries he'd collected. He taught Ricky about electricity and circuits. Not just to understand old-days electrical equipment, and repair it with existing parts when they were available—and improvise some substitute when they weren't—but to build circuits of his own. Ricky loved that, too. He soaked up knowledge and manual skills like a sponge.

And best of all—and to the despair of his parents, who after a while gave up complaining and simply chose to ignore—were the weapons. Benito taught him to hone blades, and to forge and temper them, as well. Better still, he taught him how blasters worked. And how they didn't, and what to do when they didn't. How to cut and file steel, and case-harden it, to make replacement hammers and ejectors. To wind and temper springs. To bore and cut to spec, to cut threads and tap holes for bolts. To measure, precisely and carefully.

This last didn't come naturally to Ricky, but Benito, though he never raised a hand any more than Ricky's parents had, had a tongue that cut deeper faster than any well-honed tool in the shop. Ricky learned that to enjoy the pleasure of making things—things that worked as they were supposed to; otherwise, what was the point?—he had to also learn and perform the tedious parts, without shirking or slacking.

Eventually Ricky came to understand why he needed to study boring things, too. He burned with desire to make things, to make broken things work. And the only way to learn how was to go through steps he didn't find so enjoyable. His adored yet thoroughly boring parents had been right all along.

Not that he would ever master the skills of bookkeeping.

His uncle also saw that he learned to use what he made: especially weapons. Of his many aptitudes, mechanical and electrical, the boy's greatest knack was for weaponsmithing. Tío Benito had some skill, especially with a skinning knife. He was a fair hand with blasters, too. He taught the boy what he could.

All the men and women of the ville who dealt with weapons dealt with Benito. No matter how José and María Elena felt, to keep the ville law-abiding and peaceful, the pirates had to be kept at bay. He encouraged his friends and customers to teach the boy how to handle arms—and hand-to-hand combat.

On the side, Ricky found his newfound skills useful for concocting new and marvelous traps. Not that he had much occasion to use them. He was getting bigger. And, while his fighting skills were definitely a work in progress, the local bullies had long since lost any joy in tormenting him.

Besides, the new traps he was inventing were of an exceedingly deadly nature.

He never got any chance to use any of the more lethal skills Benito's cronies and customers had imparted, but he still went out regularly on expeditions with his father and loved them more than ever. Especially when he got to talk technique with local smiths and tinkers.

His father grudgingly allowed him to handle and assess weapons he was intending to purchase. Ricky often helped him pick up broken or badly cared for weapons for little more than the cost of a fresh coconut or a mango. With Benito's skill, or increasingly even his own, these could be transformed into perfectly usable— hence salable—firearms.

But José Morales never allowed his boy to carry arms in the field. Not even a knife, beyond a Swiss Army pocketknife that had come through the shop by way of a seaborne trader. And there was seldom much actual excitement on their trips. Most of the people in this part of the island led settled lives.

The occasional fight the expeditions faced was almost always against animals of some sort, ranging from tigers to the bizarre and awful creatures that had resulted in the nickname "Monster Island." Although Ricky's mother had sadly explained that that was as much because people like his friend Ivan and his family lived in peace alongside more usual-looking folk than because of the abundance and variety of lethal mutant animals that haunted the forests, and occasionally raided farms or even the ville's fringes.

So Ricky grew up. Peaceably, prosperously, by the standards of the time, for neither he nor his family nor anyone in the ville went hungry. And, after he found his way to his uncle's shop, quite happily.

Until that morning.

Chapter Fourteen

J.B., Ryan noted with wry amusement, was staring at the boy across the fire as if he'd invented him.

"You're handy with boobies, are you?" Ryan asked.

Ricky's eyes got wide. At some point Ryan had stopped thinking of him as the captive, or even just the boy. He drank eagerly from a tin cup of water Mildred had handed him. Somewhere in there Ryan had also allowed Krysty to cut the kid's hands free, too, although he remained hobbled.

The fact was, Ryan saw no reason to doubt his story. He reckoned Ricky might be holding something back. But then, *he* would have, and he judged this boy was a sight more scrupulous and less case-hardened than he'd been at the age. He'd been a year younger, truth to tell, when an older brother's terrible treachery had cost him his eye, his family and the life he'd known as Baron Titus's privileged—if never pampered—youngest son.

"Boobies?" Ricky asked doubtfully.

"He means booby traps," Mildred said, taking back the cup with a slight twisted smile. "The kind you like to set for people chasing you. Not the other kind of boobies."

"The birds?" Ricky asked, his big eyes round and

seemingly honestly confused. Doc guffawed and slapped his thigh.

"An innocent!" he declared. "That's a rare and wondrous thing in this age. Perhaps in any, and for a fact, he would have been so even in my far more constrained and circumspect time."

"He didn't grow up during the Summer of Love, that's for sure," Mildred said, her smile turning a bit wistful.

"So, yeah," Ricky said. He was plainly adrift in their conversation, and clutching for the last solid plank that had floated by. "I guess. I did get pretty good with traps."

His face knotted like a gaudy barkeep's rag. "Not that I ever got a chance to try them out. Until today."

OVER THE PAST YEAR OR TWO, news had come that disturbed the still waters of Nuestra Señora. A leader was rising in the hills to the northwest. A man who called himself El Guapo, "The Handsome," and styled himself grandiosely as general. Once a simple bloody-handed bandit, he had managed to amass a large and growing force.

Now he claimed he was on a mission: to unite the island and save the people from the anarchy they suffered under.

Ricky had first heard about him about sixteen months previously, when José Morales's mule train reached a tiny ville in the foothills. They learned of an exceptionally large gang of coldhearts, bad enough and bold enough to attack and overrun smaller villes with ease.

From then on, news of El Guapo's conquests—and

brutality—began pouring in, first from other contacts along the trade route José followed, then into Nuestra Señora itself from travelers and traders.

A few months back a handful of men and women had arrived, following the coast on a raft. Even Ricky, who didn't know much about the sea despite living beside it, in a ville that drew much of its sustenance from it, understood that was a triple-dangerous way to travel.

The new arrivals spoke English with a funny accent that Ricky said put him in mind of Jak's. They said El Guapo's men had given them an ultimatum: surrender to his "government" or die. The people chose resistance.

The coldhearts had hit them in the middle of the night, torching their ville and boats and massacring them. As far as they knew, the five or six of them on the raft were the only survivors.

Although a big storm was approaching, the refugees had chosen to move on after only a couple of days. Soon, El Guapo and his sec boss, Tiburón, had come after them. And there was no withstanding their numbers, their firepower or their callous cruelty.

As THE BOY PAUSED to gulp down a fresh cup of water, Ryan looked around at his companions. J.B. frowned slightly. Doc had his head tipped to one side. Krysty's lips were pressed tight and colorless; her eyes were bleak. Mildred's eyes were all big and round like a startled cat's.

"So what happened next?" Ryan asked when the kid had oiled up his throat once more.

RICKY STATED THAT a couple of weeks ago a single-masted skiff had sailed into Nuestra Señora's neat little anchorage. On board was a terrified tillerman, two sec men and El Guapo himself.

Ricky had seen them bracing the mayor in the ville's plaza. He had run some cookware his uncle had mended to the García family, and was returning to the shop with a nice fresh-caught red snapper, like the ones his captors were consuming, as payment.

The crowd gathering had attracted his attention, so he hovered on the fringe to see what was going on.

Mayor Parrilla stood facing the group. The way he was sweating was unusual even for him in the midday tropical sun, and Ricky could just make out the way his eyes slid around to look everywhere but at his visitors. He was anything but happy about the confrontation.

From the mutters of adults around him, Ricky quickly understood who the visitors were. The man speaking was El Guapo's notorious sec boss, Tiburón. One glimpse and Ricky had no question where his name, Spanish for *shark,* came from: his oddly shiny gray face thrust forward into some kind of muzzle that came to a point in place of a nose. When he spoke, the words came out in a strange but carrying sibilant lisp, past what looked like rows of curved yellow teeth. He was immense, over six feet tall, bare arms fat with muscle. His sloping head was either shaved clean or naturally hairless.

He recited a list of demands in Spanish: that the ville immediately and unconditionally accept the authority of something calling itself Ejército de la Unidad Nacional—EUN for short—the Army of National Unity. That they agree to trade only with communities and individuals who had likewise sworn allegiance to El Guapo, and pay a tariff on every commercial transaction plus such other taxes as deemed necessary. That they give up their arms. And that they send regular drafts of young men and women to serve the army.

That made Mayor Parrilla sweat so furiously that it visibly weighed down his famed mustache. His Adam's apple bobbed up and down his fat gullet, and his eyes swept furiously right and left.

He clearly wanted to cave in. Though Ricky's parents were avid supporters of the mayor, and his uncle disdainfully refused to discuss or even consider politics of any sort, most people, when they spoke of the mayor at all, did so in anything but flattering terms.

The band of eight leading citizens, men and women, who stood right behind the mayor fairly bristled with the weapons El Guapo wanted them to give up. Ricky decided they had to be there, not to guard against Handsome's bandits—if they started any violence, such a small group would stand no chance of getting back to their boat alive—but to put some much-needed steel in Parrilla's spine.

But Parrilla gathered up his nerve, puffed himself up to full height and announced in a ringing voice that he had to unconditionally refuse such outrageous demands. Nuestra Señora would never surrender to coldhearts.

At his words, El Guapo's face had turned first maroon, then white. Laying eyes on the bandit chief for the first time, Ricky couldn't understand why he was called the Handsome One. He was anything but. His features were distorted horribly into unnatural grooves and ridges, and he seemed to have no nose but rather a hole in his face. But even at this distance Ricky could tell that, unlike his congenitally grinning sec boss, he wasn't a mutant. His disfigurement wasn't the result of birth, but of some prolonged work by someone with a blade and maybe something very hot. It was scar tissue, nothing less.

Tiburón never raised that deceptively gentle voice of his. "Forever is a long time, Señor Mayor," he said. "But it is something those who oppose us get to experience, quite soon. Are you sure you won't reconsider?"

Parrilla turned to look openly at the citizen delegation standing behind him. If they were afraid of the bandit lord and his mutie henchman they showed it by jutting their jaws and holding their blasters even higher.

"I will not," Parrilla said to the coldhearts, in the voice of a man sentencing himself to death.

"So be it," El Guapo declared in a ringing baritone. His voice, at least, really was handsome. He turned and stalked toward the harbor. Tiburón and the two unspeaking bodyguards followed.

When an excited Ricky brought the news to his uncle, the man's response astonished him.

"They should have chilled them all when they had the chance," he spat. "El Guapo and his vermin. That misguided act of mercy will come back to bite them on their asses. Bite us all on the asses. Mark my words, boy. Mark them well."

Ricky had been too dumbfounded to respond. In learning to fight he had wandered pretty far astray from his parents' path of nonviolence. But they had imbued their gentle values in him. The idea of killing anyone in cold blood sickened him to the core. Even a notorious coldheart leader and his right-hand man, both of whose hands were drenched in the blood of hundreds, if the stories were halfway true.

But, despite the sensation the incident caused over the next few days with the debate whispered in workrooms and shouted in the cantina, once the coldhearts had returned to their boat and sailed back the way they came, lots of nothing happened. After a week the incident was forgotten.

THE FIRST THING that penetrated Ricky's brain was his father's pleading voice. "Please, take whatever you want. But spare my family, at least!"

Sitting bolt upright in the next room, the little space he shared with his sister, Ricky realized that he'd been awakened by a gunshot when others popped in quick but ragged succession from several different directions.

People screamed.

He heard strange, quiet laughter, like a snake among leaves. "We'll take what we want no matter what, little man. But we came for your miserable lives. You dared to defy El Guapo and now must serve as lesson for everyone."

Ricky heard his mother's voice rise in a scream. It was cut off abruptly with a meaty, moist thud.

He flung himself up from his woven-straw pallet. As he ran for the warped plywood door, he heard a strange drawn-out gurgle. And then the unmistakable shrieks of his adored sister, Yamile.

He burst into the store's main room. A horrific tableau froze him in his tracks. Ricky's mother lay sprawled facedown on the planks in a pool of blood. By the front door, two bearded men held his father's arms as the huge shark-headed mutie, Tiburón, slowly shoved a machete into his belly.

Yamile writhed in the grip of another big intruder, holding her off the floor in a bear hug from behind. A fifth man was falling with one hand clapped to a pair of scissors buried to the grips at the junction of neck and chest. A pulsing red rope of blood arched between his futile fingers.

"Bitch!" snarled the man who held Yamile.

"Don't hurt her!" Tiburón snapped without turning. "She goes straight to El Guapo."

Without waiting for his sister's captor to respond, Ricky grabbed the nearest item off a nearby shelf and sprang at the intruder. He threw it, a quart jar of some sort of preserves. It struck the man in the forehead.

The man's eyes rolled up and his head snapped back. Yamile whipped her own head back, catching him under the chin and making his knees wobble. Then, slamming her bare heel up into his balls, she broke free and darted for the door.

"Run, Yami!" Ricky shouted. He jumped on her tormentor's back and grabbed him around the neck, trying for a choke hold. But even with the man half-stunned and with the breath blown out of him by the nut shot, it was like trying to wrestle an angry bear.

"Idiots," Tiburón roared. He drove the huge knife to the guardless hilt in José Morales's belly and twisted. Ricky's father screamed shrilly as his intestines flopped around his legs onto the floor of the store to which he'd devoted his life.

"Fucking incompetents," Tiburón raged. "Stop her, or I'll do worse to you than I did to this prick!"

With Ricky's father now thrashing on the floor, his kicking legs getting steadily more entangled in the slippery loops of his own guts, the pair who'd been holding his arms raced after Yamile. One tackled her across the threshold. The other landed on top of her.

"Don't hurt her, either, you idiots," Tiburón roared. "Oh, fuck me, I have to do everything myself."

Ricky still clung to the other man's back. Despairing of ever getting a stranglehold around the tree-trunk throat, he hung on with one arm and clawed for the man's eyes with the other. The man batted ineffectually at him, unable to bring his greater strength to bear against a foe clinging to his back like an angry monkey. Instead he teetered in circles, howling as if it were *his* big belly that had been ripped open.

A blur of motion caught the corner of Ricky's eye. Tiburón had carried a longblaster slung over his muscle-wedge back. Now, as his goon swung the boy toward him, he was slamming the steel-shod butt at Ricky's face.

Ricky turned his face aside, and the blow crashed into his temple. Red sparks exploded through his skull, and then a sort of black cloud swam up between him and his senses.

He was aware of falling to the floor. It seemed as if he felt it, somehow, at long distance, like hearing faint voices from far away. When he finally hit, he scarcely felt the impact, although he distinctly noticed that his body bounce-flopped three times.

Through the roiling nausea in his belly, he heard voices, growling and distorted.

"—got the slut, Tiburón," a man was saying. "What about the brat? He's a little undersized, but looks like he's old enough to draft."

"We need more blaster fodder," a second voice said. It was strained with effort. Ricky sensed vaguely it belonged to the coldheart who'd recaptured his sister.

His blood sizzled with the need to rise up and help her, but he couldn't make his limbs respond to his will. No matter how fiercely he tried.

"Let me finish the little prick," rumbled a voice that had to belong to the bear he'd been tormenting.

"No," the shark-faced man said with finality. "He's damaged goods and probably going to die, anyway. The fire'll finish him if the head shot doesn't. We have no time to waste, Mono. We still got to make sure what happens to these fuckers shows the whole fucking island what it means to dick with the Army of National Unity."

Still struggling mentally to force his body to rise and fight, Ricky heard the coldhearts leave.

Then, the world went black.

Chapter Fifteen

"Nope," Mildred said. She rocked back on her haunches and gratefully clicked off the flashlight. Pumping the flywheel that powered it made her hand cramp something fierce, but functioning batteries were scarcer than kind hearts these days. "No concussion. No sign of subdural hematoma, either, but then again, if your brain was bleeding, you'd be dead now, most likely. So you didn't actually pass out, I'm betting. Did you?"

Ricky shook his head. "I lay stunned for a while. I felt sick and dizzy for a long time, and when I tried to get up the first few times, I fell right back down." He sounded ashamed. "But then I smelled smoke and heard flames. The coldhearts had set the shop on fire, as Tiburón said they would. So I crawled first to my parents' bodies, then out into the street."

"What happened with you not being able to see, then?"

He laughed, half wild, half bitter. "That was blood in my eyes. When I rubbed my face, I could see again!"

He shook his head. "My family. My father was dead, rest his soul. So was my mother. My sister was gone. I failed. I was useless! But I will get her back. And I will chill the shark-toothed mutie, and that scar-faced bastard

El Guapo. I swear on my parents' funeral pyre, which was our store, my home, which the monsters burned around them."

"You have nothing to be ashamed of," J.B. said. "You did all you could. More than a lot of grown men could have—or would have."

"So what happened next?" Ryan said. "Where'd the fancy blasters come from?"

"I ran to my uncle's shop, down by the waterfront. The streets were filled with blood and walled with fire. Having killed and burned as much as they could the invaders had moved on to a different part of the ville.

"The shop hadn't burned. My uncle lay dead on the floor. I counted more than twenty bullet wounds without even moving his body.

"But he had sold his life expensively. Six coldhearts lay dead around him. He had continued to chill them even as they pumped him full of bullets. He only let himself die when the slide locked back on his *pistola* and his enemies were down!"

"So his shop wasn't looted?"

The boy grinned. Even as she was getting up, Mildred recoiled a little from the look in his eye and the nature of his smile. The evil mutant sec boss wasn't the only one around with a touch of the shark in him.

"Not then. Only later, at even greater cost. I retrieved Tío Benito's Para-Ordnance, as you see, and scavenged such magazines and bullets as I could find. I found the beloved DeLisle longblaster he had made with his own two hands, untouched in its hiding place beneath a worktable. So I grabbed a backpack and threw what I could inside. There wasn't much food. It doesn't keep well in our climate.

"And then, before I left, I prepared some surprises. Because I knew that even though the coldhearts weren't much interested in loot, they'd be bound to check my uncle's shop to make sure they had grabbed up all the blasters and ammo it contained."

"'Surprises,'" J.B. echoed. His voice sounded eager as a little kid's.

Ricky nodded. "I heard the explosions as I crept out of the ville, saw a yellow fireball roll up. I even heard the screams of some of those caught by the flames. The coldhearts were *very* surprised, my friends. Some, at least, for the very last time."

The wicked light died out of his dark eyes. His thin shoulders slumped.

"But it was only the beginning of *mi venganza*. Many more must pay the price for what they did to my family, my friends, my ville. And I will free Yami, or die in the attempt!"

Ryan stood facing him with his hands on his hips, then he shook his head. "So, what do we do with you?"

"Chill!" an angry voice said from the darkness to the side of the hollow.

"Jak!" Ryan snapped. "You're supposed to be on lookout. If you're listening to this, you aren't listening for trouble."

"Okay," Jak said. Ryan sensed motion. The boy was

slinking away and wanted them all to know it. Otherwise he'd have moved as quietly as a cloud across the moon.

Of course nothing would keep him from slipping right back to eavesdrop. Ryan frowned furiously and felt his cheeks get hot.

"Back to the problem at hand. What about this kid?"

"Take me with you!" the boy piped up.

"Why would you want that?" Krysty asked. "You're determined to find your sister. That's not something we're going to get involved in. You must know that."

For a moment he sat huddled and frowning. "You're going to help me find her, anyway," he said at last.

"Meaning what?" Mildred asked.

J.B. chuckled. "Meaning a group as big and well armed as us is going to attract the attention of this Handsome guy's coldhearts, sooner or later. Right, kid?"

Ricky nodded.

Mildred sensed there was more to it than that. There always was. She suspected the kid was shit-scared—he'd be crazy if he weren't. He was out on his own in the big, bad world for the first time, thrown there in the most traumatic way possible. He might be handy with weapons and tools, but she didn't see much evidence he had any skill at all at living off the land. Even a land as lush as this one.

In ways he was the anti-Jak. That made her smile. As fond as she was of the albino teen, that was not an altogether bad thing.

"So what do you bring to the deal?" Ryan asked.

The question caught Mildred off guard. He's actually

considering it, she thought. She'd taken for granted that he'd blow the kid off.

She watched as Ricky looked around at the circle of faces. With Jak's lean white-wolf features absent, none of them was hostile. Hers wasn't. Heck, she admired what the kid had done. He stood up for his family, and even if it wasn't bright to fling himself at a bunch of big coldhearts bristling with blasters, it was the right thing to do.

Even in the Deathlands, there were things that trumped sheer survival. Sometimes.

"Well, you're looking for something, right?" Ricky said.

Suddenly, the looks on the faces turned toward him got very intent.

"How do you mean, Ricky?" Krysty asked, delicately and clearly, before Ryan could get the notion of just booting the kid till he spat out where he'd learned that.

The boy shook his head and tipped it to the side, like a confused dog. "What else are you doing here? Why'd you come to the island if you weren't looking for something?"

Mildred had to grin openly at that. In her day, of course, Puerto Rico, along with the rest of the Caribbean, had been a prime destination where tourists were looking for nothing but sun and sea and a good time. These days tourism was barely a word. Certainly not a thing.

"Fair enough," J.B. said, rocking back. Of all of them, he seemed the most positively inclined toward the newcomer, which Mildred realized was only natural. With his fondness for weapons and tinkering—and lethal surprises—Ricky was cast from the same mold as the armorer himself.

"So what is it? Because I can help you find it."

Everybody looked at Ryan. The redoubts' existence was a vital secret, though at times not always much of one. The strongholds the government constructed before the Big Nuke were sometimes discovered and plundered. Usually when factors beyond the builders' control or scope of planning had broken them open, during the war and the colossal earthquakes, or the turbulent decades following.

But their real value lay in their deep dark secret, the mat-trans gateways. Few people these days knew of their existence.

They were the companions' ace in the hole. The fact that they could "jump" from one gateway to another in a different redoubt, was the only reason they'd escaped countless terrible situations with their hides still intact.

But to her surprise, even as Ryan frowned in consideration, it was Krysty who spoke up. "Why do you think you can help us find what we're looking for, whatever it is?"

"I've been over lots of the island," Ricky said. "This part of it, anyway. South-central. I know a lot of the people and villes. And many of the dangers, where the worst monsters are. I can help you get around. I can help you talk to people who know how to find what you're looking for. Really, I can! Or, anyway, people who know people who can help you."

He was clearly getting worked up by the prospect. Well, Mildred thought, he seemed like a pretty bright kid. And you'd have to be stupid not to see how hooking up with the companions could augment your odds of survival.

Ryan looked at the boy for a moment, his eye narrowed. Then he looked around at the others. Ryan was the unspoken leader and that was that. Nobody wanted it any different. But one thing that made him good at leading was that, when circumstances allowed, he gave everybody his or her say.

He was also sharp enough to realize that his companions were sharp, too, with different skill sets and knowledge and outlooks, and they could see things he couldn't. Everybody pulled their weight. It was how they kept one another alive.

"It would appear the boy's cooperation could facilitate our search," Doc said, rubbing his chin.

"Can we trust him?" Mildred asked. "I mean, he *was* trying to steal our food."

"It's not like we haven't stolen our share of grub," J.B. said. "Dark night, Mildred, the kid's hungry. You do what you can to survive."

She shrugged. "True enough. Maybe I'm still the naive one in the bunch, but he doesn't strike me the sort to stick a knife in our ribs while we sleep."

Krysty smiled. "He knows better than to try," she said. "Don't you, Ricky?"

Ricky swallowed and nodded. "That white-haired kid would spit me like a wild pig if I tried anything."

His eyes, already big, got larger. "In fact, he might do it, anyway!"

"If Ryan tells him to lay off," J.B. said, stirring the dying fire with a stick, then tossing it into the rising yellow flames, "Jak'll lay off."

He looked up at his friend, who continued to stand with arms crossed over his chest. "How about it, Ryan? What do you say?"

"Haven't heard from you yet, J.B.," Ryan said with a thin smile. "Though I don't suppose we need to. If you looked in the mirror twenty years ago, you'd see him. Except he's twice as good-looking as you ever were."

J.B. chuckled. "That's a fact. Except about the looks. He's *triple* better looking than I ever was."

Mildred couldn't resist patting his hard thigh and grinning. "I like you just fine the way you are, John," she said. "Useful as opposed to ornamental."

He blushed red to the roots of his hair, which, she had to admit to herself, was the reaction she'd hoped for.

"So everybody's ace with letting the kid tag along?" Ryan asked.

"Except Jak," Mildred said.

Ryan scratched an ear. "Can't really argue his point. We'll find what we're looking for easier with help from somebody knows the land and the locals. And the sooner we do, the better I like it. So, yeah, kid. You can tag along. For now, anyway. Don't fuck up."

"Thanks," the boy said. Suddenly he grinned. "Thanks! And, uh, can I have something to eat?"

When Krysty handed him a mango, he burst into tears. Everybody else pretended not to notice.

Mildred wondered how long the kid would be able to hold out. She hoped they wouldn't live to regret the choice to let him join. Of course, there was no way to tell in advance. It had been no less true in the world she'd been born and raised in: the only certainty was that one day you'd wind up with dirt hitting you in the eyes. Nobody got out of this life alive.

But the Deathlands always found a way of reminding you of the fact. Good and hard, and often.

Chapter Sixteen

"No. I don't know of any forbidden or secret places."

The guy looked normal enough: tall, olive-skinned, black hair, rail-skinny. All except for the split tongue that darted in and out of his mouth and made him lisp.

The morning sunlight was breaking where it hit the shallow water of the rice paddy. Its splinters flew up with considerable force into Ryan's eye.

The paddies lay in a broad, shallow valley, east along the coast and inland from the wreck of Nuestra Señora. Ryan wanted to keep clear of the actual coast. He couldn't know all of their pursuers had gone up in the explosion of the *Wailer*. In fact he knew they all *didn't,* given the encounter with Silver-Eye Chris and his two companions on the trail out of town. Where three had survived, more might. And there might be other ships with Sea Wasps on them who bore a grudge—or, for that matter, Monitors seeking the "official" vengeance of the Syndicate that ran Nueva Tortuga, and whose dick Ryan and friends had given an almighty tug.

Anyway, as a general rule, the redoubts seemed to be mostly inland. But this little ville, a huddle of grass huts upstream from the paddies, was handy, and had been on good terms with Nuestra Señora and Ricky's father. So it made sense to start their quest for information here.

The spokesman looked thoughtful. Other workers were starting to wander over. Ryan guessed that rice farming was a pretty slow-paced affair, though the labor looked backbreaking. Everybody seemed eager for a break and the diversion the visitors represented.

"What do you seek?" asked a wrinkled, elderly woman with jumbled brown teeth showing in a face-splitting grin. "Treasure? So do we all!"

"If we knew where treasure was," a slightly younger-looking man said, "would we be out here working in the sun and wading in shit all day?" And everybody laughed, including the taller, straighter spokesman, as if that was the best joke ever.

Ryan set his chin and made his mouth stretch slightly in what could pass for a smile. Mebbe. For a fact, even for him the stench of feces, so dense as to be almost visible, was nearly overpowering.

Human shit.

The organic fertilizer was why Mildred, still the most fastidious of the crew, stood carefully perched on one of the little soil ridges that divided the paddies. The rest, like Ryan, stood stoically in the midst of the stinking brown water, ignoring the clumps that occasionally nuzzled their ankles like frogs, carried by the flow from the irrigation ditches that led from the ville's communal cesspool. Even Doc, with his gentle and almost aristocratic upbringing, paid the sewage no mind. But then, being forced to wallow in human shit was one of the less degrading things forced on him by the baron who had captured him after the whitecoats dumped him in the here and now.

"If I had to guess," the spokesman lisped, rubbing his clean-shaved chin, "I'd say you should look up north in the mountains."

"That's right!" A chorus of agreement fluttered up like a flock of gulls. "The mountains are definitely where you should look."

"It only stands to reason," the elderly woman said, nodding sagely. "Odd things are always going on in the mountains. Mountains are full of secret places."

Ryan cocked an eyebrow at Krysty, who stood beside him. She quirked a grin and a slight one-shoulder shrug back. It made a certain sense in Ryan's gut. They often *did* find hidden things in the mountains, redoubts in particular.

"But there could be a problem with that," the tall spokesman said thoughtfully.

"And what might that be, my good man?" Doc asked.

The man's tongue slipped out to lick his lips. "Why, that's where most of the monsters live, of course."

"So, WHAT USE FANCY GUN, island boy?" Jak asked derisively.

"The DeLisle, you mean?" Ricky asked.

They were trudging into the foothills inland, per the advice of the folk in the nameless little rice-farming ville. They followed a narrow valley with frequent outcroppings of jagged black lava rock that climbed steeply from the alluvial plain. The walls were thickly furred in green brush. Birds called, quarreled and occasionally burst out in brightly colored flight.

"Yeah," Jak said. "So, shoots quiet. So? Anyway, can shoot?"

Krysty hung near the two youths, who walked in front of the file, keeping an eye on the interaction between Jak and the newcomer. Ricky had, she knew, made a decent impression on Ryan during the meet with the farmers. He made introductions and then stood back, not trying to push himself forward and be the center of things, the way a kid his age might. His dad, she reckoned, had taught him well.

Of course, now it remained to see if he was *too* reticent. A person had to have some spice to keep upright in this world. Especially in a crew that led the sort of lives Ryan's did.

Ricky turned his head to look at the white-haired youth. Krysty read the bafflement in his body language before she caught his uncomprehending frown. He hadn't gotten used to Jak's miserly ways with words yet.

But the way Jak's ruby eyes were fixed on him brought the message home quick.

"I guess I can shoot some," he said with a certain pride.

"Why not show us?" Ryan said, closing up to Krysty's left from behind. "Up ahead there, where the granite juts out and the other valley flows into this one."

"Those monkeys?" Mildred asked. She followed Ryan. Behind her walked Doc, smiling vaguely and humming to himself. J.B. brought up the rear, shotgun in hand and eyes well skinned for danger.

"Mutie monkeys," Jak hissed, stopping short.

Halting, mainly so as not to walk into either of the two boys, Krysty peered up the path. They were headed pretty much north right now. She had to raise her left hand to shade her eyes from the sun. It was going to disappear behind the ridge to the west before two more hours passed, plunging the valley into early mountain twilight.

She'd noticed the monkey troop perching on the rugged gray boulders sticking out from the near side of the confluence of valleys. They were big ones, though not huge. Rhesus monkeys, she thought. Big enough, smart enough—mean enough—to threaten humans in a pack. There were perhaps twenty of them. Could be a problem, she acknowledged.

And looking closely through the glare, she saw Jak was right, as he usually was about the world of the senses. The creatures had what looked like yokes of spines bristling up from their shoulders and backs, reminiscent of porcupine quills. Even at this range, a good sixty or seventy yards, she could tell they were heavier than usual, and bleached white.

"Monkeys with bone spikes?" Mildred said. "You have *got* to be kidding me."

"If those spikes are bone," Doc said, "they cannot be firmly attached to the skeleton. Note how the beasts seemed to lower or erect them when interacting with one another."

It was true, Krysty quickly saw. Though Doc's blue eyes looked weak, they were still quite sharp, more befitting his actual age than his apparent one. And while he didn't have Jak's overwhelming intuition for the natural world—or at least the wild one, since so much of today's world couldn't be called remotely natural—he had an encyclopedic knowledge of it.

Usually Krysty felt far more in sympathy with Jak's perspective. Sometimes she saw the use of Doc's, though.

"Wonder if they can shoot those things," J.B. said. "Like porky-pines do."

"That's just an old wives' tale," Mildred said promptly. "Porcupines can't shoot their quills."

Krysty looked back to see J.B. take off his glasses and polish them with a handkerchief. He showed her a bland smile. "You haven't come up against the porcupines I have."

Mildred blinked at him, then she scowled. "John," she accused, "you're making fun of me."

The armorer put his specs back on and blinked at her through the round lenses, the very image of innocence.

"Why, Millie," he said. "Would I do a thing like that?"

"Yes."

"Normally I'd chase them off myself with this," Ryan said, raising the Scout Tactical longblaster he carried. "But I'm interested to see what you and that Denial of yours can do."

"DeLisle." J.B. and Ricky corrected him in unison.

"Whatever," Ryan said. "Show us, kid."

Ricky took his time cinching up his left forearm in

the carbine's shooting sling. From his hesitant posture, Krysty guessed he was wondering whether to kneel or sit to get a more stable shooting platform. Then, straightening his back slightly, he brought the longblaster's buttplate to his shoulder. It had adjustable iron sights, but the boy didn't bother with them. One way or another it wasn't a prohibitively difficult shot for a longblaster, even one as short as his. Although she wondered if the fact it shot a handblaster round made a difference.

Clearly—at least to her—Ricky guessed he was most likely to impress his audience if he took the shot standing up. Boys, she thought.

Then with a grin, she mentally amended that to men. They never grew out of it entirely. Not even Ryan, although he'd long since learned to rein in the urge to showboat. The one exception she could call to mind was J.B. He didn't seem the show-off type. As fond as he was of Mildred—and the rest of them, of course—he was his most demanding audience. Nobody else would hold him to anywhere near the standards of skill he demanded of himself.

When Ricky fired the stubby carbine, it made a muted thump, like a fist hitting someone's thigh. Krysty didn't see how hard it kicked or how the boy handled it. She was focused on the mutant monkeys sitting and grooming one another downrange.

The biggest of them sat a bit above and apart from the rest, eyeing the landscape with stern grandeur. He was apparently somewhat myopic, since he gave no sign of spotting the humans yet. The wind blew down the valley, bringing the musky tang of the monkey tribe to Krysty's nostrils, rather than human smell to him.

The troop leader's body jerked as if a thought had struck him.

But it had been something a little harder than a thought, if perhaps not so fast. He pitched off his rock, to land on a flat granite ledge twelve feet below. The wind brought the plop a beat later. It was only a little quieter than the carbine had been.

The other monkeys sitting on the outcrop looked at one another, right through the space where the pack leader's butt and shortish tail had been a breath before. They did an almost comical take of surprise before turning almost as one to stare down at the fallen alpha, lying on his face with his rump slightly elevated and clearly a chill.

Krysty heard the muties chitter to one another. One hopped down to sniff at the fallen leader.

The DeLisle thumped again. The inquisitive monkey flopped onto its far side. It beat the air with fists and feet for a moment, then went limp.

Krysty looked back to see that Ricky had the shrouded barrel of his piece back down online from the recoil. He was jacking the action to chamber a cartridge for the next shot.

"Okay," Jak said a little glumly. "Not bad."

Ricky shrugged and grinned shyly. "Thanks."

"Not bad at all," Ryan said.

Ricky looked at him, a little anxiously. "Is that, uh, enough?" he asked. "I don't— I don't want to shoot more than I have to."

Even Krysty half expected Ryan to sneer at his soft-heartedness. Instead, he proved that you could never take the man for granted—and made her love him all over again.

"Only a mad thing chills more than he needs to," he said. "And only a stupe wastes ammo."

"Bastards're still in our road, though, Ryan," J.B. said.

Mildred laughed. "They don't have any idea what happened to their friends," she said. "Shit, they don't even know we're here yet." Then she winced as a blaster shot cracked off nearby.

Krysty blinked as the side-blast from Ryan's SIG-Sauer smacked the side of her face. He'd drawn his Steyr and fired a shot in the air.

As the echoes chased each other up and down the green-and-black valley walls, the monkeys turned to stare at the humans. With a swirl of tails they vanished, as if into the rocks.

"They *parlez-vous* blaster," J.B. said in satisfaction.

"Most things do," Ryan said, "that live."

To Ricky, who was looking an obvious question at him, he said, "My nine ball's easier to find than your .45. What're we standing here for? Let's move, people."

He holstered the piece, grabbed the wrist of his long-blaster stock and strode forward with long legs eating up the sloping trail. The two boys had to scamper to avoid him brushing them off the narrow path.

"Are those unsightly creatures edible, young man?" Doc asked.

"Huh? Yeah. Not bad. Mebbe a little gamier than, you know, normal monkey."

"Muties!" Jak spit. "Not eat muties. *Tainted*."

"That's more for the rest of us, then," J.B. said jovially. Coming up alongside Mildred he fetched her a comradely slap on the shoulder. "Isn't that right, Millie?"

She blanched and swallowed hard. "Whatever you say, J.B."

As they neared the juncture of the two valleys, Jak took off at an angle, up the slope to their right, vanishing briefly into the brush before reaching the top. He reappeared a moment later to wave an all clear before melting out of sight again.

As they came up on the dead monkeys, a chunk of dirt and dead grass flew up from right beside one of the little lifeless bodies.

A moment later the unmistakable crack of a big-bore longblaster reached Krysty's ears.

Someone was shooting at them!

Chapter Seventeen

Ryan brought up his Steyr and snapped off a shot. If it hit near the party of heavily armed men who had just rounded a bluff a hundred yards up the valley's far side, he didn't see. Much as he hated to waste ammo, the other side had the edge on them right now. If he made even one of them hurry a shot, that was one thin sliver of survival his burning a round had bought them.

Fireblast, bad luck that I was looking the wrong way when they spotted us first, he thought. But that was as far as that went. Regret was useless.

Especially now, when only action, fast and hard, could save their hides.

"Up the other valley!" he shouted to his companions. "Fast!"

"What about you?" Krysty asked.

"I'll hold them!" He got a flash sight picture through the sights and fired.

The coldheart went down, but Ryan wasn't fooled. The man was spooked, not scared. He got the sense he had pulled a fraction to his left, probably stinging the enemy with a burst of black lava chips from the rocks beside him.

"Go!" he shouted again.

He sensed the others in rapid motion. He knew they didn't like leaving him to face at least a dozen well-heeled enemies all on his lonesome.

But they did what he said, and it wasn't as if he planned to sacrifice himself covering their escape.

Ryan ducked behind the outcrop the mutant monkeys had been sitting on as a flurry of bullets kicked up more dust from the trail. One of the dead monkeys rolled over as slugs slammed into it.

More bullets cracked off the hard granite and screamed as they tumbled away across the valley. Ryan found a sort of natural step that allow him to pop up, prop an elbow on jutting stone and brace for a quick shot. He snapped down the built-in folding bipod and went for it.

This time he used the long eye-relief scope, mounted well forward, among other things, to keep it from stamping a bloody circle around an unwary shooter's eye. It wasn't high-power, but was more than enough.

Especially now. He lined up the pointed bottom post on the chest of a man standing bolt upright firing an M-16 from the shoulder. Then he lowered his aim point to midgut. He didn't owe this bastard an easy out, and he wanted the dude's buddies to think deep, unhappy thoughts about what they were doing.

He squeezed off the shot. The lightweight polymer stock kicked him in the shoulder. The short muzzle rose sharply.

Before the longblaster settled back on its bipod he'd chambered a new round. Even as the weapon bucked up he'd had his eye out of the glass, looking for his next target. There were at least twenty coldhearts in sight now, most firing their blasters with no idea of what they were shooting at. Shots crackled down the valley to his left so hard and fast it sounded like a big bonfire built of green wood.

He didn't bother glancing at his first target. He'd aimed so close to center of mass it'd take a serious miss not to hit flesh somewhere. The coldheart's screams told him he'd planted the bullet in the man's belly, where he wanted it.

He shot another enemy. As the Scout recoiled, Ryan saw the man jump and drop his rifle; he guessed he'd winged an arm.

The one-eyed man ducked. Taking two shots in a row from the same position was crowding it. These bastards had ammo to burn and were doing just that.

The rough rule of thumb Trader had taught him, long ago and far away, was that past 150 yards, even a lot of people shooting at you full-auto would hit you only by your own bad luck. Unless they were shooting an MG on some kind of mount, in which case you were already in dreck to your neck.

Unfortunately, inside about 100 yards, where these coldhearts were blasting from, the odds of one of them getting lucky went way up. Especially once they all got dialed into the general vicinity of where their target was.

Not all of them had autoblasters. Even if they were the Army of National Unity—and if they weren't, El Guapo and his people had lots worse things to worry about than Ryan and his band of unwilling armed tourists—it was unlikely they could scrape together enough to arm everybody with automatic weapons. He could hear the louder, flatter barks of bigger-bore blasters as he scouted quickly for another sniping position. Single shots meant bolt-action blasters or even lever actions.

Most of the coldhearts with nonautomatic weapons didn't aim any better than the ones rocking and rolling balls-out. Even if they could, it took more presence of mind than most random sec men had to mark their shots carefully when the hot sizzle of the chase was firing up their blood. Even when no one was shooting back.

But Ryan wasn't about to take it for granted they didn't have at least one good marksman. Or one with the self-control to line up his piece on the spot where Ryan had been shooting from, and wait to pick him off when he stuck his head up for another shot, like a Deathlands dirt farmer popping a prairie dog out of his bean field.

He didn't see an appealing platform for a fast and steady shot, short of the mostly flat top of the outcrop. He scrambled up the slope beside it, then flung himself belly-first against the sun-hot stone. It cut into his skin through his shirt as he brought the bipod down on the top. He could smell rank monkey shit and felt sliminess between him and the rock.

Even as he'd sprung into position, he'd kept his eye on the enemy, trusting his flash impression of his destination and his superb body control to bring him safely where he needed to be. They did, with a little scrabbling of his right boot when the first foothold rolled out of place from beneath. It was the sort of thing he could correct without looking, by feel, and did.

He was already lining up a shot on a coldheart with an armband who was furiously waving his men forward and shouting. That made him an ideal target.

Because the coldheart had his head stretched around on his neck, and the motion of his arm was rhythmic, his head was a more stable target than people's heads usually were. Ryan lined up the post on his right temple and squeezed off.

This time he watched the dark spray puff out the far side of the man's head as the weapon reared up. The coldheart dropped like an empty sack.

A couple of men raced forward along the trail leading down the valley's far side. Some ran down into the valley itself, which was neither steep nor deep, with only a little splash of stream running through it. Those could eventually be trouble, but not for a while. The hill he'd seen Krysty and the others go up was taller and steeper than most around here.

Ryan dropped back almost to the trail, set up on the first rock he'd used as a brace, shot the lead of the two men running toward him. The guy sprawled face-first, his longblaster flying from his hands to bounce down toward the stream. He snapped a second shot at the guy's partner, but missed. The second man had flung himself into the brush on the far side.

Even without the one leader type Ryan had chilled, somebody was starting to coordinate fire toward Ryan's rock clump. It was still more enthusiastic than accurate.

He could hear ricochets zinging in all directions as well as shots continuing to crack past in open air, missing the outcrop completely.

His companions were likely safe by now. They knew how to find cover. With the added advantage of a guide who knew the country, they should have either found a spot where the pursuers would have a hard time finding them, or holed up somewhere they could defend.

Still, Ryan was reluctant to quit his sniping and follow. This seemed to be a young army. He still hadn't seen more than twenty guys. But he'd chilled a couple at least, and wounded several more. That was high casualties for even the stoniest of coldhearts to absorb. It would normally make them go to ground and wait for him to go away, if not just turn tail and run.

Maybe this Handsome guy had a stern sense of discipline. But even if it involved getting boiled slow in a pot, deferred punishment seldom trumped having bullets crack close by your ears. Especially while your buddy moaned and howled and clutched at a belly full of guts turned to bloody pulp.

They had to break, and soon. It was just a matter of keeping up the pressure, bouncing between spots and taking quick shots until they just plain had enough. Which Ryan continued to do as he held the internal debate with himself.

Oh, and not get shot. There was that. If nothing else, the hypothetical supersharpshooter didn't seem to have made the trip today. They were all pretty crap shots.

I just don't want this many of them on the trail of

Krysty and the others, he thought, as he popped up over the top of the outcrop and snapped off a quick blast. This time he saw blood fly from the leg of a kneeling shooter, who squalled, grabbed himself and fell.

Ryan slid all the way to the bottom again. He crouched behind the rock, catching his breath. And suddenly there were bullets cracking all around him.

He sucked into a tight crouch as sharp shards of lava rock stung his face and hands. Ricochets screamed. He felt something tug the left shoulder of his shirt.

The firestorm paused. Ryan looked up to see a couple of shooters silhouetted atop the far side of the valley. Another man stood a few feet away. He and one of the others were aiming longblasters in Ryan's direction. The third man, up on the ridge, was half-turned, frantically signaling someone behind him with his right hand.

Now Ryan knew why the coldheart squad was so hard-core in the face of casualties: there were more of the bastards.

He swung the Scout to his shoulder, acquired his target, then fired at the man slightly down the slope as the muzzle of the coldheart's longblaster sprouted yellow fire.

He felt a sting on his left cheek as the shot cracked by. The coldheart dropped as his left shin was plucked right out from under him. He tumbled down the ridge, losing his bolt-action longblaster as he did so.

Ryan threw himself into a desperate rear somersault away from the outcrop that had sheltered him from the first wave of enemies. He was deep in trouble, and he didn't need anyone to tell him. Even as the two still on their feet on the far slope blasted rock splinters from the space he'd just occupied, he could hear the triumphant cries of the first wave as they surged forward.

He'd gone and gotten himself flanked. It was about as tight a crack as a person would fit in. The odds were long against him getting himself out.

If he tried bolting to cover, or straight up the hill, he was asking for a bullet in the back, which would leave his companions at the mercy of their foes. He wouldn't do that.

All he could do now was to sell his ass dearly and discourage pursuit.

He fired again before he came out of his roll, the blaster bucking in his hands like a live thing. Once again he hoped to throw off the coldhearts' aim long enough for him to take down at least one more.

The shot flew wide, as expected. As he came up to a kneeling position and raised the longblaster to his shoulder, he saw something that hit him like a round in the gut.

There were more men silhouetted against the far ridge. They weren't shooting at him yet, but soon would be.

And even if they all missed, it was only a matter of minutes before the first group closed in to blast him like a rabid dog.

Suddenly the head of a man trying to sight in on Ryan with an M-16 jerked back. He fell on his back flopping, grabbing the attention of his cohorts.

Ryan shot the remaining member of the first trio through the chest.

One of the men on the far ridgeline toppled backward out of sight. The remaining newcomers looked at one another and rabbited back down the far valley wall.

"Ryan!"

The shout came from the slope above him. The voice was momentarily unfamiliar.

"To your west! They're crossing the side valley!"

He recognized the voice now: Ricky Morales. He suddenly realized why he hadn't heard the shots that took out the two coldhearts.

He flung himself back to his first perch near the base of the outcrop where the two mutant monkey bodies still lay in pathetic huddles. Four of the original enemy unit were indeed scrambling down the far bank of the side cut and crossing the dry streambed at the bottom.

Ryan shot the nearest man in the face. He was only twenty yards or so away, so his head burst like an overripe cantaloupe hit with a sledgehammer.

As he toppled, the man right behind him triggered an AK blast from the hip. Even as Ryan brought his longblaster back online that man was cut down by another shot from Ricky Morales.

Another man sliding down the bank fired to reverse course, but took Ricky's next blast in the hip. He went down screaming.

The survivors sprinted back toward the rest of their patrol, who themselves were pulling back out of sight the way they came.

"This way!"

Ryan looked up the slope to see Ricky grinning at him from a bush.

"*¡Andale, señor!*" the kid called.

Without a second thought, Ryan raced up the slope toward him.

They started moving fast through the brush up the hill. The kid made more crunching and rustling noise than Jak would have, or even than Ryan did. But Ryan didn't think it'd make much difference. No enemy was near enough to hear them. At least, not one in shape to do much about it.

The scrub wasn't cover, but it was pretty fair concealment. The only way an enemy would be likely to hit them was to blanket the area with fire.

But the group that had run into them headfirst had shown no taste for any more of Ryan and his companions. It was always possible they would rally and come right back, if they fetched up against some kind of leader with the balls and presence to kick their asses back into action. But odds were this was an independent patrol. And even if somebody did get them turned around in short order, it was triple-sure they wouldn't be pursuing his friends any too eagerly.

"Where're the others?" he asked Ricky.

"Safe," Ricky said. "Up about half a kilometer, hidden. I, uh, came back on my own."

"Thanks," Ryan said. "One thing, though."

"What?" The kid sounded scared at being judged by his new comrades' formidable leader.

"That last little demo impressed me a shitload more than shooting some mutant monkeys."

Chapter Eighteen

From somewhere out in the night, someone coughed. It sounded like a plaguer trying to hack his lungs up, but magnified four or five times.

Ryan looked around sharply from the bonfire where he squatted. The crude grass huts of a small ville stood in a ragged circle around him, his companions and their hosts.

"What was that?" he asked.

"Tigre," the ville boss replied. You couldn't call him a baron. Not without laughing, anyway. He was a little middle-aged guy with pipestem arms and legs and a pot-belly hanging over a greasy loincloth. And his domain was about sixty people living in fifteen or twenty huts in a clearing in the heavy woods.

"You mean, some kind of mutant tiger?" Mildred asked. She was gnawing the roast rodent on a stick some-one had handed her.

"Oh, no," the ville boss said in Spanish, grinning. "Just a tiger. They roam these woods."

Mildred looked around in alarm when Ricky trans-lated.

"What?" Jak demanded. "Feel better if mutie tiger?"

"Well…no," Mildred admitted, relaxing slightly.

"Now that you mention it. It just gave me a turn. I suppose they—their ancestors—must've escaped from zoos after the war. If they made it through the skydark somehow, the climate would suit them pretty well."

"We should be safe here," the ville's senior woman said. Ryan wasn't sure whether she was the headman's wife or sister. He wouldn't even assume she couldn't be both. She was taller and sturdier than he was, built like a cinderblock, in fact, as well as visibly younger. But not that much different to look at. "They won't come near the fire."

"Even *chupacabras* don't like fire," the boss said with a cackle.

"Shit," Mildred said. "Not *chupacabras*."

The ville woman shrugged. "We don't get them much down here these days," she said. "Not like when I was a little girl. They mostly stick higher up in the mountains."

The boss tittered. "After we taught them a sharp lesson," he said. "It was during a year the rains didn't come they started getting bold."

Ryan took a healthy swallow of the local palm wine they'd given him in half a coconut. Coconut shells seemed to serve these people for all vessels, mugs and bowls alike.

Mildred tried a sip, but the stuff made her stomach roll over on its back and beg. For mercy. It was sour, vile, and slimy. She suspected that like a lot of quaint third-world bush types, the locals helped the fermenting process along by chewing the components and spitting them into the pot.

But her companions were slugging it down without batting an eye. Just as they'd devoured the stew of boiled rice, mashed bananas and some kind of stringy meat they'd been served earlier. She suspected the meat was monkey, which was never going to be her favorite, but it was better than, say, rat.

Mildred didn't know if the monkeys the villagers had stewed up had spikes or not. She didn't ask. She was hungry after their third day on the trail. She noticed that Jak didn't ask, either, despite his distaste for "tainted" flesh. That gave her a chuckle.

The other villagers squatted around them in a big-eyed, respectful circle, allowing the elder pair places of honor with the guests by the fire. Either the common tribesfolk had eaten earlier, or would later. Only the chief, the woman and the visitors were served food and drink.

Lucky us, Mildred thought, holding her breath and knocking back another swallow of the wine. It coated her tongue in nasty sickness. Her gag reflex fought it all the way down.

"That was the year the rainy season didn't come till late," the woman agreed. "The drought was worse in the mountains. Usually the mountains get more rain higher up. Not that year. We had a lot of animals coming by the ville. They gave us a lot of trouble. Some ate our crops. Some ate *us*. Especially the monsters, obviously. The mountains teem with them."

"The *chupacabras* are worst, though," the man said, as she nodded agreement. "They organize, see. Like monkeys. Mebbe smarter." He shrugged and took a drink of wine.

The ville elders continued their assessment of the *chupacabras'* tactics. Normally the goatsuckers hunted by stealth—and alone. But that year, driven from their mountain realms en masse by drought, they ran—and attacked—in packs of twenty or more.

"First they started taking people who were out alone after dark," the woman said. "That's always dangerous. We try not to do it. But you know how people are, no? A month or two goes by without a monster attack, we get careless. Lazy. Then a *tigre* or a *gato armado* or the scorpion dogs or spike monkeys grab some poor person walking back from the fields alone, or some drunk farmer stumbling outside his hut to piss in the middle of the night.

"Then they started invading homes by night. The *chupacabras* often raid huts, so it didn't seem so bad at first. No worse than any other time. We just had to be on our guard more.

"But even after we caught and killed one trying to snatch a baby from a crib, the night invasions didn't stop. Then packs started attacking small groups going out after dark. Then even people working the fields or hunting in the daytime."

The man shook his head. "It was a terrible time. We and the other villes of the valley lost many people, as well as dogs and other valuable livestock. It got so nobody dared venture out in groups of less than five or six, armed with spears, clubs and cane knives.

"Next the monsters started attacking whole villes, in force, at night. They all but wiped out one ville half a day's walk upstream. They stopped being afraid of fire. They'd attack people gathered around fires."

"They don't like having flaming torches stuck in their ugly faces any better than anyone else," the woman said in satisfaction.

"So when they got that bold—"

"That *desperate,*" the woman said.

The man nodded. "Then we had to get cagey ourselves."

"What did you do?" J.B. asked.

He had been knocking back the horrible palm wine as if it were actually good.

"We set up a trap," the headman said. "We stood watch around the ville with torches and weapons in hand, night-long vigils for one whole week. Sometimes we saw eyes shining back from the bush, which we'd cleared back to forty or fifty yards to make it harder to sneak up on us. Sometimes the eyes were big and widely spaced—*tigres* or armor cats. They gave us trouble, too, but nowhere near the goatsuckers. They might be cunning but they're more like animals, you know?

"But most of all, we saw the nasty slanty glows of *chupacabras'* eyes. We could feel their hunger and their hate. We pissed them off, keeping watch like that. They had no chance against us. They were smart enough to know it."

"So after a week of no attacks—" the woman took up the narrative as the man stopped to wet his whistle

"—we had a big party to celebrate. We danced and sang and got drunk and went off into our huts to screw and sleep off the wine."

Ryan got an especially wolfish grin on his harshly handsome features. "You set them up."

Their round, dark faces split into grins. "Of course!" the woman said. "They were smart, these monsters. Smart enough to see their opportunity. Smart enough to see we had gotten overconfident. They waited until mebbe an hour before dawn—"

"When folk are always most vulnerable," J.B. said. He could see where this was going.

"*Si,*" the headman said. "Then they hit us from all directions. There must have been a hundred of the muties. Usually they attack silently. Not that night. They were chirping and screeching to one another in their eerie voices as they came. They were enraged, and they were famished. And they were going to slake their hunger for vengeance as well as for the meat on our bones."

"And of course we had been drinking water," the woman said, "and only pretending to drink ourselves triple-stupe. We lay awake waiting. We planned to sleep in shifts, to stay as fresh as possible, but no one *could* sleep. And we kept waiting until they started ripping open the huts."

The huts here were more substantial than most of the ones built closer to the coast, where hurricanes could get an unobstructed shot at them. They actually had walls of sorts, although these seemed more like mats woven of sticks and grasses than anything more solid.

"We laid into them with everything we had. We even had friends and cousins from other villes hiding with us. Plus refugees from isolated huts and villes they'd attacked, survivors.

"And so it was we, not they, who took our vengeance. Ah, but that was a lovely bloodletting! We stabbed and beat and hacked them. We were wild things ourselves. We knew no fatigue, any more than mercy. We knocked them down and then ran after the ones who could still flee, while the children and the old ones beat the wounded muties to death with rocks and sticks. We chased them through the brush, across the fields, into the woods.

"They were too surprised and terrified by the hot reception we gave them to try to turn back and ambush us. And only the fastest—or mebbe the first to flee—got away."

"We counted a hundred and thirty bodies the next morning," the woman said. "We stuck twenty or thirty on sharpened stakes around the ville to rot, far enough out not to give us the black shits or other sickness. The rest we piled up in the middle of the ville, right where we sit now, and burned. Oh, how nasty it smelled! Yet wonderful, too."

"After that," the man said, "it was over ten years before any *chupacabras* were seen in our valley at all. Even the other monsters seemed to get the message. We had little trouble from any of them—even the scorpion dogs who fear nothing—until the rains returned to the mountains and they all went back to their heights."

J.B. stood up and spanked dust off the back of his trousers. "Now, that's the kind of bedtime story I like," he said. "But if it's all the same to you good people, I reckon it's time we hit the hay. We've got miles to walk in the morning."

Ryan nodded agreement. "Thanks for the hospitality," he said. "And the story. I'm a sucker for happy endings, myself."

"If we could only trouble you for a place to sleep, please," Krysty said, sidling up to her man and slipping an arm around his narrow waist.

"Of course!" the headman beamed. He gestured grandly at the hut directly behind them. It was easily the biggest in the ville, about twenty feet in diameter and a couple of feet taller than the rest. "You can have our hut for the night. We insist!"

"Thank you kindly," Ryan said. He had his arm around Krysty's shoulder.

"There is one favor we ask in return," the woman said. "We are a small ville, as you see. The other villes nearby are small, as well, and most of the people who live in them are our cousins."

"And we don't get many travelers through here," the man said. He had a glitter to his eye, Mildred noticed. She had no idea where this was heading.

"So it's hard to get new blood," the woman explained. "But we need to. Otherwise we start getting kids with too many fingers and too few eyes, you know? As bad as muties, interbreeding."

"Um," Ryan said. "Oh."

Mildred had to laugh out loud. Maybe it was the palm wine speaking through her. It didn't have a high alcohol content, she was pretty sure, but she wasn't used to drinking much, either. But it delighted her to see Ryan at a loss for words, for once.

"We see, of course, that two of your males are paired," the woman said matter-of-factly. "We respect that, of course. We know the rules of hospitality. We are not *jivaros*."

"Jivaros?" J.B. asked.

"Legendary cannies," Ricky said. "Some say they're a real tribe on the mainland, down south. It just means 'hicks' here, really."

"But three have no mates," the woman went on. "The old one and the young ones. We ask therefore that they do us the honor of sleeping with some of our unmarried women."

A pair of giggling young women appeared beside Doc. He looked around in bewilderment as they tugged him unceremoniously to his feet by the sleeves of his frock coat. Obviously premarital sex wasn't a problem in this ville.

Doc straightened and brushed off his sleeves. "When in Rome, they say. Lead on, ladies! I am entirely at your disposal."

Chapter Nineteen

"Chupacabras," Mildred said. "I thought there weren't many of those in our world."

The elder couple's hut was capacious, containing a central pole, woven sleeping mats scattered around and not much else. Light from the bonfire outside, which had been allowed to burn low and was being tended by a couple of kids, flickered through the open door, giving a shifting, uncertain illumination to the interior. The door was a rolled-up mat that could be unfastened and allowed to hang when necessary.

Aside from the slight scent of stale sweat, human grease and smoke, apparently from when it was too rainy to build fires outside, it didn't stink hardly at all. Krysty had slept worse places in her life. Lots of them, in fact.

"Mebbe they're different *chupacabras,*" Krysty said. "Not like the creatures in San Juan."

"Turns out we were wrong," Ryan said. "What difference does that make? They're fucking muties. They'll try to kill us if we run into them—like everything else that lives in the direction we're going, apparently."

"Why not try another direction?" J.B. asked.

"Two reasons," Ryan said. "First off, I'm guessing this Handsome guy is concentrating his island-conquering efforts on the coast, for the time being, anyway. Just stands to reason. Most of what's worthwhile, ports and trade goods and that, they're all on the ocean. If he gets hold of enough of those, he'll control this whole region, or the parts worth having, instead of spreading his troops out trying to subdue every little rad-blasted valley."

Ryan looked across the circle to Ricky. For some reason, the kid hadn't availed himself of the opportunity to go with one of the young women, despite their urging. From the way he looked at them, licking his lips and swallowing, he liked them fine; that wasn't the problem. Krysty wondered if he was just shy.

"That square with what you know, kid?" Ryan asked.

Ricky nodded. He sat cross-legged with his hands on his thighs, rocking back and forth slowly and staring at something nobody else could see. Krysty reckoned she was just as glad she couldn't.

It wasn't likely anything she hadn't seen before.

"That was the idea we got from what the travelers and refugees said," he said.

Ryan nodded.

"What's your other reason, Ryan?" J.B. asked. He and Mildred sat side by side, just touching. They were a lot more restrained in their displays of affection than Krysty and Ryan were. But they couldn't hide from Krysty that they didn't plan on going right to sleep after the palaver was over.

"Well," Ryan said, "it's like this. The monsters have to love the mountains for some reason. They aren't likely hanging up there because they like the scenery. So what are the odds they've got some kind of connection to the…place we're looking for?"

Krysty glanced at Ricky. He didn't respond. It wasn't as if they could keep secret that they were looking for something. But they couldn't ask for hints on how to find the mat-trans without revealing something about it. So Ryan had decided to tell people they were looking for some kind of special cave or hidden place, and let them draw their own conclusions about what they wanted with it.

The odds were good they'd never imagine anything close to the truth.

J.B. nodded. "Does make sense." He looked up, grinning ruefully. "Damn it, anyway. If that's right, the closer we get to our goal, the more monsters we've got to wade through."

"Well," Ryan said, "I might be wrong."

But he didn't sound optimistic, nor did Krysty feel that way herself.

"So," Ryan said, turning to their new friend and tipping his head to one side so the curly, shaggy hair hung down over his weather-beaten face, "Ricky. Why are you hanging with us, exactly? I thought you were fixated on finding and rescuing your sister."

"Yes," Ricky said slowly. He didn't look up or even seem to focus his eyes on the here and now. "I want to find her. I will find her. And then I will make the *coños* pay!"

That didn't seem likely to Krysty—not the finding his sister part, because she had no idea. But the part about making El Guapo, his shark-toothed sec boss or really any number of his henchmen pay for abducting her. Not that he hadn't exacted a down payment when he'd shot several of them, rescuing Ryan from their flanking maneuver several days before. But still, it was a pretty tall order.

Of course Ryan didn't buy that any more than she did.

"Okay," he said, drawing the word out long. "So, then, we're headed into the mountains. Away from the coast, where you say this El Guapo is hanging and banging. And if we find what we're looking for, we're not going back that way anytime soon."

Ryan shook his head. "At first I thought mebbe we might sign on with him. You know, a man like that, building an army like that, he's got to rely heavy-like on mercies. He'll always be hiring."

"You wouldn't!" Ricky burst out. He snapped upright and stared at Ryan with frightened-cat eyes. "You couldn't! They're coldhearts! Monsters!"

"Son," J.B. said gently, "you don't know us. You don't know what we've done to survive. You don't know what we'll do to keep on doing that thing. Fact is, we were also thinking seriously about taking up with a gang of pirates not so long ago. Doubt they was much better than this Handsome fella of yours."

Ricky looked at him, first as if he thought the armorer was joking, then with a look of outrage so intense Krysty almost laughed. Truly, the boy had to have led a sheltered life, in a prosperous family, in a happy ville. Whose very prosperity and happiness obviously doomed them, in the end, despite their willingness to fight to keep both.

"Why didn't you join them, then?"

J.B. shrugged. "Same reason we aren't likely to sign on with El Guapo anytime soon," he said. "Before we could reach the negotiation stage with the pirates, we kind of got crosswise of them. Wound up putting holes in a few of them, truth to tell. Mebbe more than a few."

"Plus the ones your boobies blew sky-high, J.B.," Ryan said with satisfaction.

"There's that, surely."

"Wait," Ricky said, staring at J.B. with his outrage turning to awe. "That big explosion in the harbor a few hours before I met you. I didn't see it, but you could've heard the blast on the other side of the island, and I saw the black smoke rill up into the sky. Was that you?"

J.B. nodded. "It was."

"*Magnífico,*" the boy breathed.

J.B. dipped his head self-deprecatingly. "Things sort of came together, you know? Anyways, looks like now we gone and crapped the bed where this El Guapo's concerned, too."

He reached up to scratch his head under his fedora. "The fact is, we got a way of rubbing people the wrong way. Shame, sometimes."

Ricky shook his head in wonder. "I knew I was right to join you."

"Actually," Mildred said drily, "you tried to rob us."

"I was hungry! After that, I mean. And that's the reason I stay with you. I want to stay alive, you see. I need to, if I'm ever going to find Yami!"

Ryan scratched his upper lip with his thumb. "Well, we do have a knack for surviving," he admitted. "But we also have a knack for getting into places where that is far from given. And fireblast, kid! We got a way of being hard on people who travel with us, I got to tell you."

Ricky shook that off as if trying to dislodge a biting fly from his ear. He's young, Krysty thought. He doesn't believe him. He probably didn't yet believe he'd ever really die. Kids that age just didn't. Even though he'd seen just how fragile life was, up close and in the most horrifying way possible.

"All right," Ryan said, hunkering down so he was at eye level with the boy. "What's the real reason?"

To his credit, and a bit to Krysty's surprise, Ricky didn't try to dodge. He swallowed hard, and in the bad light looked as if his olive skin got a shade or two paler. But, after that hesitation, he answered straight.

"It's like this," he said. "El Guapo will never let you and your friends roam free about Puerto Rico. He must neutralize you."

"How do you reckon that?" J.B. asked. "Dark night, he's got an army! There's just six of us. Okay, seven, counting you and that fancy whisper-shooting blaster of yours. Even if his army's just a few hundred strong, like it's liable to be, we aren't a trickling piss in the mighty ocean by comparison. Ow, why did you elbow me in the ribs like that, Mildred?"

Ignoring the glare she gave J.B., the boy smiled broadly.

"El Guapo means to be the big man on the island, you know? The top man. The only man. But you, Señor Ryan, you are *muy macho*. Your friends are *muy especial*. El Guapo will never be the only real man on the island as long as you're on it. Nor will he be the biggest.

"You've made your presence known to him. So El Guapo must deal with you and your friends—recruit you, or kill you. And after our meeting with the EUN, he will now want to see you die slowly. He does not like frustration, this man."

"No," Ryan said slowly. "I reckon he doesn't, at that."

Ricky beamed. "So you see, the Handsome One will hunt you. He *is* hunting you. He can't bear the thought of a man such as you roaming the island, giving the lie to his claims of being the biggest, the baddest, the most powerful. So where you are, there El Guapo will be, sooner instead of later. And then I will find my sister and set her free!"

Ryan sat down, arching a brow. "Mebbe," he said dubiously. "It's still hard to believe he'd take time off from his important business of conquering the nuke-sucking island to take a chance against a raggedy-assed bunch like us."

"You will see I'm right," the boy said. "Just wait."

As Ryan had feared—and expected—the clues they got led them deeper inland into the mountains.

"My cousin, *señor*," the man in the battered hat said.

"She knew a man—a lover, to tell the truth, which is a scandal to her poor mother—who said he saw a curious cave opening into some rocks. It wasn't so easy to spot. An outcropping hid it. He happened to be out hunting, and came at it from across a hill on the other side of the valley at just the right time for the light to strike it."

"So what did he do?" Mildred asked.

The trader shrugged. "He said a monster attacked him then. So he ran away. Nor would he ever go back, or even tell anyone about where he found the cave."

"What kind of monster?" Ricky asked, sounding more excited than he should have.

Ryan was scouting around, not looking at the little dusty trader or his loaded donkey. The trail they were following ran along a jagged-back ridgetop, with sparse vegetation. It gave him a pretty good look in all directions. The problem was, it also gave everybody in all directions a good look at *them*. Some heavy forests grew nearby, so people in them had the edge in seeing without being seen.

"That, he would not say. He did say he saw many more monsters there than he had ever seen before in his life. He said more than one chased him before he got away. Truly, his experience terrified him. He was so scared his hair turned white."

"That doesn't actually happen," Mildred began.

"Shut it," Ryan said sharply. "We're here for information. Not debate."

Mildred scowled mutinously, but she shut it.

"Muchas gracias, señor," Ryan told the man. "Good journey."

"Buena viaje, señores y señoritas." The man hauled on the braided leather rein fastened to his donkey's halter. Reluctantly, the little beast pulled its snout out of a clump of grass and followed him down the trail, chewing placidly.

"I think that was a load of B.S.," Mildred said. "Getting scared doesn't actually turn a person's hair white."

"Do I care?" Ryan said. "What does anybody think who isn't fixated on this damn hair-color thing?"

"I think," J.B. said, taking off his glasses and polishing them with a handkerchief, "that guy had a tail. Hard to see. Tip just sticks out the bottom of that long shirt thing he's got on."

Ryan didn't even look after the trader with the big hat and the tiny beast of burden. "Anybody think anything that might, you know, actually load us some magazines?"

"How can we trust him?" Mildred said. "I mean, if he exaggerates about—"

"Mildred."

"Sorry, Ryan. Shutting up now."

"Notwithstanding the veracity, or lack thereof, in certain details of the man's account," Doc said, "in broadest outline, what he told us is much of a piece with the rest of what we have been hearing."

"What that mean?" Jak demanded.

"It means," J.B. said, "that just because he might have

miscounted the number of rivets on an undercarriage, doesn't mean a wag didn't run over him."

Jak grunted. "Big help."

"So, what do you think, lover?" Krysty asked.

"The one place we need is the place that's swarming thickest with monsters, on a place called Monster Island," Ryan said. "I think that sucks."

THEIR QUESTIONS CONTINUED to evoke mostly blank stares and fearful evasions, but also tantalizing hints from the people they met. One hint led them west into a lower region, an area of hills and broad valleys. It rained frequently there, through some freak of the Carib weather, disordered by the Big Nuke and skydark and still not settled.

It was raining now, in fact, fat, hot drops that burst like tiny water grenades off the companions' faces. They trudged along through a break in the trees. A true canopy rain forest had grown up here, with enough breakage in the upper foliage to allow dense undergrowth to sprout in places. They were following a trail, an animal track, really.

Behind Krysty, Doc was softly singing "Sweet Adeline" to himself. When she glanced back through the rain she saw him smiling dreamily. His watery-blue eyes were distant. He was off wandering again, following a path that had nothing to do with his long legs and big feet going up and down in the physical world. He's back with his wife and children when he smiles like that, she thought.

She smiled, herself. She was glad Doc had that escape from the hard realities of the world from time to time. She did fear, though, that someday he'd stray off down some mental pathway and never find his way back.

Ryan brought up the rear, longblaster in hand. The weapon didn't quite have the long-range punch his older Steyr had. But the sniper rifle was just that: a specialized tool that wasn't much use at closer ranges. If anything jumped out at them from the dense walls of rain-wet vegetation, he was ready to blast the hell out of it.

J.B. had point for a change, with Ricky walking right behind him, then Mildred. J.B. toted his Smith & Wesson M-4000 scattergun. The local boy had his peculiar longblaster. Neither Mildred nor Krysty had weapons in hand.

Jak was doing what he usually did in unknown country: ranging out front, along their flanks, hanging back to keep their back trail clear. He'd been especially edgy about that the past few days, although he wouldn't explain why.

Not even Ryan pressed him. Jak had a feeling. If he *knew* anything, he'd say as much. And while he was far from stupe, expressing himself in words wasn't his strong suit. When he just felt something, and people tried to pump him for specifics, he got sullen and defensive and clammed up.

She smiled. They were a family, as tight-knit as any she'd known. Yet they were also a unit, in the old military sense. Each had a role, each functioned smoothly in it, and they all knew one another well enough that they anticipated the others' actions without much need for words.

Mildred compared them to how a jazz band played. When the time came to improvise, any one of them might take the lead, confident the others could follow. Krysty had never heard a jazz band herself, but she caught the drift.

Krysty frowned. Something had just tickled the edge of her peripheral vision. She felt the hairs prickle at the back of her neck.

She didn't have Jak's senses, honed taut as a wildcat's by a life prowling in the bayou, hunting the deadliest of beast, human and mutie prey. But she had her own bond with the natural world—with Gaia—a sense of connection to earth and what lived on it.

"Ryan," she said softly over her shoulder. She felt a strong desire not to speak aloud. She didn't want to alert whatever was out there that she was aware of it. She would have passed the word through Doc, but the old man was still in his own little world. "Something's out there."

"Triple-red, people," Ryan said, in the soft speech that was much more stealthy than a whisper's hiss. "Stay sharp."

A shape appeared beside J.B. One moment the armorer was shouldering past a branch that ended in a clump of leaves like a sharp green shellburst. The next heartbeat he had something right alongside.

Krysty had already started slipping her snubby hand-blaster out of its holster at her belt. Ahead of her, Mildred already had her heavy ZKR held muzzle-up in both hands. Then she relaxed—a hair. It was Jak.

"Something," he said softly to J.B. without looking at him. "Hunting."

Unfortunately Ricky Morales wasn't yet attuned to them. "What?" he asked, his voice shockingly loud in the rain and all this still. "What's going on?"

With a loud rustle of brush a hairy shape leaped on him from the right. He yelped and went down beneath its weight.

Before Krysty could react, something sprang from the right, jaws wide and yellow teeth gleaming to tear out her throat.

Chapter Twenty

Krysty turned and shot. She didn't need to aim. The lunging shape was almost touching the short barrel of her .38-caliber handblaster when she triggered it.

The little revolver bellowed. She caught a whiff of scorched wet fur then heard a squeal of pain and rage as the bullet punched home.

The creature hit her in midchest. The rotten-meat stench of a carnivore's breath filled her nostrils. A furry muzzle snapped at her face. She grabbed the animal by its breastbone and threw it over her head, using its momentum as well as her own strength to hurl it shrieking and writhing into the surrounding jungle.

It was a dog, the size of a big coyote, about thirty or forty pounds. Feral dogs were a widespread menace in the Deathlands.

Snarls and barks crackled through the sounds of raindrops hitting leaves and limbs. Gunshots boomed as her friends blasted the attackers lunging at them from both sides.

"Pack!" Ricky screamed.

The boy was lying on his back, his attacker nowhere in sight. Ricky's face was flushed with sudden violent effort beneath the coating of sweat the humid jungle heat had lathered over all their skins. She guessed that, like her, he had thrown the beast off, probably with his legs.

"Protect yourself," he shouted. He scrambled to his feet and butt-stroked a snarling attacker across the muzzle with his DeLisle. "Don't let them bite you."

Reacting instantly, she swung her pack off her back. She heard the roar of Doc's shotgun.

The charge of buckshot took a dog in midleap, striking its breast bone and peeling it open in a spray of blood. The dog fell yelping and gasping into the foliage from which it had jumped.

Krysty got her pack clumsily in front of her just in time to catch something whipping toward her belly. It struck with a fistlike impact: a brown-and-yellow knot at the end of a dog's jointed tail. The creatures looked like German shepherds or small wolves, with rough, shaggy hair that spiked around their raised hackles and shoulders. But their tails looked like a scorpion's.

The creature snarled as it tried to tug its stinger free. The tails were longer than the torso and head combined, allowing them to strike targets to their front, again, like a scorpion. She shot the animal in the face.

The bullet ripped off the front of its muzzle. Squealing, it cringed away.

"Run for the tall timber!" Ryan yelled. "Now!"

She glanced back to see him slamming his Steyr like a riot baton horizontally into the gaping maw of one beast springing for his face.

"Ryan, behind you!" she screamed. But he had the sixth-sense of a stray tomcat. He was already spinning, his left hand coming off the longblaster's foregrip. As a stinger arced over to inject its load of venom into his leg, Ryan sidestepped and slashed through the tail with a savage stroke of his heavy-bladed panga.

The tip fell beside him. Ocher liquid dribbled from the raw stump. The needlelike sting tip was black, and a brighter yellow fluid pulsed out of it.

"Get a move on, girl!" Doc thundered up hard behind her with his long gangly legs pumping comically high. He held his swordstick in his left hand and his big handblaster in his right. As usual, crisis had snapped him back to reality.

Krysty could only turn and obey. She held up her heavy pack in her left hand, her S&W 640 in her right. At least she could hold her pack up one-handed and swing its mass to bat away another scorpion dog, which sprang straight back into the bush.

Ahead of her, Mildred was pushing forward, holding up her pack with both hands and clutching her wheelgun at the same time. She wasn't able to shoot that way. But she was probably smart all the same, since she could use the pack as Krysty had, both as shield and weapon to knock attacking muties away.

The problem was, no amount of hiking could ever make Mildred's legs, powerful as they were, a millimeter longer.

She was still making respectable speed, though. Krysty bit down an impulse to bolt, and instead shot a dog that tried to hamstring Mildred with a snap at her heel.

The monsters were all around them. It was a big pack. They were yipping excitedly now, trying to coordinate attacks. With the branches close enough to brush the party's shoulders, dumping loads of accumulated rainwater down their backs and sides at every step, the scorpion dogs could keep attacking from close range.

Whether the spiky growths at their shoulders were just bristles or actual spines like the mutie monkeys had, Krysty couldn't tell. One way or another, the creatures seemed able to slide through the brush like eels through water. Their numbers made them brave and lethal. Those venom-packed tails made them extremely dangerous.

J.B.'s shotgun boomed from the front of the little column. He was using it to blast the dogs that got close and bash the ones that got closer. Behind him, Jak ran shoulder to shoulder with Ricky, his white hair streaming behind him.

Jak parried tail strokes with his bowie knife in his left fist. His Python was in his right hand, vent-ribbed barrel pointed skyward. He preferred blade to blaster when the chips were down.

Ricky held his fat-barreled carbine in his left hand, using it mostly as a shield. In his right, he carried his big handblaster. As Krysty watched, he fired the Para-Ordnance to his right at something she couldn't see.

Ahead of them soared the big trees of the rain forest, their broad-leafed crowns a hundred or more feet above the forest floor. Krysty was only vaguely aware of them; her attention was on keeping her front—and Mildred's back—clear of the attacking muties. And not tripping over a root or twisting her ankle on a rock slimy with rain and decomposing vegetation, which would get her quickly dead and probably doom Doc as well when he tripped over her.

After furious running and more furious fighting, J.B. and the rest broke from the dense jungle growth into the rain forest.

"Twenty yards in and form circle!" Somehow Ryan found the breath to bellow the command from the rear.

J.B. put on a burst of speed. His sprint took him well out in front. He reached a spot roughly sixty feet in, wheeled, knelt and brought his M-4000 to his shoulder.

It bucked, vomited noise and yellow fire. Ahead, to Krysty's left, a scorpion dog squealed. Briefly.

The two teenagers dashed free of the brush and took up positions flanking J.B.

"Don't shoot your pals!" the armorer snapped. The two raised their weapons and aimed straight back along the path. Even running and fighting for her life, Krysty felt a flash smile as she caught the shamefaced expression they shared.

She knew what to do. Throwing her pack into the face of a dog that tried to dart at her legs—she thought she heard a skinny leg snap, and the creature gave a piteous shriek—she accelerated. She grabbed Mildred's right arm as she dashed past and towed her, in a sort of high-speed forward stumble, across the mostly open forest floor, past Ricky's left shoulder.

She let Mildred go. Yelping, the physician tumbled, landing on her face in the slimy mulch of decaying leaves. She slid a good ten feet, plowing a furrow in the sludge.

Krysty slipped around to just behind Jak's right shoulder. Then, holding her .38-caliber blaster in both hands, she shot down a dog that was running on Ryan's left, looking for a chance to strike. Doc ran past on the far side of J.B. and Ricky.

Then Ryan reached the circle in the open ground.

And that was the key: open ground.

It offered little concealment for beasts the size of the scorpion dogs. Especially against seven humans who had blasters and knew how to use them.

They'd laid a ferocious hurting on the pack on their desperate dash through the undergrowth, but the monsters pressed their attack.

The companions were a tempting target. This much meat would last even a pack this size for days, before their chills liquefied completely in the high-speed rainforest decomposition process, and the last of their nutrients drained into the humus in a reeking yellow ooze.

A half dozen scorpion dogs went down howling in the volley the group fired when they formed a circle in the relative open. And that ended it. The survivors turned chitinous tail and fled.

Krysty heard them barking to one another as they receded into the distance. They sounded disappointed.

"Hold steady, everyone," Ryan said. He knelt facing away from the brush wall, into deeper woods. They needed to maintain a circle in case the pack decided to return. "Sing out—everybody fit to fight?"

Though Mildred and Doc sounded down to their last breath, all were.

"Nobody got stung?" he asked. When all confirmed they hadn't, he said, "Now we wait to make sure the bastards are really gone."

"Good call, Ryan," J.B. said. He sounded hardly winded from his exertion. He might not look like much, but he was tough as boot leather. And not just in his wiry little body. "Bastards might be up to tricks. Just waiting for us to let our guard down."

No, Krysty thought. They're done. They had taken their best shot, and like any hunting pack, they knew when it was time to cut their losses—and slake their hunger on their own chills and crips, likely.

But she said nothing as she broke open her snubby handblaster and ejected the five cartridges into her palm. They were all emptied out and still warm from ignition. She tumbled the brass into a shirt pocket and was reaching for her pack when she realized she'd jettisoned it in the brush. She'd retrieve it later. Instead, she took a speed-loader from another pocket and injected five live rounds, then sealed the piece.

Waiting to make sure the monsters are gone may not be necessary, she thought, but it's a good habit. And keeping up the right habits, she knew, made all the difference between being on your feet—and, thank Gaia, unpoisoned—and staring lifelessly up at the faraway green ceiling.

"YES," THE HEADMAN SAID, nodding gravely. "I know of that place."

The ville was a handful of huts that seemed to Mildred to consist mostly of bundled grasses and brush, cleverly bound together and connected by intricate basketwork. It clung to a steep mountainside of dark purple dirt and red-tinged black lava, with green tufts and blue flowers sticking out here and there. Some terraced fields, mostly given over to lettuce and bean plants, straggled up and down the slope.

The grandest building was a kind of longhouse in the middle of the ville, with walls and roof beams of hardwood cut in the forested valleys below and dragged laboriously up winding trails. The headman had been sitting there at his ease, smoking a pipe that smelled suspiciously of ganja, when the party entered the tiny ville.

"I, myself, saw such a cave, in my youth. I was more adventurous then, and had not yet taken on the responsibilities of a chief."

He spoke Spanish, which Ricky duly translated for those who needed the help. It was a bit hard to understand him, not because of any accent, but because a scalie's mouth was shaped differently from a human mouth.

Mildred wondered if it gave her friends the same creeps it did her, to stand here surrounded completely by scalies. These were a fairly advanced variant of that mutation, roughly four feet tall when adult, with large patches of scales on skin that had a greenish cast in the hot morning sun. The chief's eyes were huge wet gleams in the shadow of what Mildred couldn't help thinking of as a coolie hat, although she suspected that was racist. Not that anyone alive today would have the faintest conception what she was talking about if she brought that up.

From Ryan's frozen expression, Mildred suspected he found the situation no more natural or comfortable than having a yellow jacket perched on his nose.

If the scalie headman noticed the humans' unease, he gave no sign of it. Mildred guessed that, even if the mutie understood human expressions and body posture—as he might from regular dealings with the breed—he still might not get that *he* was the cause of Ryan's discomfort, as opposed to what he was saying, the humid heat or jock itch.

In the days they'd been here, they'd definitely gotten to see up close and personal both reasons the outsiders called the place "Monster Island." Humans and muties, or the high-functioning humanoid branches who at least approximated human intelligence, coexisted so commonly and smoothly that the island's inhabitants might well find the mainland's pervasive fear and hatred of muties incomprehensible.

"We have a ritual of passage into adulthood," the ville boss said. "Our young must prove their worth by making a journey up into these mountains. To the very heart of the monsters' lair."

"I'm hating where this is going, okay?" Mildred said to no one in particular. "Anyone else with me on this?"

"Shush," Ryan said evenly.

The senior scalie ignored them both. "I was there in the valley, at nightfall, hiding. And I saw the creatures coming out of the very rocks above me as if the earth herself was giving birth to them. I was able to creep up behind a pile of rocks and climb a rock face, where the horrible things would surely expect no one to go. And I saw them coming out of a hole in the mountainside. But it was no normal cave, my friends. Oh, no. Inside the narrow crevice I saw a rectangle.

"It was a door. There could be no mistaking. Someone made that entrance into the earth. And now the *chupacabras* dwell there!"

Ryan sighed. "Bingo."

"So why are we just assuming," Mildred asked, "that where we're going is the same place these freaking *chupacabras* hang out?"

"That's how our luck runs?" J.B. suggested helpfully.

They labored up a steep path on a forested mountainside. It was midday, and the broad-leafed green trees to either side offered little shade from the sun.

Krysty resisted the urge to flick a look back at Ricky Morales. The boy was bringing up the rear with his De-Lisle tightly gripped in both hands, his head seemingly on a swivel and a stern yet proud expression on his narrow face. This was the first time Ryan had allowed him the important duty of rear guard.

The kid was justly proud. It was a sign of trust, and

he knew that Ryan Cawdor was a man whose trust was anything but easy to win.

That brought a question to Krysty's mind: what did they tell the boy when they reached the redoubt—the gateway? What did they do about him?

In the end, she knew Ryan would make the call. And as always, he would make the call that best promoted his and his companions' chances of survival.

Because she liked the boy, that worried her. Ryan wouldn't hesitate to abandon a person who wasn't actually part of their close-knit circle. He'd done it before.

"Last time we hit Puerto Rico," Ryan said, "the *chupacabras,* so to speak, came from a redoubt. What are the odds of the same thing here? Look good to me." He was currently walking point.

"But why would there be two facilities working with *chupacabras?*" Mildred asked. "Especially on the same island?"

From her posture, Krysty could tell Mildred was staring a hole through the back of Doc's head. He walked directly in front of her, head high, jauntily twirling his ebony swordstick. The time-trawled professor had more intimate experience of the shady—and to Krysty's mind, infinitely evil—types involved with the redoubts, and the secret science that was performed inside them, than anyone else in the party. For which she heartily thanked Gaia.

But Doc's only response was to laugh.

"You can't expect whitecoats to think like normal people," Krysty said.

Mildred turned to give her an exasperated glance. Her brown eyes went wide in her round, smooth face.

"Behind us, people!" she gasped. She pointed back along the trail.

Krysty's snub-nosed .38 was in her hand when she turned, but the physician wasn't pointing to immediate danger on their back trail, nor anything else nearby.

What had caught her attention was the plume of dirty-white smoke billowing up into the mostly cloudless sky above the trees to the south and east.

"Shit," Ryan said. "That's the ville we just left this morning."

"Coincidence?" J.B. asked.

"I wish," Ryan said grimly.

Chapter Twenty-One

It took a triple dose of chilling to chill a scalie.

The scalies of the little mountain ville had died hard.

"Shit," Ryan said.

The village stank of burned grass and charred flesh.

The muties smelled worse than humans did when they were burned. That actually took some doing, since the smell of incinerated human flesh tended to hit humans in the core of their being, instinctively revolting them. The humanoid mutants gave off the porky-sweet stink human flesh did, plus some kind of weird chemical reek that stung Ryan's eye like tear gas.

Unlike Nuestra Señora, the little ville had been built of highly combustible materials. It had burned so fast and thoroughly that there was little left but smoking ashes by the time Ryan, Ricky and Jak returned to it in midafternoon.

The chillers of the tiny mutie ville had been thorough. Dead scalies lay everywhere: sprawled on the paths between the mounds of ash that had been their homes, their deflated corpses showed the marks of blades and bashing as well as bullets. Others lay in the ash heaps, green flesh peeking hideously through cracks in the char. The terraced fields had been uprooted and trampled, and bean frames tossed on bonfires.

"El Guapo," Ricky said, picking something up as they passed through the sad smoldering huddle of incinerated huts to the middle of what had been the tiny ville. "He did this."

"Guessing," Jak said.

"An ace guess," Ryan replied.

"No guess," Ricky said, straightening. "Triple-sure."

He held something out to Ryan. Frowning, the one-eyed man took it.

"Cigar butt," he said. "End still wet. So?"

"So, it is a *cigarro cubano,* my friend," Ricky said. "The Cuban barons grow prime tobacco in their villes, and have their slaves roll the cigars by hand. They are prized throughout the islands. And among the whole Army of National Unity, El Guapo alone has the privilege of smoking them."

Ryan grunted. He and his companions stopped in front of an *X* of big wood beams in front of the burned-out ruin of the ville chief's house. Apparently the cold-hearts had yanked it out of the ville's only permanent structure before giving it the torch and put it to distinctive use.

Scalies died hard. The ville had died hard. And the ville boss had died hardest of all, to judge by the big nails, apparently scavvied from his burned-down home, that held palms and feet to the rude timber cross. Or the way his belly had been carved laboriously open and his guts unwound.

And then all cooked in a big bonfire, the remnants of which mingled with the overdone sausage links of scalie intestines at the foot of the cross.

"Bad," Jak breathed.

"Triple-bad," Ricky said.

"We've got to shake this ville's dust off our boots and triple-fast," Ryan said through a throat that seemed seared. "Before worse lands on us."

"So EL GUAPO'S HOT ON our heels," J.B. said. "Dark night! That's all we need."

"He seems to have a positive taste for disembowelment," Doc said thoughtfully.

"He likes to make real vivid examples," Ricky said. "At least, that's what the people who took his side in Nuestra Señora used to say back—back before he made an example of them. Me, I think he just gets off on hurting people."

"Lots of barons do both," Ryan said. "Sec bosses still more."

Krysty frowned. It was late afternoon. They marched on looking for a spot to hole up for the night.

Her belly churned inside her. It took a lot to make her feel sick that way. She was Deathlands born and bred, after all, not some innocent plucked out of her own time and dumped in the nuke-waste like Doc and Mildred.

"He's been following us all along, hasn't he?" she asked. Her throat was dry, though the air along the mountain forest trail was humid.

"Since that little run-in we had with the EUN back in the valley," Ryan said, "yeah. I reckon he has."

"So we've brought the same horror down on everyone we talked to?" Krysty asked.

Ryan was walking by her side as he and Ricky told their story. Jak, who wasn't long on talking, had prowled off into the brush to ghost along beside them and try to protect them against surprises. The trail was relatively wide, probably an old service road of some kind.

Possibly it had been paved once, which didn't mean that much. Even though they weren't in a rain forest and jungle setting up here, closer to the high rocky spine of the island, growth as vigorous as the trees and scrub around them would have broken up the asphalt in a couple of generations and effectively swallowed it back into Gaia. Krysty reckoned the only reason the trail still existed so distinctly was that people made regular use of it, though settlements seemed few and far between on the steep up-and-down ground. Mebbe this was a pass-through route from here to there.

Like the ones Ricky, who trotted behind them with a distinct green pallor to his skin, would've traveled with his father's trade caravans.

Ryan laid a hand on her shoulder. "Regret won't load any blasters," he said.

His voice was gruff, but the look in his blue eye told Krysty that the brutality in the nameless little ville had hit him where he lived.

Something tickled the edge of her peripheral vision.

She whipped her head around, felt her sentient hair curl up tight against her scalp as the skin tingled.

"Ryan," she said under her breath. "Something just moved in the brush there. It didn't make any sound but I saw it. Like a shadow."

She felt chagrin at responding so overtly, but she was upset by the story Ryan and Ricky had just told them. It set her nerves so far on edge they acted like trip wires.

"Yeah," he replied, as if she had just told him it was a pretty day, which it was, with a few fluffy clouds drifting aimlessly across a brilliant blue Carib sky. "We noticed something shadowing us on the way in. Even in the scrub and rocks of the hillside, not even Jak could get a square look at them."

"Chupacabras!" Ricky blurted.

"No way," Mildred said. "It's daytime. They're stealth hunters. They're nocturnal."

"But the people back at that one ville said that when they got upset enough, they come out in the day," J.B. observed. He was walking the trail with his shotgun in his hands and a thoughtful look behind the round lenses of his glasses.

"What would they be that upset about?"

"If strangers were coming into their home territory," Ryan said, "that'd probably rile them up."

"You think they really do live, uh, where we're going?" Mildred demanded.

Ryan shrugged.

"Evidence is looking strong that that's the case, Millie," J.B. said.

"Whatever they are, there's a bunch of them," Ryan said. "And they're working together pretty tight, keeping close tabs on us, but not so close Jak can get a clear look at one of them."

"That sounds like intelligent behavior," Mildred protested. "They're just animals."

"Clever animals, dear lady," Doc said from behind her.

Beaded plaits swinging, Mildred turned her head to give him what Krysty thought of as the fish eye. "Doc," she said, "you can accuse me of being many things. But 'dear' isn't one of them. Not in that sense, anyway."

He drew himself up to his full gawky height. "It is a figure of speech," he said in tones of injured dignity.

"Wolf and dog packs manage to communicate pretty well, coordinate their stalking and attacks," Krysty pointed out. "As the scorpion dogs did with us. And when we ran up against them before, the *chupacabras* showed some pretty unsettling signs they might be smarter than regular animals."

"Why aren't they attacking us, then?" Mildred asked.

"If they get hungry enough," he said, "or pissed enough, they will."

"If I may be forgiven for speaking bluntly," Doc announced, "do we not find ourselves in danger of ignoring the rhinoceros in the sitting room?"

"Speak plainly, old man," Mildred said, annoyed.

"I shall endeavor to do so, then. Must we not assume that El Guapo now operates with as much knowledge of our destination as we ourselves have?"

"Well," Mildred said, "he can't know what we're looking for."

"He'll figure it out," Ricky said, then added almost cheerfully, "I have!"

Everybody looked at him. His eyes got wide.

"How do you mean, boy?" J.B. asked in a deceptively gentle voice. Krysty knew he was never more dangerous than when he spoke softly. And no poisonous snake was more lethal than J. B. Dix when he figured there was chilling to be done.

"Well," Ricky said, drawing the word out. Clearly he sensed he was in a very narrow place here. "It's like this—you want off the island, right?"

"Yeah." Ryan clipped the word off.

"So, what do you need? You lost your ride when you got here. Señor Dix blew it up with all the pirates aboard in his wonderful trap."

"Well, not quite all of them," J.B. said. But he looked pleased nevertheless.

"You need treasure!" Ricky caroled. "You got to buy passage to the mainland. Or mebbe even buy a boat. You need jack and trade goods. Valuable stuff, not bulky.

"So, where can you find such a treasure, of portable yet precious items, all gathered together? Where but in a cache of predark goods, which the Old Guys hid when they saw the end was coming? And now I know what brought you here. Clearly you learned of this treasure, and that it was worth taking fearful risks to possess it."

Ryan turned his face forward, sweeping his blue eye

across Krysty's emerald gaze as he did. She thought the hint of a smile quirked up the edges of his lips.

"You read us like a book, kid," he said. "What now?"

"Well," Ricky said, puffing out his chest. "I hope I have served my new friends well enough you'll think me worthy to share in the treasure that you find. If you can take it from El Guapo, of course!"

"Big 'if,'" Mildred muttered.

"You've earned consideration, yeah," Ryan said. "Tell you what. Any plunder we find, we'll let you grab a share right off the top."

Krysty looked at him with relief flooding like sunlight into her body. If they found treasure—and there could be an abundance of scavvy in the redoubt, guarded by secrecy as well as the *chupacabras* who seemed to nest there—Ryan would be willing to let the kid have all of it. *If* they could just get to the mat-trans unit and jump out while he was filling his pack and pockets with the loot.

Then he could think whatever the nuke he wanted to. But he wouldn't have any inkling of where his new friends had gone off to so suddenly.

She felt a bit of a pang over that. He'd saved their lives a couple of times over. It would be hard to abandon him.

"But first," Ricky said gravely, "you must take it from El Guapo."

"That's if the ville boss talked," Mildred said.

"Wouldn't you?" the boy asked.

She widened her eyes and tipped her head to the side.

But she said stubbornly, "Scalies are tough. We know that as well as anybody."

"Somebody would've talked before they got chilled," Ryan said. "Seems to me like this Handsome dude likes to torture friends and family as a way of getting to the holdouts."

Ricky nodded. "He has that reputation, *si*."

"We got to assume the worst, in a case like this." J.B. shook his head gravely. "That's just plain sense."

"You're right, J.B.," Ryan said. "El Guapo's going to stop at nothing to get his hands on loot like this. He's a man with big dreams. However many soldiers he's got, he's going to need more. And that takes jack to buy them, and gear to outfit them."

"Is your sense, then, that he's going to follow us to the, ah, the treasure trove, my dear Ryan?" Doc asked.

Ryan shook his head. "No. He doesn't strike me as the type to bide his time when he doesn't have to. He's an action guy."

Which was, Krysty knew, an assessment Ryan was as well qualified as anyone to make. He was a man who preferred action to waiting, and was good at taking action.

"Anyway," Ryan said, "what does he need to follow us for now? Like J.B. says, we got to assume he knows what we know. And it's not like he won't have people who know the ground. At least as well as our guide here does."

Ricky set his lips briefly before admitting, "My father and I never came this far into the mountains of the interior together. I know nothing more about the area than you do."

"You've been a big help to us, though," Krysty said, "helping us get this far, and getting folks to open up to us."

The boy beamed at that.

"How do we handle it from here, Ryan?" J.B. asked. "Fast? Or cautious?"

An eruption of blasterfire, so loud it sounded as if it came from everywhere at once, answered the armorer's question.

Chapter Twenty-Two

"That answers that," J.B. muttered as they broke for cover to both sides of the trail.

Ryan dived to the left. He hauled out his SIG-Sauer handblaster in midleap and was shooting when he crashed into a bush covered in waxy oval leaves.

He hated to fire blind. That was the same as wasting ammo—most times.

But he heard Trader talking to him in his mind, clearly as if his mentor were standing right beside him and shaking his head. *You walk into an ambush, boy, your survival depends on your ambushers not being competent. Since they were smart enough to mousetrap you in the first place, you can work out the rest yourself.*

As, indeed, Ryan had. And what he'd worked out— before he and Trader parted ways, in fact—was that when the enemy had you locked up in his sights, anything you could give him to think about other than chilling your stupe ass worked on your side. And not getting his own hide punctured was a thing that might tend to distract an ambusher.

Ryan had no idea if he hit anything but trees before he was getting whipped by skinny branches and falling hard on a ground just barely cushioned by a mulch of rotting leaves and twigs. Odds were better than good he hadn't. He did see a couple of muzzle flashes blazing from a place where the road turned right to pass around a hill about twenty yards ahead. He thought the shooters might be sheltering behind a fallen log. One flare was the unmistakable flicker of a full-auto blaster, some kind of AK by the deep, choppy roar.

He heard cracks from across the trail and behind as his friends opened up. He hoped they'd all gotten clear. There was no time to check.

Something had made the ambushers jump the gun and open up before the group walked right up to their concealed blaster muzzles, where even half-assed peasant conscripts could barely miss them. And he suspected this bunch was a higher cut of coldheart beef than that.

He rolled away from the trail. Jamming his handblaster back in its holster he squirmed his longblaster off his shoulder and into a firing position. He could just see where the blasters' flashes continued to blossom ahead through the leaves.

Ryan tried to sight on one through the ghost ring. Of course, when he fired he'd give his own position away, but if he could cut their odds by even one shooter, that'd be worth the risk.

From somewhere ahead and off to the left he heard the sharp bark of a .357 handblaster. He actually saw some of the flash past a rough-barked tree bole. Somebody screamed and thrashed behind the moss-grown log.

Another figure reared up, swinging a remade Kalashnikov right, to bear on the sudden flank attack. Ryan twitched his sight onto the shape and fired. The figure fell away out of sight. The one-eyed man thought the longblaster dropped from his victim's hands, but couldn't be sure.

A person ran up the road, yelling. A blast of full-auto fire drowned the wordless battle cry. It was from J.B.'s Uzi machine pistol, which he was shooting from the hip in ripsaw bursts.

Then Jak launched a sudden attack on the ambushers' right flank and changed the game completely. From having the hammer hand, the coldhearts were suddenly caught in a crack themselves. Ryan knew from his own brutal experience there was no nastier kick in the balls than that reversal.

The ambushers may have been more than grunts dragged out of the cane fields and bean farms a couple of days ago by EUN "recruiters," but they'd had balls of vanadium steel not to flee from a madman with an autoblaster and an unexpected assailant who fired up their asses from a totally unexpected direction.

Ryan stayed where he was, looking for targets of opportunity to help his friends. As crazy and fast as J.B.'s move was, Ryan knew his friend and right-hand man seldom did anything without careful calculation. J.B.'s keen tactical eye and quick insight had told him this was the best shot they had.

He'd been right. An ambusher leaped up without a weapon in hand, and raced away in pure panic. Ryan swung his longblaster right to take him down, but another three-round burst ripped out from J.B.'s stubby machine pistol. Ryan saw dust fly from the back of the guy's shirt. He screamed as dark blotches appeared on the fabric, clutched at his kidneys and fell.

Jak ran up to the log where the ambushers had lain in wait. Fire blossomed from the barrel of his big stainless-steel Python, straight down.

Voices began calling from off to the west, from behind where Jak had crept up on the ambushers. They sounded pissed.

"Fireblast!" Ryan exclaimed. "Time to power out of here! Head east, everybody, now!"

Ryan saw that Doc, Mildred, the new kid and Krysty were all fit to fight and had a head start on him.

He didn't look left at Jak and J.B. He knew what they were doing.

Same thing he was: running for their lives.

"So," Ryan said. "Burnin' ammo to chill the wounded?"

Lying nearby him between some purplish head-sized lava rocks that sprouted bushes like bad hair plugs, Mildred frowned. She was squinting at the far slope, west across the heavily wooded valley. As if her unassisted eyes were going to spot anything Ryan's big longeyes wouldn't.

They had fled east, away from the second force of ambushers. That was predictable, but necessary. But, contrary to Mildred's intuition, rather than doing the sensible thing and heading north toward where their goal allegedly lay, Ryan had headed the party south, adding perhaps a half mile to their total journey. But in a race against the EUN, and adding in a delay to shake off pursuit, that could make all the difference in whether they reached the lost redoubt first, or El Guapo did.

"Didn't want any of them coming back to life suddenly," the armorer said, "and blasting us in the back. I didn't have time to check them close, so I figured I'd just make sure. Reckon Jak saw things the same way—passing up a chance to finish off a coldheart with his blade, like he did."

"Shame." Jak's voice floated down from above, as soft and colorless as ash.

"So why *didn't* we head north while we put distance between us and the bad guys?" Mildred demanded, unable to keep it in anymore. "Why did we wind up going the wrong damn way?"

"You may not believe this, Mildred," Ryan said, "but I thought of that, too. Right off the mark. We could use the opportunity to slip at least a hair closer to our target. Simple. Easy. Obvious."

He paused a moment to let that last word bore into her skull.

"I haven't lived as long as I have," he said, "by thinking I'm smarter than my coldhearts. I thought of that. That means Tiburón could, too, if I guess right and he's the man in charge of this little surprise party."

His eye had never twitched from the glass.

"Oh, he is, Señor Ryan, be assured," Ricky said. "You and your friends—I mean, *our* friends—are a most valuable prize. El Guapo wouldn't trust a lesser man than his sec boss. And he wouldn't trust any man at all, not even his filthy pet shark, to find the treasure ahead of him."

Ryan nodded behind his longeyes. He shifted the device to the left. It was braced on his backpack. The man lay on his belly on that razor-toothed uncomfortable rock, same as the rest of them. Jak, however, squatted under a pink-flowering bush a few yards upslope of them, making sure nobody caught them from behind.

"And speaking of Shark Boy," Ryan said suddenly, "I got a good ten men moving through the trees over there. Mebbe a dozen. And… Yeah. Shaved head, gray skin, more snout than skull. Big fucker."

"De veres," Ricky said. "It is truly Tiburón you see."

"Can't you take him out?" Mildred asked, a trifle more shrilly than she would have liked. "You know, snipe him from here?"

Ryan shook his head. "No chance. Too long a shot to make reliably. Only thing it would do is give away our position."

"It's just as long a shot for them as it is for you, Ryan," J.B. said. "And it would make them go to ground. Slow them down just that additional little bit to give us a chance to lose them."

"It would," Ryan agreed, "if this Tiburón hadn't split up his force. Least two wings, I reckon, north and south of the main group."

J.B. blinked, then nodded.

"Do you see them, lover?" Krysty asked.

"No. It's just what I'd do, if I was a coldheart boss."

He studied the distant hunting party a minute or two

longer. Mildred felt her skin begin to crawl with nervous anticipation. What if he's right? she wondered. What if there are more of the bastards, heading out to surround us? What if they're closing in on us right now? What if they're creeping up even as we dawdle here beating our gums?

She realized she'd hear the same thing from pretty much all her companions, maybe even Ricky, wet behind the ears though he was: we fight, we run. We win. Or we die.

Standard operating procedure.

"What's so funny, Mildred?" Ryan growled, easing himself back down out of sight behind the rock and the bush.

She realized she had to have chuckled out loud. "Only me, Ryan," she said. "Only me."

RYAN HEADED EAST to increase the distance from the cold-hearts as shadows lengthened and the sun sank toward the early end of a mountain day. The terrain that way was up and down, mostly wooded but with patches of open space and heavy brush.

"I'll take us north or south, whichever feels right," he said as they trudged up a rocky slope. It exposed them to observation from a lot farther away than he liked. But whatever he did, there'd be trade-offs.

"Any particular reason we're headed right up this steep hillside?" Krysty asked. "Instead of around?"

"Yeah. I want to avoid the obvious high-speed routes.

If we keep them guessing which path we take, it gives us better chances to slip away clear."

He glanced back over his shoulder at the sun. "I'm looking to make it until nightfall," he said, "then shake the bastards off for good. Tiburón doesn't have him any ace trackers, does he?"

Ricky said he didn't think so.

"What happened to always assuming the worst?" Mildred asked.

"If the worst happens," Ryan said, "we're stone chilled. Why plan for that?"

"Don't you ever get tired of being right?"

"It hasn't been a problem so far."

He didn't mind the banter. If they got to feeling so beat down they couldn't speak their minds, they couldn't help one another survive.

Ryan was a bit more concerned about Jak. The teen had been less than stoic when Ryan told him to keep an eye on their path and stay out in front. That was the direction pursuit was least likely to come from, which was his beef. Jak wanted to be the first to spot the danger to his friends. And perhaps the first to dig into danger with one of his pet knives.

But the threats they knew about came from behind and left and right. It was keeping an eye skinned for the danger you *didn't* know about that kept dirt from hitting you in that selfsame eye.

Jak acted a tad testy. Krysty said he was feeling threatened by the new boy. Ryan would have thought maybe the kid would like somebody to talk to who was more his own age. But apparently that made him get on Jak's nerves more.

Still, Jak would learn to adjust. He was a survivor.

He was also ace as a scout, but there was only so much he could do. As quickly became clear when a bullet cracked by Ryan's head. From the report a heartbeat later, he could tell it came from his left. Off to the north.

One of Tiburón's flanking patrols had spotted them.

Even before he glanced that way, Ryan shouted, "Run!"

"But, Ryan!" Mildred yelled. "I see them—"

"No!" he shouted before she could say *shouldn't we shoot back?*

Under normal circumstances, the answer was *yes!* Take cover and teach yet another bunch of bullies that they couldn't miss fast enough to catch up with dead-aimed shots. But these circumstances were in no way normal. Even Deathlands normal.

"You want to get caught between fires?" he roared. "Run, for fuck's sake!"

That, he reckoned, was enough to remind everybody that if Ryan had been right about Tiburón sending out the one patrol, he was definitely right about the pincers' second jaw. Too close to bet your life against. And the southern team would be homing in on the ruckus right now, practically drooling in blood lust.

The main force didn't concern Ryan much. He was fairly confident they'd left it well behind. The companions had taught the EUN some sharp lessons about getting frisky with them. And why bustle into an ambush when Tiburón had patrols out to hunt the quarry down and pin it so he could finished it off at leisure?

Ryan never looked back. At this point, his companions would follow. Or they'd die.

More shots cracked off from their left. He heard shouts. Glancing far enough ahead to be sure he wouldn't put a foot wrong and twist his ankle, he finally looked that way.

The ground here was broken by short, steep hills and narrow valleys.

The EUN team was coming over a ridge he judged was a shave less than a hundred yards off. Actually, it was a pretty long sight line in this kind of country; bad luck the pursuers had gotten such a long glimpse at them.

Or was it? Ryan realized he'd much rather the enemy spot them at long range and let the usual coldheart chase reflex take over, causing them to hoot and holler and fire their weapons without much chance of hitting what they fired at, rather than announce their presence with a volley of blasterfire at powder-burn range, the way the first bunch had. His companions couldn't keep riding their luck forever.

The trail led them through low scrub and grass, and jogged right around what looked like the end of a lava flow, higher than their heads.

When he dodged around it, he saw Jak's face peering at him from a pink-flowered bush several yards ahead. The kid was heading back to lend his friends a hand.

Wrong call. "Go on!" Ryan shouted, waving at him. "Lead the way east! Make sure we're clear. Go, go, go!"

They needed speed now, not another blaster. Jak would just be another rabbit in the trap if the closing jaws snapped tight. Nuke it, if they *did* get pinned down they might have a jolt-walker's chance if one of their people stayed free to do some well-placed back-shooting—or, being Jak, stabbing.

But Ryan preferred not to find out.

They pounded up a slope, risking brief exposure crossing a bare hilltop. That drew blasterfire from the south, even farther away than the bunch that was now northwest of them. The two patrols were burning lots of powder, but that was to be expected. Even for a half-way army like the EUN, good fire discipline usually meant they might let off single rounds or short bursts instead of blazing through a whole mag every time they touched a trigger.

Then Ryan was pounding down the far side. He crashed through a shin-high bush, judging that gave him less chance of putting a boot wrong than vaulting it. The rest of the way was open with loose gravel down to a trickling stream about twenty-five feet away. But his sense of balance could manage that.

He risked a look back. Krysty was helping Mildred down the scree. He was glad to see neither woman had a blaster drawn.

After Krysty and Mildred came Doc, holding his swordstick by the middle. His eyes were clear and his cheeks were flushed by the afternoon heat, though the humidity had finally dwindled as they worked their way higher up into the *cordillera*. But he didn't seem to be laboring or breathing hard. His endurance was one thing that hadn't suffered during his travails. Then again, the miles they'd hoofed over the years since he joined up, some at similar rates of speed, would either keep you fit or chill you.

Ryan led them down the stream. No point in avoiding obvious routes right now. The coldhearts knew where they were, close enough to be all over them in a heartbeat if they slowed. He was hoping to gain distance.

The converging EUN teams were still shooting and shouting. At what, Ryan had no clue. None of them was currently within eyeshot of their prey, although that could change in a heartbeat.

Where the stream dribbled into another, slightly more enthusiastic one, Ryan cut to the right. He saw Jak jump out of a weather-twisted scrub tree at the crest of the next rise and crouch at its base. He was staring right at Ryan.

A red mist of anger boiled up inside of Ryan, and he opened his mouth to yell at the albino teen for his disobedience. Ease up off the trigger, a reasonable voice said in his head.

The adrenaline crackling in his blood had him hyped up and on the razor's edge. Fortunately, some keen part of his brain was always working. Jak had a rebellious nature but tended to follow Ryan's orders, especially when the shit-hammer was quickly descending. The only reason he'd have headed back from breaking a safe trail for his companions was if he'd run into something up ahead that was even worse than what was fast coming up behind.

What, Ryan couldn't think of.

But Jak's soft one-word call gave him his answer in spades.

"Monster."

Chapter Twenty-Three

"Fuck me," Ryan murmured, more to himself than the albino youth lying up at his side. "Will you look at that bastard?"

Time pressed hard. Their friends were holed up in the rocks at the top of the outcrop where Jak had come back to meet them. With any decent luck they'd pulled out far enough ahead of the pursuit that the coldheart teams had flowed together into one, chasing straight after them. Even if they got the same luck the Deathlands usually dealt—bad—they had decent cover as well as concealment on three sides and could stand off both jaws of the trap.

For a spell.

But the sight that greeted Ryan through a scraggly wisp of bush was the sort to give the strongest man pause. And it did.

The beast stood on a high brow of bare granite.

"Armor cat," Jak said quietly.

"Yeah. A big one," Ryan said.

Even at a good sixty yards, its mere presence was terrifying. It was huge, the size of a wag. It was built more like a wolf than any cat Ryan had ever seen, with a deep chest and high back. But its face was clearly feline, like a bobcat's. Or a tiger's.

True to its name, the bastard was armored. Really armored. Its body, face and limbs were covered in dark brown plates that shone like metal in the sun, but Ryan thought they were more like a bug's chitin. The plates looked thick and tough, accentuated by little tufts of fur that bristled out of the joints here and there. Ryan felt a sinking surety that those plates would shed even the pointy-nosed copper-jacketed bullets that left his long-blaster as easily as a duck's ass shed drizzle.

The cat also had sharp, bony spikes protruding from its shoulders. Just in case it looked too cute and cuddly without.

"Bastard must go a thousand pounds without even allowing for that shell of his," Ryan said. "Don't know how you'd even down something like that, without a wag-chiller missile. My best advice would be to aim for an eye and hope for the best."

The eyes were big and yellow. Standing still, the creature was an easy shot for Ryan at that range, even with a fairly brisk breeze blowing crosswise down the sliver of valley that separated them. But the monster's head never stayed still, and the armor plates that formed its brows looked extrathick. All the cat had to do was lower its head and there went your eye shot. A creature that size generally had a skull hard enough to shed a glancing shot, even without all that hard shell.

"What do?" Jak asked. He was practically quivering

with eagerness. Ryan wasn't sure for what. To run? To fight the thing?

Both, mebbe. Ryan quirked a grin. "Listen close," he said. "I've got a plan, if you're crazy enough to try it...."

JAK WAS, OF COURSE.

He had crept to the base of the slope above which the armor cat still stood, arrogantly surveying its domain. It hadn't yet seemed to notice him. Fortunately, the wind still blew crosswise, meaning it wouldn't carry his scent to the cat. Otherwise he'd have been attacked already.

The albino teen judged it was trying to figure the meaning of all the noise going on off to the west. The shooting had gotten more concentrated, somehow. Jak could tell it was now going both ways. His friends were shooting it out with their pursuers.

He didn't fret about them. They could look out for themselves, and they had Ryan with them, which shifted the odds in their favor.

Anyway, he had all the worrying he could handle about his *own* skinny ass. Especially since he was about to lay it on the line in the most triple-stupe manner imaginable.

He stood up.

"Hey, fuckface!" he shouted, waving a hand over his head.

The monster looked down at him, an almost puzzled look on its face.

Stooping, Jak grabbed a chunk of lava and threw it

at the creature. The rock bounced off its low, armor-plated forehead.

"Pussy!" he yelled.

The big yellow eyes blinked once, slowly, then the armor cat roared and sprang.

It was an impressive leap, a terrifying leap.

A fatally surprising leap. The mutie's enormous mass flew the whole thirty feet straight to where Jak had been standing and taunting it.

Fortunately, Jak had not only moved the instant it did, but his reflex was to move at an angle away from the axis of the armor cat's jump, the way he'd avoid a punch or knife thrust by dodging at right angles.

He actually felt the earth shake as the creature crashed down right where he'd stood, by which time he was flying down the narrow valley at top speed.

The armor cat bounded after him. Jak dodged through a stand of saplings, hearing them splinter as the monster rushed into them, hot on his heels.

The cat could easily run him down. But Jak could change course like a rabbit, which the thing proved it couldn't when it slammed side-on into another boulder pile. Shaking off the torrent of lava rubble and dirt that fell on its head, it roared in annoyance and launched after him again.

Also, while it could run him down like a coyote taking a three-legged gopher on the flat, that didn't seem to be its preferred mode of hunting. It liked to get close and spring. The cat couldn't be bothered to take less than a good twenty-five feet at a shot, which gave Jak, who kept glancing back over his shoulder, ample time to change course while the beast was in midflight and couldn't switch direction.

Hunter as he was, he could see why. When the mutie cat fell from the sky like that, it would just pulp anything less sturdy than, well, itself. Or maybe a light war wag.

He sensed frustration in its snorting, panting breaths and the way it kept shaking its head, as if trying to loose a horsefly from an armored earhole. Just when he reckoned it had finally figured out its strategy wasn't working, Jak ducked behind a big moss-grown granite boulder.

The monster blundered past, its huge clawed feet digging giant furrows in the purple dirt as it realized its quarry had vanished.

Jak, meanwhile, had scrambled up and over the rock and gotten a head start. "Missed!" he yelled over his shoulder.

The mutie cat bellowed with rage and bounded after.

The albino teen led the chase around to the north of the heights where his friends were. If sound were any clue, they were holding their own in a brisk firefight. It sounded to Jak as if the two pursuing forces had, in fact, joined up; most of the shots seemed to come from the same general area southwest of him. It was only a matter of time, though, before whoever was in charge of the combined patrols sent out a squad to flank the now-pinned-down party and deliver the kill shot.

In fact five men were just setting out around the north side when Jak burst out of the brush several yards in front of them, running directly toward them. Beyond the men, he could see the rest of the party firing up at the promontory from behind rocks and stunted trees.

Their faces lit with sadistic glee as the slight albino youth suddenly appeared, running right up on their blaster sights with his white hair flapping behind like a banner in a breeze.

Their abrupt shift from triumph to pants-filling terror gave him his cue. He dived to his left into a bush. Putting down a shoulder, he rolled and came up with his Python in his left hand and his big bowie in his right.

It was a gesture of utterly futile defiance; whichever foe he wound up facing would make short work of him.

But he wasn't facing any enemies at all. As he expected—hoped—the armor cat had caught one glimpse of the coldhearts and thought that many prey were better than a single skinny one. When Jak came up on one knee, the armor cat was already in the air, trailing a joyous snarl.

Jak watched in fascination as the men, frozen solid in terror, gazed up at the armored bulk of the monster falling on them like a meteor.

Jak's estimation of what the armor cat landing on an enemy would do turned out to be far weaker than reality. Basically, all five coldhearts burst like big, ripe bags of blood and guts when the creature came down on top of them. They were so completely squashed the monster didn't slow down, although its claws slipped a little in the blood and guts as it charged straight into the remainder of the EUN patrol.

Jak watched a moment in happy fascination. Then, making sure to keep out of the way of a stray round, he trotted back around the rise where his friends were holed up. The sweet sounds of futile gunshots and even more futile shrieks was like his own personal fanfare.

"Something."

Mildred came awake to Ryan's soft word. He was hunkered down between her and Krysty.

She sat up. By reflex she had her ZKR 551 revolver in hand.

"El Guapo's bunch?"

Ryan gave his head a shake as Krysty sat up. "They'd be crawling all over us if it was them. Those boys aren't subtle."

He gave Krysty a quick kiss and straightened. He had his Steyr in one hand. On the far side of the camp, Doc was still sitting in his bedroll, yawning and stretching.

J.B. was squatting by their fire. To minimize their chance of being detected, they had kept it small and banked it when they turned in. Now, as the yellow flames began to grow and crackle, Jak materialized out of the darkness between Mildred and Krysty.

"Out there," he said quietly. "Watching."

Skeletal fingers walked down Mildred's spine, leaving frost.

"Who? What? How many?"

"Not know."

They had pitched the camp just down the north side of a ridge. Trees screened them from below. Clumps of rock and brush hid them from the sides. Of course, as it meant that they couldn't see an approaching enemy until he was right on them, either, they always had someone on guard duty.

"Up there." J.B. pointed his jaw at the top of the ridge.

Ryan stood with a brand burning in one fist. He raised it high. Even before he got it all the way up; two circles of red light gleamed back at them from the crest.

"Chupacabras!" Ricky hissed. He started to raise his carbine.

"Hold on," Ryan said.

"Why?" Mildred said. "Why not shoot it?"

"I want to see what it's doing," Ryan said. "Jak, keep your eyes skinned to back and sides."

"Right." The youth didn't sound resentful. He'd *seen chupacabras.*

Mildred wondered if he suspected—as she unhappily did—that the others he sensed out there watching in the night were the mutie's kin.

The brand flared as a soft mountain breeze fanned it. Mildred saw the creature clearly now.

"Why not just chill it?" Mildred asked again. "It might attack."

"That's why I have all of us except Jak pointing blasters at it," Ryan said.

The creature was about the size of a small man or teenager, with long powerful back legs, a scaly tail, smaller arms. The limbs ended in wickedly curving black talons. Its shape and dimensions vaguely suggested a kangaroo gone horribly wrong. The eyes were big and seemed to glow red.

The creature looked as if it had been gene-spliced out of nightmares.

The hair rose on the back of Mildred's neck as she heard curious trilling sounds from several directions. They might have been night birds. Or bugs. Even up here in the cooler, drier mountains, Puerto Rico never seemed to lack for bugs. But Mildred couldn't make herself believe that was what was making the sounds.

The *chupacabra* began a strange sidling dance, left and right, erecting and lowering the long black spines that covered its body. The motion was hypnotic, which was the mutie's intent. If it could mesmerize its victim, then it could strike without opposition, sink fangs into flesh and drink living blood.

J.B.'s M-4000 scattergun roared. The creature rocked back on its tail then toppled to the ground, as the buckshot pistoned into its chest.

But the heavy, densely grown spines provided the *chupacabra* a rough-and-ready form of armor. The creature hissed and sprang onto its big hind legs again. A forked tongue darted from between tooth-lined jaws.

Mildred's shot blew out its left eye. The narrow spine-crested skull snapped back. A heartbeat later a .44-caliber slug from Doc's huge handblaster smashed into its narrow chest.

It went down with a limp finality that made it seem unlikely the monster was playing dead.

Shadows began to move visibly around them. "Form a circle, everybody," Ryan said. "Blasters up."

That trilling—insistent and sinister—grew louder.

As though the blackness was taking solid form around them, *chupacabras* began to appear from the night.

Chapter Twenty-Four

"Go away, you!" Ricky shouted. "*¡Salgan!* Get out of here! We don't want any trouble, but we'll sure finish it!"

He shouted more in Spanish, probably just repeating the same thing, but too fast for Mildred to catch.

"What are you doing?" Ryan said. "Have you lost it?"

"Listen!" the boy said. "They're talking to each other, can't you hear? Anyway, that's what the stories say. That they're smarter than just animals."

"That's just a superstition," Mildred said primly.

"Isn't that what people in your time said about *chupacabras?*" Ryan asked.

The comment about Mildred's time passed by Ricky.

Mildred frowned and gave a grumpy grunt.

J.B. guffawed. "You're too smart to think you can get one over on Ryan, Millie!" he stated. "Not with words, fists or firearms—well, mebbe with your ZKR. Best wait till he's laid up with colic, and you can get your own back by giving him an enema."

"Joy," she said.

A sidling shape moved toward her. Putting her left hand on her hip, Mildred turned her right side to the monster and extended her arm.

The creature came up short and did an almost comic take, then it slipped quickly into the night.

"Knows what a blaster is, that's for sure," J.B. said.

"Any animal learns to recognize a blaster," Ryan said. "Or they don't live to breed." But Mildred thought she heard a note of doubt in his voice.

Keening, the *chupacabras* closed in on the fallen mutie. One, bigger than the rest, stooped and picked up the dead one with its short forearms. Then, still making that thin whine, they turned and began to half walk, half hop away in that weird way of theirs.

"Well, now, *that* was different," J.B. said.

"Eat good tonight," Jak said with a grin.

But Ryan shook his head, his black brow beetled thoughtfully.

"If they got hungry enough," he said, "mebbe. But this time, I don't reckon so."

The creatures blended back into invisibility. Ryan blew out a long breath through pursed lips.

"Let's move on," he said. "If they change their minds about trying us on, we don't want to make thing easier on them than we have to. Plus the coldhearts will have heard all that blasting. This isn't a good place to be."

THROUGH THE GATHERING gloom of the early evening, Krysty saw red embers arc upward on the far side of the valley. Someone had already reached the cave the scalie ville boss had told them about.

"Well, isn't that our luck all over," J. B. Dix commented.

The evening air teetered on the edge of cool. A breeze blew up the valley from the left. Krysty couldn't help but wonder at the site of the hidden redoubt. The rocky, brushy, windswept height they were perched on overlooked the ridge into which it had been built. She guessed the military had its reasons.

"So this Handsome bastard beat us here," Ryan said. He drew in a deep breath and let it slide out through pursed lips.

"What will you do now about the treasure, Señor Ryan?" Ricky asked.

"Figure out how to take it away from him."

He passed the longeyes to J.B. "Scope it," he said.

The armorer adjusted the focus and studied the position carefully, as well as the surrounding rocks. A jut of granite would normally almost completely hide the redoubt entrance from their position. The incautious sentry with the fire, though, might as well have lit a signal flare.

"Looks like two men on watch," the armorer said thoughtfully. "No sign of anybody else."

"So how do we get in?" Mildred asked. She sounded bitter and defeated. They were tired, still nervous about Tiburón's patrol hunting them, though they hadn't seen their pursuers since introducing them to the armor cat the evening before. Also, they were on edge because of the shadows slinking near them in the gathering dark.

"We can't assault a redoubt full of heavily armed coldhearts," Mildred said.

J.B. passed the longeyes back to Ryan. "Seems to me like the sentries aren't expecting any company soon, either. From how this Handsome guy acts, he'd probably put that fire out with the guy's head to, you know, encourage the others."

"You answering me, Ryan?"

"Ease off the blaster's trigger, Mildred," Ryan said. "He just showed us the way in."

"How do you mean?"

"I believe, my dear lady," Doc said, stretched out on his stomach on a slab of rock still warm from the sun, "he means that if the guardians expect no one to emerge from the interior in any short period of time, it strongly suggests two things—*primus,* that there's no one inside near the entrance, and *secundus,* that the rest of the party, however large, and presumably including their esteemed leader, is otherwise occupied somewhere within."

He raised his head and lifted an eyebrow at Mildred. In the poor light, Krysty thought she saw a bit of a smirk.

Mildred scowled. "I went to med school, you grizzly old coot," she said. "I know what *primus* and *secundus* mean."

"Of course you do."

"What *do* they mean?" Ricky asked.

"They mean El Guapo and his coldhearts are busy exploring, looting or both," Ryan said. "Fireblast. This sucks glowing night shit."

"Except it presents us with a sterling opportunity," Doc said.

Ryan nodded grudgingly. "Yeah, I reckon. Not like we really need—"

He broke off with a quick flick of his eye at Ricky. Peering avidly at the half-hidden redoubt entrance, Ricky quivered like a dog eager to show its master how loyal and useful it could be.

"It just bugs my ass that the bastards are getting the pick of the plunder before us," Ryan said. The falsity in his tone rang clear as silver-washed pewter in a tin cup to Krysty's ears. Ricky continued to seem oblivious.

"But yeah." Ryan turned and grinned at his comrades. This time it was genuine. "I see a way we can put the wood to him after all. You're right, Doc. If we take care of those slack-ass guards, we can slip in easy as you please."

"There aren't many places to hide when entering a redoubt," Mildred said dubiously.

"No, but once we're in, there are if the doors aren't locked," J.B. said. "If they're looting in there, they must be getting into places where loot may be."

"We just need to get in the front door," Ryan said. "Between us, I reckon Jak and I can chill those sentries quickly."

Jak was squatting on his haunches down behind the rise, watching their backs. He nodded.

"What about me?" Ricky protested. "I can chill them from here, easy!"

"You can chill one, mebbe," J.B. said. "His buddy might not hear the shot, sure. But you reckon he *won't* notice his partner fall down, and raise a squawk before you can cycle that bolt, line up the next shot and silence him?" He shook his head. "I'm not willing to stake my life on those odds, for sure."

"Nobody's going to," Ryan said gruffly. "Kid, we need you to stay up here, watch our backs and make sure to let us know if something goes south over there. Think you can handle it?"

Ricky nodded eagerly.

Krysty knew perfectly well where Ryan was heading. But the boy was an ally, even if he wasn't one of them. An ally who had saved their lives repeatedly. She felt she owed it to him to say, "What about the *chupacabras?* What'll they do if we leave Ricky alone up here?"

"They getting any closer, Jak?" Ryan asked.

"No," Jak said without turning. He had his arms wrapped around his knees. "Keeping distance. Afraid."

"Reckon they are," J.B. said. "Mebbe they're smart enough to savvy man-talk, mebbe they aren't. But they speak blaster, right enough, and they respect us after what happened to their pal last night."

Krysty could sense it, in communion as she was with Gaia. Although these creatures were probably not, strictly speaking, Gaia's children, they acted the part of wild animals, even if perhaps more intelligent than the general run. The ones out there in the night around them...knew.

Something had raised an almighty fuss, even as they'd made their final creep up to this vantage point overlooking the redoubt entrance. Krysty had heard an angry yowl, changing to hissing and squalling, accompanied by a rising chorus of the chirps she'd come to associate with the *chupacabras* of the mountain zone. Whether they'd chilled the creature or not, the commotion had ended after a wild minute or so and hadn't been repeated.

Mildred wondered aloud if it might have been an armor cat. For her part, Krysty doubted any number of *chupacabras* could bring down a leviathan such as the one Jak had lured onto the coldhearts so quickly. Not without taking losses so terrible that even animals would have to take note.

Ricky had reminded them that the ville boss had said many different monsters were known to frequent the vicinity of the lost "cave." Krysty hadn't found that especially comforting. But at least, as Doc observed cheerfully, it meant that the *chupacabras* shadowing the party were also protecting them.

Now Ricky said, "I can take care of myself. I'm not afraid!" If he'd been standing up, Krysty reckoned he'd have puffed his chest out.

"Right," Ryan said. "So here's how we run this deal...."

"I'M AFRAID OUR BOY might be a bit of a stupe," J.B. said as they made their way up the far slope. About a hundred feet above them, the redoubt entrance was completely hidden by the ledge in front of it. "He took that hook without so much as poking at it first."

Ryan sniffed the air. He could smell the tang of tobacco smoke from the sentry's cigarette. The man was a smoking fool. Emphasis on *fool*.

Well, his father's healer had always said the habit would kill you. He grinned.

"He trusts us," Krysty said.

They spoke softly, knowing the breeze that now blew briskly up the valley would carry the sounds they made away from the sentries' ears.

Krysty sounded reproachful. Mentally, Ryan shrugged. They'd do what they had to do. Like always.

She'd cope. Like always.

"What do you mean?" Mildred asked.

"Haven't you worked it out yet?" Doc asked. "We're abandoning the boy. We jump out and leave him here." He shook his head. "Sad. Harsh to treat him so. Yet a kindness, in a way, to spare him our extended tour of the deepest circles of hell."

"Not like," Jak said.

"What's that, Jak?" J.B. said. "Thought you couldn't stand him. 'Chill him,' being your last word on the subject, if I recall."

The albino shrugged. "Got backs."

"Yeah, well," Ryan said, "he's not the first person who did us a good turn we've had to walk away from. Anyway, Doc's right. He'll do better back here at home than tagging after us. Plus he's still hot to find this sister of his. And if El Guapo's men haven't raped her to death, she'll be with him. And we, with any kind of luck, will be somewhere else."

"What if we should run across the gentleman in question?" Doc asked. "Or our young friend's sister?"

"We steer clear of both," Ryan said. "Got no beef with

El Guapo worth dying over. And she's not *my* sister, or one of yours. Remember, we're trying to sneak our way to the mat-trans and jump out without anybody noticing."

"What do you reckon our odds are of doing that, Ryan?" J.B. asked.

Ryan laughed quietly. "Better than our odds trying to take on a whole redoubt full of El Guapo's men," he said. "But if you'd rather take your chances out here with the monsters?"

"Lead the way," J.B. said with an answering grin.

RYAN MOVED AS QUIETLY as a stalking panther, and he made no more noise than the panther's shadow.

While their friends crouched twenty feet below the ledge, well out of sight of the guards, Ryan sneaked up to the left of the entrance, and Jak headed to the right. In keeping with their general slackness, the two lookouts stayed back in the vestibule formed by the rock that concealed the entrance. Ryan had the easier go, since he could get almost on top of his man around the big narrow jut of rock that screened the opening.

It meant he'd attack him from the front, but he didn't intend to give the man much chance to defend himself. Or even sing out.

Once in place, his back pressed to the still-warm hardness of the granite outcrop, Ryan drew three deep, deliberate breaths, keeping the exhales noiseless to avoid alerting his prey. Then he peeked past the edge of the tall stone to where Jak crouched on the other side. Holding up three fingers, he counted down: three, two, one.

Go.

Panga in hand, he whipped around the boulder. The man on his side was just lowering his cigarette. His hand descended but did not interfere with the backhand slash that opened his throat to the neckbone.

Even as he cut the man's gullet with his heavy blade, Ryan continued to step to his left past the man's right shoulder. That helped put him clear of the vast jet of blood from the severed neck. Not that he was squeamish, but being soaked in drying blood got itchy and inconvenient when it started to get tacky, and also tended to leave drip trails if not glaring red bootprints.

With his free hand, he grabbed the man by the back of his jacket. Clumsily, he had to catch hold with the knife hand, as well. The man's deadweight was tough to handle, even for someone of his strength.

He heard a scuffling sound and looked over to see the other sentry drop to his knees. Jak had managed to leap up on his back and wrap strong legs around his waist, while yanking the man's bearded chin back with one hand and slicing his big bowie side to side through the sentry's throat. The blade's bell was outward: a single powerful push cut jugular veins, carotids and tough windpipe with brutal efficiency. As the sentry collapsed, deflating from instant blood loss as had Ryan's victim, Jak rode him down, got his feet planted and used the strength of his core to lower his victim silently to the stone.

"Odale, hombres. ¿Qué tal?" a voice said from between them.

Chapter Twenty-Five

Ryan froze. The worst possible luck had just kicked him and Jak squarely in the balls. Another coldheart had strolled out to pass the time with his buddies on sentry duty. And with Ryan and the albino youth both still occupied controlling their dying but still-moving victims, there was no way either could stop him from raising the alarm—if he didn't blast them first with the AK he had slung muzzle-down over his back.

Ryan heard a thump, like knuckles softly rapped on an oak tabletop. The EUN coldheart's eyes started to widen as his brain tried to process the utterly unexpected sight in the vestibule.

Now they bulged halfway form their sockets. Literally. A hole had appeared above the arched brow of the right one.

The man pitched forward. The space was so narrow that Ryan, still holding his man with one hand, was able to catch one arm of the head-shot sec man. Jak caught the other. Ryan's shoulder strained in its socket, but they managed to ease him down along with his dead comrades.

Jak slipped into the entrance. After a moment he popped his head out and nodded. All clear.

Ryan stepped to the edge. He saw his companions' wide eyes turned up at him. He made a "come on" gesture, then stepped hastily back to stand against the smoothed-off stone beside the actual door into the redoubt.

He held up a hand and waved a thank-you salute at the lonely boy watching their backs from the far crest. The lonely, *betrayed* boy.

"Ricky saved our asses again," J.B. muttered as he slipped past Ryan into the redoubt with his shotgun leading the way. "Bet you feel like a bastard, 'long about now."

"Yeah, well." Ryan moistened his lips. "What else is new?"

Last came Krysty, giving him a quick kiss in passing. He followed her inside the cave, unslinging his Scout longblaster as he did so.

The vanadium steel door was wide-open, which signaled something was wrong with the controls. There was a brief interval of unlit hallway to minimize the light that showed outside. Past that, the usual concrete walls were illuminated by the usual fluorescent lighting.

The redoubt surroundings were familiar to Ryan, but he stayed on edge. Though there was no sign of them, in all likelihood EUN coldhearts swarmed throughout the stronghold. His companions' only realistic hope at this point was that the coldhearts were overwhelmingly occupied below, where the best scavvy was liable to be found.

The corridor was about twelve feet wide and about

eight tall. Doors were set to either side. It ran to an apparent T-junction, perhaps fifty yards along.

J.B. stood side by side with Jak, across the group from Ryan, where they could take the lead.

"How do we play it?" J.B. asked softly as Ryan joined him. "Clear each room as we pass?"

Ryan shook his head. "If a door's open, second person in line can stick their head in and give a quick but careful check while the rest of us power on. Then catch up at the end of the line."

J.B. nodded. "We don't want anybody popping out a door and blasting us in the back."

"Lots of things I don't want," Ryan said. "First and foremost being on this bastard island in the first damn place. Even less do I want a whole squad of coldhearts catching us in the middle of this bare metal corridor while we lollygag along. After stealth, speed gives us our best shot at seeing the sun come up tomorrow. Wherever."

"Gotcha," J.B. said with a nod. He turned and touched Jak's shoulder, gingerly, so as not to slice his fingers open on the sharp bits Jak sewed onto his jacket. "Lead the way, Jak."

RICKY LAY ON HIS BELLY on the ridgetop, concentrating with his entire being on watching the valley, with no more light than that of the tropical stars overhead.

It kept him from thinking about the rustling and chirping of the restless bloodsucking monsters around him.

But, so far, they continued to keep clear of him. He

doubted it was because they were all that scared of a skinny kid with his blaster. More likely they'd just decided he wasn't much of a threat. And they clearly had something more pressing on whatever passed for minds in those narrow, quill-crested skulls than making him their dinner.

He wondered how long he was going to have to wait up here in the wind. It was getting chilly—at least, to a boy who'd been raised in a humid coastal ville. Would they signal him from the doorway? Send somebody across the valley to fetch him, to make sure he got the word and came in safely?

Or did they expect him to hang out here all night while they looted the place at their pleasure? They couldn't expect to grab more than a few kilos of the choicest scavvy with El Guapo and some sizable chunk of his army inside. So Ricky reasoned it couldn't take them *that* long.

Then he glanced down the valley and saw disaster bearing down on his new friends at a fast swagger.

THE COMPANIONS WORKED their way deeper into the redoubt. They saw some signs of hasty ransacking on the way, but fortunately they didn't run into anybody.

It was a big facility, bigger than the standard redoubt. Clearly this one had fulfilled some major purpose other than weathering the Big Nuke. Ryan had taken up position right behind J.B., who followed Jak with his scattergun ready. Next came Mildred, then Doc. Krysty pulled rear guard.

The rooms they passed were mostly offices or small labs. Some might hold valuable scavvy. But of course Ryan and company couldn't afford to stop and check.

What they were trying to salvage in this redoubt hive was their asses.

Jak slowed to approach the next stairwell. He had his big bowie in hand, in hopes of chilling anybody they ran into quietly. Discovery was their biggest fear.

They'd descended five stories by now. Mat-trans gateways were usually located near the bottom level of redoubts, which was generally the most secure location.

Several stairwells plumbed the depths of the giant facility. They'd passed by a centrally located bank of elevators several times as they descended. It was tempting to hop in and ride right to the bottom, but the elevators were potential death traps so they ignored them and hoofed it.

They knew the entrances to the stairwells were their biggest risk zones. The heavy doors would keep them from hearing the sounds of enemies approaching from below or above.

Sure enough, when Jak had crept within ten feet of the steel door with the wire-mesh reinforced window, it swung open to reveal a pair of EUN coldhearts, smoking and joking with longblasters slung.

FIRST RICKY SAW THE GLOWS, bobbing up from where the valley twisted out of sight below to his left. He initially froze, wondering if all the myths he'd disregarded growing up were true, that the spirits of lost dead souls really did haunt the land by night as free-floating balls of fire: *luz mala,* "evil light." Such sightings were reliably reported on a regular basis in the coastal regions, but Ricky's father and uncle both dismissed them as fool's fire. They were lights caused by the gases of dead plant matter decomposing in marshy regions, spontaneously catching fire. Certainly Ricky was too firmly rooted in the real and practical world of making and fixing things to believe in ghosts.

Until now, cold, alone on a windy mountaintop, surrounded by monsters unmistakably real as he was himself. Not that any modern Puerto Rican would dismiss monsters as legendary. They were much too common for that.

Then he realized he was seeing something worse than ghost lights: torches. Held up by a party of men who didn't give a glowing night shit if anyone saw them or not.

That could only mean one thing: EUN coldhearts, either a returning patrol or reinforcements come to join El Guapo in his new treasure house.

He had a small pair of binoculars his uncle had given him, scavvy he'd bought cheap from someone who thought them broken when all they needed was a good lens-cleaning. Ricky aimed them at the train of dancing lights and dialed in the focus.

He saw what he knew he'd see: armed men. There were at least twenty of them. And though the little lenses didn't give him a very clear picture, he couldn't mistake the bald, slanted head and evil snout of Tiburón himself.

El Guapo's sec boss was dragging his ass and his

straggle of survivors back to their leader to report failure in catching or killing the fugitives El Guapo had sent them to hunt. The Handsome One didn't take disappointment well.

But then again, Tiburón was his valued right-hand man, and while he'd probably receive a virulent ass-chewing, the horrid weight of any physical penalties that occurred to a furious El Guapo would doubtless fall on a scapegoat or two.

Ricky lowered the glasses. The head of the little column was already starting to climb what appeared to be a random trail up the slope, no different from any other of the thousands that ran up and down through the island's central mountains. Nervous energy filled Ricky like an army of soldier ants on jolt, so that he could barely lie still.

I have to *do* something, he thought. They're going to realize something's wrong when they find the sentries chilled or missing.

He laid the binocs aside and shouldered his carbine. He knew what place Tiburón had in the file of men now angling up the far slope. Shooting at night was a tricky business, but he was sure he could do it. He lined up his sights on the tall misshapen figure, drew in the shooter's deep breath, let out half, and caught and held the rest. His finger began to tighten slowly, steadily on the trigger.

Then Ricky stopped. He shook himself like a wet dog, sighed out the last of the breath and rolled away from the longblaster.

If I chill Tiburón, he thought, what then?

If he missed, there was a chance nobody would notice the heavy bullet striking the ground. Unless, of course, it bounced off a rock and went howling off into the night. But if Tiburón or any of them went down suddenly, no way would the rest of the patrol fail to notice right away. It wouldn't take them more than a moment to discover the victim had been shot.

And that would doom his friends as much as if he'd walked into the redoubt and pulled the alarm himself. Even if El Guapo and his men were too deep within the cave to hear the inevitable storm of blasterfire, Ricky couldn't shoot fast enough to ensure nobody dashed up the trail to the entrance and ran inside to alert them.

Rage blazed up inside him like wildfire. The man who had so horribly murdered his mother and father before his eyes was in his sights. He wanted to blast the mutie more than he'd ever wanted anything in his young life. He wanted vengeance.

But his rational mind poured water on the flames of his passion. Chilling Tiburón would chill his friends. And Yami would be lost to Ricky.

He shook his head. Frustrated tears rolled hot down his cheeks as he watched the torches climb toward the hidden entrance, from which he fancied he saw the faintest hint of glow.

What do I do? he wondered, sick with fury and fear and indecision. *Madre, padre,* what can I do?

WITH A COUGAR LEAP, Jak was in the face of the man on his right, jamming his knife hilt-deep in his big belly.

At the same time, he clamped a white hand over the his victim's mouth.

The other man's eyes went wide in a round, bearded face. He opened his mouth to shout as he fumbled at the sling of his longblaster.

But J.B., while lacking the incredible speed of the albino youth, was nobody's slow-foot. He moved forward and slammed the steel buttplate of his M-4000 into the fat coldheart's face before he could get a sound out. The warning cry turned to a moan that turned to a gargle as the blood from his mashed-in nose and teeth filled his mouth and poured down his throat. The man toppled backward into the still-open stairwell door.

Ryan was in motion himself by then. Jak's guard was struggling furiously. The noises that escaped around the albino's white hand were as angry as they were agonized. The skinny coldheart was bastard tough, or perhaps adrenaline had taken away the edge of the pain from the knife twisting in his entrails. Either way, he was struggling furiously, and Jak was in a poor position to hang on. He'd even have trouble hanging on to his knife, with the man's blood flooding hot and slippery out over the hand that gripped it.

Ryan dashed past the wounded guard to the right. As he did, he swung his panga backhand. It was a risky move—a miss with that heavy, razor-keen blade could take Jak's left hand off. But even that was a better outcome than the bastard being able to scream his lungs out.

The panga struck true. The big, heavy knife sliced

through the neck vertebrae to sever the spinal cord. The coldheart jerked once, as if a charge of electricity had shot through him, then fell.

J.B. straightened from crouching over the supine fat man. As he did, he wiped the angled tip of the folding knife on the man's trousers. The guard wasn't dead quite yet, but any breath he might have used to cry out now wheezed and bubbled through the blood that welled from his cut throat.

"Too close," J.B. said, as Jak jumped back from the pathetic, blood-drenched crumple that had been his opponent a few heartbeats before.

Ryan just looked at him and shrugged. It was going to get worse before it got better.

IN AN AGONY OF INDECISION Ricky Morales watched the last torch vanish behind the tall jutting boulder that helped hide the cave entrance. As it did, he heard angry shouting from somewhere just inside.

He couldn't make out the words. It didn't matter. He knew what they meant.

He got up to one knee, stuffing his compact binoculars back into his heavy pack and shrugging it on. Then he picked up his longblaster.

He hesitated, sensing shadowy predators close by. Oddly, he felt no threat from them. He knew that the strange, horrific beings who had been sidling and chirruping around him the whole time had frozen because he had moved. They didn't know if he might threaten them.

"Listen, monsters," he said, first in English, and then Spanish. "Listen well and fast, if you want to get your home back…."

DOWN THE CORRIDOR, twenty yards to the right, a door opened. A man walked out, swigging from an upturned bottle. It fell from his hands to shatter with a crash on the concrete floor when he saw half a dozen heavily armed strangers bearing down on him.

J.B. took a step toward the left wall to clear Jak, shouldered his shotgun and fired. The man screamed even before the fléchettes struck him in the upper chest and neck in a splash of red.

As he fell backward, other doors flew open. His fellow coldhearts jumped into the corridor with blasters blazing.

Chapter Twenty-Six

Cautiously Ricky peered around the edge of the open redoubt entrance, his shoulder pressed to the cool steel framework. The corridor was empty. As expected, he saw no bodies, but a door standing open a few yards down the concrete corridor on the left showed Tiburón and his men had quickly found their missing comrades. Not, he suspected, that it mattered much.

Tiburón was a devil, but he was cunning. He would never have become the sec boss for a man like El Guapo—much less survived in the role—without being smart. His finely honed paranoid instincts would have screamed alarm the moment he found the sentries missing.

And no matter what his brain told him might have happened—that they had snuck off for a smoke or a drink, or even to watch each other's backs while they pissed—the sec boss's gut would have told him instantly what had happened, in no uncertain terms.

Ricky was far from worldly despite his yearly trade trips with his father. But just from hearing the traders talk on the trail, or the travelers who came to his uncle's shop to buy gear, or have theirs repaired or even just to shoot the breeze, he knew quite well that no sec boss believed there was any such thing as coincidence.

Tiburón knew perfectly well who had snuck into what appeared to Ricky to be a stronghold. And the fact that he hadn't raised the alarm himself only gave Ricky a clammy, cold punch to the gut.

It could only mean the shark-faced sec boss planned to make up for his failure to chill Ryan and his friends by hand-delivering them to his commander.

Clutching his carbine to his skinny chest, Ricky ran. He doubted anyone would be left behind to spot him and bar his way; Tiburón would want every man on the hunt lest their pesky quarry give him the slip again. But he didn't care.

All that mattered to him was saving his friends. And Yami.

If only he could pretend he had a moth's chance in a furnace of reaching them in time....

THE BARE WALLS GAVE BACK shattering waves of noise as J.B. ripped off a burst from his Uzi.

"Dark night," the armorer said as he stepped back into the room where he and Ryan had ducked to find shelter from the horizontal bullet storm outside. "Why haven't they punched up the alarm yet?"

There were about half a dozen men just ten yards down the hall, themselves ducking in and out of side rooms to loose off a burst or two.

As far as Ryan could tell, his companions were all fit to fight. Jak was in the office across the corridor. Krysty had shouted that she, Mildred and Doc were holed up in the next room back on that side.

At least two inert forms lay down the hall where the coldhearts were. Moaning came from one of the rooms the EUN men were ducking into and out of, suggesting Ryan's group had tagged at least one more. The problem was, they were in a stalemate.

"Puerto Rican standoff," J.B. said with a smile as he stood with his back to the wall inside the doorway. He dropped a spent magazine and rammed in another.

"You read my mind," Ryan said sourly. He peered out around the jamb from the other side of the door. Seeing nobody, he aimed his SIG-Sauer P-226 down the corridor.

A moment later, a man jumped into the corridor with a triumphant shout and some kind of longblaster leveled from his waist.

Ryan double tapped him, center mass. The man fell over backward, his boot heels drumming the floor futilely as Ryan ducked back inside.

J.B. wasn't smiling anymore. "Of course—" he began, then paused as a thunderous volley of full-auto shooting broke.

"That's not really right," he continued when the firing subsided, as coolly as if nothing had happened. "All they got to do is hold us here until reinforcements come up, and we're toast."

He frowned thoughtfully. He and Ryan had found themselves in a fairly large space, about thirty-five feet by twenty, that looked like a cross between some kind of metal shop and a lab. There were heavy worktables with steel-plate tops and legs bolted to the floors, and other smaller tables that seemed to be flat granite slabs, polished smooth beneath a coating of purplish dust. There were racks of what he knew were calipers and micrometers on the walls, and weird man-sized shapes spaced apart, hunched beneath plastic shrouds that had yellowed with age.

The distinctive boom of Doc's .44 LeMat replica echoed from right behind. After a quick glance, J.B. ducked out and fired a blast.

"Damn," he said without heat. "Nuke-sucker was trying to get lucky. Reckon he did, too, because he got his ass back out of the corridor before I could blast him."

He shook his head. "Wish we had some grens. We'd shake some shit up then."

"Yeah," Ryan said. "And if wishes could fly, we'd all be fucking screamwings. Anyway, let's just hope *they* don't have grens. Which they might, being an army and all." He glanced around the room. "Krysty," he called.

"Here, Ryan," he heard after a moment. Blasterfire broke out from the EUN coldhearts, who apparently thought their targets would be stupid enough to stick their heads out when somebody called.

Ryan waited out the spatter of blasterfire. As it died off, he heard a flat bark he thought was Mildred's handblaster. A squeal of pain answered from down the hall, followed by a thump and the sound of thrashing.

"Keep the bastards' heads down, but don't take chances."

He heard the ear-shattering roar of Jak's .357 Magnum Colt Python from across the corridor. He reckoned he hadn't told the coldhearts anything they couldn't work out on their own.

Anyway, what were they going to do about it—shoot at them? Their only other options appeared to be to turtle up and wait for El Guapo to come see what the fuck all the noise was about, or make a screaming kamikaze frontal attack on Ryan's group, which was fine with him, since if they charged right down the open corridor the coldhearts would make it convenient to kill them.

The back and forth blasterfire continued outside. Prowling around the room, Ryan tuned the racket out, even though the reverberating echoes and nasty supersonic harmonics were making his head hurt. But a little pain wouldn't chill him. Fireblast, a *lot* of pain didn't, so what was a headache?

An idea hit him as J.B. fired his scattergun with a boom around the corner.

"Running low on loaded mags for the Uzi," the armorer reported.

"Got a full one?" Ryan asked. The little man nodded.

"Slap that bastard in. I have got a plan."

Low-voiced consultations flew among the scattered companions, then Krysty counted loudly to three.

A terrific clatter of blasterfire broke. Hearing the three-count, the EUN coldhearts had cut loose with everything they had, expecting to scythe down a sudden assault.

Instead, their shots went banging and singing off along the walls of the corridors, leaving bright red smears of copper jacket or gouging out cement dust.

When their blasters ran dry and the roaring dropped suddenly into almost dizzying silence, Ryan roared, *"Now!"* and began pushing for all he was worth.

He had no idea what the machine under the tarp was. He suspected it was some kind of fancy whitecoat measuring device, but he had no way of knowing. It was a head shorter than he was and a little bit wider than his shoulders, more or less square. The covering was draped over something round on top, for whatever that might say about the thing's actual shape or nature. All Ryan cared about was that much of the body seemed to be solid metal.

The bastard had to have weighed half again what he did, even with the overstuffed pack on his back. It was on casters, but that mostly meant it could be moved, not that it was easy to get all that mass moving. Though he tightened up his gut and put his legs and hips into pushing, sharp metal corners cut into his palms, and the muscles of shoulders and back creaked from the effort.

He shoved the machine out into the corridor. He half expected to be met by a withering blaster firestorm. But instead the EUN coldhearts had ducked out of the way of the anticipated counter-barrage.

Ryan swung to the side of the bulky object away from the enemy, then he put his back into pushing. J.B. emerged from the door behind him as he passed.

A bearded head wearing a black beret popped out a

door to the left. Ryan winced as an earth-splitting bang and dragon's-breath heat went off by his left ear. J.B. had lit off the M-4000 shotgun he held by the pistol grip in his left hand.

The face disappeared. Ryan didn't know if its owner managed to yank it back in time to avoid it getting filled up with the fléchettes J.B. had loaded or not. He didn't much care.

Blasterfire snarled from up ahead. It was the higher-pitched, faster fire of an M-16 on full-auto, as opposed to the deeper, more deliberate noise of an AK. Ryan felt the rolling shield he shared with J.B. vibrate from multiple bullet strikes, but nothing touched them.

J.B. ripped an answering burst from the Uzi in his right hand. Neither of them were light weapons, the machine pistol and the scattergun, but the armorer had plenty of wiry strength in his deceptively light frame.

From ahead came shots, shouts, screams. Someone bolted out of a doorway and ran away down the corridor. Blinking to clear his eye of the stinging sweat that blurred its vision, Ryan wasn't sure which of his friends' shots brought the runner down with a despairing wail, to slide ten feet on his face along the floor.

The machine's little wheels hit something that yielded slightly but didn't give way. The thing tipped forward about an inch, then settled back and refused to budge.

Guessing it had served its purpose, Ryan shouted, "Moving!" so nobody'd blast him in the back, then swung around to the right, whipping out his panga.

As he suspected, the heavy machine had fetched up

against a body lying across the corridor. A door opened a little ahead. Someone came out swinging up a long-blaster from the hip.

Ryan sank the panga's blade into the coldheart's head with a backhand swing and a meaty thunk. He wrenched the big blade free as the man melted to the floor in the doorway, his longblaster falling from his hands with a clang.

"Freeze where you are, motherfuckers, or I'll chill you all!" a voice roared from behind him.

As much because of the sudden threat as in spite of it, Ryan started to turn, reaching for his holstered SIG-Sauer with his left hand.

"Ryan! *No!*" he heard Krysty cry. Desperation rang plainly in her voice.

He froze. And yeah, it felt as if his heart had turned to ice inside him.

"Put the weps down," the voice rasped. "Then hands up and turn around slowly."

"Ryan," he heard J.B. murmur.

"Do it," Ryan said. He knew that this wasn't the time to make a move.

Whether or not that time would ever come, he had no clue.

Bending at the knees, he laid the panga on the floor. He heard gentle, almost musical pings as J.B. laid his shotgun and autoblaster down with reverence. He treated his weapons gently when he wasn't bashing people in the head with them.

Slowly Ryan stood and turned in place, raising his hands.

He had never seen the big man close up before, but there was no mistaking the big mutie: the rough corpse-gray skin and the unnatural jut of snout from the bald head told Ryan he was seeing Tiburón before the sec boss opened his mouthful of snaggly teeth.

"You fuckers caused us a bunch of trouble," he said. "Glad to meet you at last, you know?"

Seven or eight of his coldhearts backed him up. They were aiming their weapons at the rest of the companions from a few feet up the corridor.

"We figured out right away what must've happened to the boys on watch up top," the Army of National Unity sec boss said in the weird lisp his inhuman dentition gave him. "So we came hunting. And once we heard the shooting down here, we approached real quiet, and what do you know? You couldn't wait to jump right out into our laps."

"I say we chill the motherfuckers," said a tall, rangy man with one dead eye.

"Easy, Angel," Tiburón said. "We've got nothing but time."

"But they wasted a load of our friends," Angel protested. "Anyway, they're trouble. Let's chop them down and haul the stiffs to El Guapo."

The sharklike face wasn't very mobile, but it could muster a scowl, especially with an accompanying hunch of those huge, sloping shoulders.

"El Guapo's gonna want to hurt somebody," he said.

"Triple-bad. First, because we didn't ice these pukes out in the hills the way he told us to. Second, because they got clear down here into his shiny new HQ. You know how he gets."

He narrowed his eyes, which looked like matte steel marbles, showing no more sign of life than Angel's milk-white orb.

"I reckoned he'd be able to take his anger out on the prisoners. But if you want to have the satisfaction of chilling them, go right ahead. Then you take their place, understand?"

The dead-eyed man went pale behind his thatch of black beard. "No, man, never mind. Forget I said anything, okay?"

"Yeah," Tiburón grunted. "Tie 'em up."

"Good choice, my friends."

Ryan turned his head at the sound of the new voice from behind, the way he and his friends had been heading before they ran into the enemy band.

It was another tall man, leanly muscular. Unlike most of the EUN coldhearts he had no beard.

Possibly he couldn't grow one. His face was the most hideous mass of twisted scar tissue Ryan had ever seen on a human being.

"El Guapo," Ryan said.

"No fucking kidding. And you're the dirtbags who've been giving me such a pain in the ass, aren't you?"

He turned a hot black glare on his sec boss. "And what are they doing in the middle of my new fucking fortress?"

Tiburón showed a literal shark's smile. "Surrendering."

For a moment Ryan thought—hoped—the hideous mutie sec boss had overplayed his hand with his even-more-hideous master. But then the Handsome One laughed.

"All right, cousin. Point to you. Congratulations. You get to live."

He laughed again. He had a good strong laugh. A good strong voice, deep and assertive. Ryan could see how he got people to follow him. You couldn't just terrorize people into doing that. At least, not the sort of hardcases with blasters and machetes who did a baron's dirty work terrorizing the peasants into submission.

Mebbe those awful fucking scars work for him, Ryan thought, despite the companions' predicament. Bastard's got to be titanium-tough for a fact, to survive getting them in the first place.

"What would you like to do with the prisoners, *jefe?*" Tiburón asked. Ryan heard more than a trace of grovel in his raspy, sibilant voice, which brought home just how stone a badass El Guapo had to be.

El Guapo looked Ryan up and down as if thinking about bidding on him, Then he passed the same scrutiny over the others. Ryan couldn't help noticing how his intense obsidian eyes lingered on Mildred's form— and even longer on Krysty's.

"Torture them to death publicly, of course," he said with a shrug. "After I mebbe get to know the bitches a bit better."

"Now?" Tiburón asked.

"Of course not, asshole. Right now I'm headed back upstairs. We passed some rooms up there that look like mebbe they're some kind of command posts. Or at least sec stations. Mebbe work a way to get the elevators running. And also to open up the cargo doors that open out onto the valley floor, so we don't have to hump all the weps and meds up eight flights of stairs. Plus air the place out some from all these nuke-sucking monsters that've been fucking and shitting everywhere for two hundred years."

"So what would you like us to do with them now?"

The Handsome One swept his captives with that chillingly appraising stare once more. He shrugged.

"Whatever the fuck you want," he said. "Just don't chill them, don't break nothing, don't mark them up too much."

He stalked past the captives to grab a pinch of his sec boss's gray, leathery cheek.

"Remember, if one of them's not healthy enough to put up a good show when I give them their public send-off to educate the masses, you're his stand-in. Or *hers*. Which you'd probably like even less, you know?"

Chapter Twenty-Seven

Tiburón had a fist just like a twelve-pound sledgehammer. At least that's what it felt like to Ryan when the ugly sec boss swung it full force into his gut.

All the air came out of Ryan's naked body, and he sagged at the knees. His legs simply couldn't support his weight.

The hard hands clamped on his biceps held him off the floor of the lab. With his hands tied behind his back, his own deadweight wrenched cruelly at his shoulder sockets.

"You like that?" Tiburón held up his fist and kissed it, then laughed. "That's nothing. You're weak, *hombre*. You need to be better, you know what I'm saying? Make a braver show when El Guapo starts cutting and burning parts off you."

Ryan raised his head, which felt like it weighed only a little more than the mountain they were inside. He glared at his tormentor with his good eye, which wasn't so good right now by reason of being swollen half shut.

He spat a string of ropy saliva, red with the blood of a split lip and loosened teeth, straight at that shark snout. Unfortunately he couldn't force enough air out to send it far enough. It dropped just shy of the big mutie's combat boots.

"Pathetic," Tiburón said. "Piss weak."

He rocked Ryan's head around on his neck with a backhand so hard it felt as if the vertebrae struck sparks off one another, bright yellow sparks, that shot right through Ryan's brain, blazing trails of pain.

He feigned being weaker than he was, just hanging in the arms of the men who held him. He let his head loll, looking around the room, searching for an opening.

Not that one looked likely to open up anytime soon.

Two burly dudes likewise held J.B. by the arms while Angel, who appeared to be Tiburón's second in command, kicked the hell out of him. Like Ryan—like all of them—the armorer had been stripped buck naked.

Jak and Doc lay trussed like game animals, wrists and ankles bound, tossed in a corner. The right side of Jak's thin face was one huge bruise, ugly green against his paper-white skin and now going purple and yellow around the edges. He'd resisted and gotten a longblaster butt in the face for his pain.

Doc had done more than resist. He looked like a such a befuddled, harmless old man that the sec men hadn't taken his swordstick away while they stripped him down. He'd just docilely gone along. For a while…

Now a fat sec man lay in the corner, gasping and whining with increasing feebleness, knotted around Doc's sword blade, which had run through his belly and out his back. His buddies, disgusted at his idiocy, hadn't bothered to tend his wounds, put him out of his misery or even pull out the sword. They just shoved him in another corner and left him to moan until he bled out.

The women had it worst. Of course. Laid out on their backs, Mildred and Krysty weren't much scuffed yet, except for a few palm prints on their faces. Krysty had a handprint on her left boob as well, looking as if it had been painted there, pink against her pale, perfect skin. Somebody'd gotten frisky, reckoning the boss wouldn't notice. Or that the mark would fade before El Guapo saw it.

Their hands had been stretched out beyond the heavy wooden legs of two different worktables and tied together, trapping their arms behind their heads. EUN goons squatted on the women's ankles, pinning their bare legs to the cold concrete floor. One of them, even more grossly obese than the one Doc had run through, seemed fascinated by the helpless women, almost as if this were his first time in a minor position of power. He kept running his fingertips along Mildred's skin despite her struggles, snarled protests and hurled spit.

Tiburón himself had yelled at the sec man to knock it off a few times, then he'd gotten more involved with beating Ryan and seemed to forget.

Now the nightmare-headed sec boss stood leering down at Ryan with fists on hips. He was broad around the middle, but it was muscle, not flab. He looked like he could lift a wag one handed.

"You're so piteous it's not fun pounding on you anymore, One Eye," he said. "But I think I know something you'll like."

He walked slowly over to Krysty. She shied away from him. He caught a handful of her red hair with one hand.

Then he jerked it back. "What? Fuck, your hair moves?"

She glared green laser death at him. He laughed.

"You're a mutie, too, then, aren't you, Fire Hair? Well, give me some of that sweet red stuff. Us muties got to stick together, no?"

Along with fury Ryan read resignation in Krysty's face. In extreme circumstances, she could summon the power of Gaia, the Earth Mother whom she worshiped and claimed communion with. It tended to leave her drained and sometimes unconscious, which was why she used it only in emergencies. But she was clearly trying to call on the power now.

And failing.

Tiburón squatted beside Krysty and grabbed her right breast. She grimaced in revulsion as he kneaded it.

"Let her go!" Ryan surged to his feet. He might not have the power of Gaia, but suddenly he had the power of being hotter than nuke-red.

But it wasn't enough. He was on the point of busting loose of the sec men who held his arms when a third stepped in and pile drove a steel-shod longblaster butt into his kidney. He went to his knees in a heap of pain and helpless rage.

Through a red haze of agony Ryan watched the terrible teeth close on his lover's flawless breast. Krysty's muscles stood out from her smooth skin as she tensed in horrified anticipation.

"How about I give you just a little love bite, Red?" the sec boss asked.

Krysty went ice-cold.

"Go ahead," she said, shaking her writhing hair from her face. "I wonder how El Guapo will respond to your disobeying his orders. After failing him so badly already."

For a moment she thought she saw fear in those ball-bearing eyes, but then he laughed.

"I could just, you know," he said, "cut you some. A few bandages, throw a shirt on, Handsome wouldn't have to know."

She felt his needle-sharp teeth glance across the sensitive flesh of her captive breast.

Gaia, why have you forsaken me? she wailed in her mind. If she ever needed the Earth Mother's power, if ever her companions needed that help, it was now.

But she felt cut off, somehow. She didn't know why. She had never called upon Gaia within the safety of a redoubt. Could it have anything to do with the thick concrete walls blocking her communion with Gaia? She had no idea.

All she knew was that her natural strength wasn't enough. She could only, helplessly, let Tiburón have his way.

He licked her nipple, which immediately hardened.

He pulled back. Though it was hard to tell from his horribly misshapen face, she knew he was grinning.

"See?" he said. "You like Tiburón. Mebbe you shouldn't judge him so fast, Fire Hair. Mebbe El Guapo let Tiburón play with you, you know, at the end. Give you some pleasure before the pain."

He settled back on his powerful haunches with his hands on his thighs. The great muscles threatened to burst through the strong fabric of his pants.

"You're too white," he said. "You mark up too easily. But I know someone who won't."

He whipped aside and snapped at Mildred's left breast.

The physician shrieked. For a moment, Krysty thought the sec boss had gone too far and actually bitten her breast off. But he let her go and rocked back into a triumphant posture.

"Bastards!" J.B. shouted. "Leave her alone!" He thrashed mightily, but warned by Ryan's near break, a couple of other sec men had stepped in to help hold him down. They already knew he was stronger than he looked.

"You're okay, Dark Meat. No harm, see? A shark knows his own teeth, slut. I know how to make mine hurt you without drawing blood, you know?"

He shook his slope-skulled head reluctantly and stood up.

"But I better not play around anymore. I have to stay professional. But my boys, they can have all the fun they want with you bitches."

"*All* the fun?" asked the fat guy who sat on Mildred's right ankle. He'd gone so pale when Tiburón lunged in his general direction, Krysty thought he'd shit himself. Now she was glad he hadn't; she wasn't fastidious, but the ventilation in the room wasn't that great.

"I mean just fuck 'em both, Rebozo," Tiburón said. "Just don't leave marks. Don't make me break your fingers again."

"All right, Tiburón! Whatever you say. But can somebody else take her leg? I want first crack at that good stuff!"

Tiburón sighed. "All right. Miguel, you take the fat boy's place."

"But what about my turn?" protested the runty guy Tiburón had gestured at.

"I'll tell you when you take your turn. If you'd like to have a chance at *getting* a turn—and mebbe to have something to take your turn with when you get it, if you catch my meaning—you do what I say. Fucking *now*."

"Yes, Tiburón!" the man said hastily. He actually stumbled trying to walk the few yards across open floor to take the place of the fat man, who jumped eagerly to his feet, fumbling with his web belt.

The two men holding Krysty's ankles scooted her legs wide. Angel stood over her, grinning down. She couldn't stop staring at his white dead eye for some reason.

Mebbe if I concentrate on that, she thought, I can ignore what he's doing to me.

He dropped his trousers. He had a rigid hard-on already. His dick was so skinny it put Krysty unpleasantly in mind of some kind of giant jungle stick insect.

"Don't judge me, Red," he said. "It ain't the meat, it's the motion."

He dropped to his knees and got into position.

Please, Gaia, she thought, at least give me the strength to break my legs free and crush him when he enters me....

His hands grabbed her thighs like claws, and he leaned down. A trail of saliva fell from his pendulous lower lip.

She drew in a deep breath. I will not scream, she commanded herself, wondering if she could obey.

As he lifted himself to plunge inside her, his head abruptly changed shape.

Chapter Twenty-Eight

It was as if Angel's head was wax and had suddenly half melted. His whole face seemed to distort, grow longer at a weird angle—right to left, front to back. His live eye bulged from the socket.

And then a piece of his forehead broke free from the rest of his deforming head and flew past Krysty on a column of dark fluid and pallid clots. He fell off to her right.

She was only slightly less surprised than Angel. Then she heard the distinctive clack-clack of a longblaster bolt being expertly and rapidly thrown, and knew what had just happened. Knew who had done it. And knew that it was the steel door to the room that had sealed her off from Gaia's loving, vengeful energy.

The door that was now open.

The power blasted through her body as if electrodes had been fastened to her wrists and ankles. She sat up with the strength of a world.

As she did, she raised the table she was bound to and lifted it over her head. The bolts that held its legs to plates in the concrete floor failed with little musical pings.

She swung it like a hardback book, over and forward and down.

The two men who pinned her ankles had been goggling without comprehension at the twitching body of their comrade. The table knocked them back away from her bare feet and squashed them to the floor like roaches.

She tore her hands free of the nylon ropes that bound them as if each were a single strand of spring-green grass. She stood up.

Then blackness filled her head. She was aware only that she fell....

RYAN DIDN'T KNOW how it could possibly be happening, but he heard the unmistakable sound of a big-bore bullet hitting the back of Angel's shaggy skull and saw him go down with the limp finality of the head dead.

Off Krysty. She was saved.

Blubber-bellied Rebozo reacted faster than anyone else in the room to Angel's sudden demise. With a squeal of sheer terror he threw himself to the left, away from Mildred, whom he'd been on the brink of raping. Even as Ryan's mind registered the metallic clatter of an Enfield-style longblaster bolt being thrown, dust and blood flew from the fat man's right shoulder. He rolled under a table, crying and spurting blood.

And then Krysty smashed the two guards holding her legs with her table as if it were a flyswatter.

The guards holding Ryan and J.B. let them go to grab for their blasters. It wasn't a bright move, but they were clearly panicked.

Ryan's hands were tied behind his back. Now he did something his captors' constant attention, and near-constant rain of blows, hadn't let him do: he skinned his bound wrists down his back, over his buttocks. Then, sitting on the cold concrete, he quickly slid his legs through the circle of his arms.

His hands were still tied tight at the wrists, but now they were in front of him.

Tiburón happened to be standing near him. The huge mutie seemed as taken aback by the unexpected turn of events as anyone.

Ryan swept the legs out from under the sec boss with a vicious scissors kick. Tiburón hit the ground hard, his head bouncing off the concrete floor with a crunch. Ryan rolled over and scrambled toward his pack, lying against one wall with his weapons beside it.

With a roar, Tiburón scrambled up onto all fours and hurled himself after the one-eyed man.

His roar changed to a steam-whistle squeal of pain as Ryan whipped around and buried his panga to its grip in the mutie's muscle-ribbed stomach.

Pain paralyzed Tiburón momentarily. Grabbing the grip with both hands, Ryan twisted the big blade in the man's belly. Ryan let go with his left hand to ward off the clumsy but desperate blows Tiburón launched at his face. Then he wrenched the panga free, spilling Tiburón's intestines in greasy coils on the floor.

Tiburón uttered a gobbling gasp and vomited blood onto Ryan's chest. Energized by rage and vengeance Ryan slid around the sec boss's side, then he leaped up onto the monster's broad back and wrapped his arm around Tiburón's neck, squeezing with all his strength.

Ryan was aware of shouts, shrieks and shots all around. He saw Mildred, her hands somehow freed, rise up screaming and throw one soldier against a steel-topped table so hard his back broke with a snap. He saw Doc dancing, stabbing enemies with his sword; saw J.B. shoulder an M4 carbine and squeeze off loud single shots at foes who screamed and sprayed and died.

With Ryan's arms throttling him, Tiburón struggled mightily. But massive blood loss had weakened him so quickly that he couldn't stand up. He swatted at Ryan, weakened rapidly and died.

The sec boss toppled forward on his snout and stayed there. Ryan swung off him, then hacked through the back of the bull-shark neck with a single downward panga stroke to make sure the bastard wasn't playing dead.

Then he looked around, dripping blade in hand.

The fight was over. Mildred knelt beside Krysty, helping her sit up. Doc steadied a still-groggy Jak on unreliable legs.

And standing in the doorway, legs braced, high-capacity handblaster fired to lockback in both hands, silenced carbine slung, was Ricky Morales. His eyes were wide.

"That there's some ace shooting, boy," J.B. said with overt pride. He walked up to a sec man who lay stirring feebly. When J.B. shot him, the exaggerated muzzle flash filled the room with the stink of singed hair and cooked human flesh.

Krysty went to Ricky, unselfconscious in her nudity,

and hugged him. The boy turned so red Ryan half expected his head to explode. Ryan had to turn away to hide his grin.

"We, ah, I mean, ah, thanks," Ricky stammered. "Now we better move. Like fast. Triple-fast."

"Why's that?" Ryan sat down on the hard, cold edge of a table, suddenly feeling weak. He'd been beat to crap and then battled a monster to the death. He needed a breather.

"I, ah, I sort of let the *chupacabras* in," Ricky said. "That is, I told them if they followed me into the redoubt they could get their home back. And they seemed to go for it."

"You mean those sidling horrors are heading here?" Mildred asked.

Ricky nodded

"I'm guessing they're not going to bother trying to tell us from the EUN," he said. "Fireblast, it's not like we've given them reason to love us."

"Probably they won't," Ricky agreed. "They left me alone as I came down. I don't know how long that'll last."

"Uh, Ryan?" Mildred stood holding her own clothes in a bunch. "Pants?"

"Hurry up and get dressed," he said. "We've got to get out of here. We don't want to get caught between angry goatsuckers and an angrier EUN. And I *don't* wanna run through the fucking redoubt barefoot. Might be broken glass."

Operating on the same wavelength, J.B. had already grabbed his clothes and was donning his sturdy work boots. He then searched the dead men and stood up brandishing something like a metal apple.

"Grens!" he exclaimed with a happy grin. "This'll help."

"Yeah." Ryan looked around. He noticed the fat guy, whatever the hell his name was, lying with his face to a wall. He was trying to look dead, but his blubber was still jiggling. It looked like he was suppressing sobs.

"Haul him over here," he directed. Doc, who had draped his frock coat over his bony bare shoulders like a cape, stalked to the wounded man. Despite the sec man's bulk, he dragged him twenty feet by the collar to dump at Ryan's feet.

"Sir," Doc said with a bow, then hastily began to dress.

"Listen, stupe," Ryan told the weeping man. "I've got no time to fuck with you. So tell me straight and fast and I promise I won't chill you."

"Anything!" the injured man blubbered.

"A room with colored glass walls," Ryan said. "Six sides. Sound familiar?"

"Oh, yes," the fat soldier said. "Two floors down, above the floor with the vats and—and nests. You must believe me, *señores!* I don't know what else to call them."

"All right," Ryan said, stepping back and nodding. "We're square."

The gunshot actually made him jump. A handblaster was loud in this small room. Rebozo's head jerked to the side and blood streamed out. His boot heels hammered the floor briefly. Motionless eyes bulged sightlessly at the ceiling.

"What the fuck, Mildred?" Ryan yelled.

Mildred stood with her handblaster tipped toward the ceiling, a thin trail of smoke wisping from its muzzle. "*I* didn't promise not to chill him," she said. "Now *we're* square. He got a little too goddamned free with his hands. I don't enjoy killing, but he needed it."

"Okay," Ryan said. "Fair enough."

He looked at Ricky, who had reloaded his handblaster and tucked it back in its flapped holster. Sharp kid, but Ryan knew that. They all did.

"Where did he say El Guapo went?" the boy asked.

"Upstairs, my lad," Doc said. "In search of some kind of control room."

"Listen to me, kid," Ryan said, picking up his pack. "Listen tight. I haven't been square with you. I'm dead square now. We're getting out of this shithole, and we're not taking the stairs or the cargo doors. And we aren't going to fight our way past all the monsters on the radblasted island. We have a fast way that will take us to the mainland. I can't tell you how, but I want you to come with us."

"We all do," Krysty said. "You've earned it."

"But what about Yami?"

J.B. approached Ricky and put a hand on his shoulder. "Face it, son," he said. "She's chilled. And probably better off for it."

"No." Ricky shook his head, then he frowned. "Well, I

don't know. And I *need* to know. If she's alive, she needs my help. I promised to give it to her."

Ryan shook his head. "You do what you have to, boy," he said. "We're headed for that six-sided glass room you heard us ask the meatbag here about. Once we get there, we'll wait ten minutes for you. Or as long as we can hold. Be there or make your own way out. Final offer."

The kid was already gone.

When Ricky was halfway back up the stairs a rumbling, grinding sound ran through the whole redoubt. It echoed up and down the winding stairwell.

He looked up and down the area, but he could see no source. It seemed to come from all around.

The *chupacabras* who had been slipping down the stairs never paused. They seemed to recognize the sound. They weren't bothering him; they might give him a yellow-eyed glance as they ghosted past, but they either recognized him as the one who'd led them back into their home, or knew he wasn't the threat they were bent on dealing with.

They didn't bother much with the stairs. They seemed to prefer to leap from railing to railing, a whole landing at a time, catching themselves with claws, feet and prehensile tails before launching down again.

The vibrations died away. Shaking his head, Ricky continued his run up the endless steps. He should have been exhausted, but the heavy pack felt like nothing on his back.

Yami, he kept thinking. Yami, I'm coming.

AT THE DOOR TO THE STAIRS to the next-to-last level Ryan paused to catch his breath. They hadn't met many EUN sec men on the run down. The *chupacabras* hadn't gotten down here yet, and the coldhearts seemed occupied elsewhere. Probably looting.

Ryan and his companions had given the slip to a few, chilling a four-man team they couldn't dodge.

A strange vibration came up through his boot soles. A booming squeal, hinting of vast metal movements, rose up around them like water.

"What that?" Jak asked, leaping around and looking in all directions with wild ruby eyes. "Earthquake?"

"No," J.B. said. "That's machinery. Mega-machinery."

"Fireblast!" Ryan said. "That baboon-faced bastard Handsome's got the garage door open!"

"Might be an armored vehicle we could use," Mildred said. "If we can take out the sec men."

But J.B. was frowning and shaking his head. "No," he said. "That's armored doors closing and opening. The blast doors."

"Coming from up, down, all around," Jak agreed.

"What the fuck? Is El Guapo trying to figure out the controls? Opening doors at random?"

"Seems pretty simultaneous for that, Ryan," the armorer said.

"I know!" Doc said. "I know the minds of the men who built this place! The evil minds!"

"Doc, you're losing it," Mildred said quietly.

But Krysty shook her head. "He does have intuition

into how the whitecoats who time-trawled him think, Mildred," she said. "You have to give him that."

Her expression and tone made it clear she didn't envy him that insight. There wasn't much to envy about remembering the process that had made him the way he was.

"Spit it out, Doc, and don't walk all around the barrel of the blaster."

"Those are automatic doors. Opened by timers at night. Closed by those selfsame timers each morning. We can access entry and exit via the keypads, but the automatic timers are for another purpose."

"You lost me there, Doc," J.B. admitted, scratching the back of his neck.

The old man smiled. "Do you not see? The doors open to allow the monsters bred here to stalk the land at night. And then come home with the sunset!"

"Which means—" Mildred said, then stopped, her face taking on an ashen hue under its own coating of sweat.

"The monsters the EUN ran out of this place are all going to be swarming back in," Ryan said. "And not just the nuke-sucking *chupacabras*."

"Right," Jak said.

Ryan glanced down the corridors. Was it his hyperactive imagination, or did he see a dark shape duck into an open doorway?

It didn't matter. They *would* see them, if they hung around long enough.

"Go now," he said, pushing open the door to the stairs.

FOR SOME REASON RICKY saw no *chupacabras* when he finally reached the entry of the redoubt. He suspected the ones who had crept up the hillside behind him had all headed down to their lair, to judge by what the guard said before Mildred iced him.

Which suited Ricky. He didn't recognize the man as having personally hurt any of his family or his friends, but the EUN armband was enough for Ricky to wish him a worse send-off than he got.

The sound of muttering voices sidled like *chupacabras* between the walls.

Voices. Ricky's blood ran cool despite his exertion. El Guapo—if that was indeed he—wasn't alone.

Softly Ricky stole down the corridor. He held no weapons. If he encountered *chupacabras,* especially a pack of the hissing, black-spiked, red-eyed monsters, he reckoned his best chance at living lay in not looking like a threat.

When he got alongside the open door from which the low, intense conversation came, he drew his .45. The whisper-quiet blasting of the carbine didn't outweigh the advantage of an Enfield longblaster's famed fast bolt-action. A room's occupants would notice if one of them suddenly went down, no matter how hard they were concentrating on the task at hand. He would need to shoot fast.

And not miss.

He pressed the backs of his shoulders against the concrete wall. Holding his Para-Ordnance right-handed with its muzzle toward the ceiling he fished inside the open collar of his shirt and hooked a thin, light chain.

From where it hung against his breastbone, he drew a small silver medallion, the size of an old quarter-dollar coin. It was tarnished, nicked, so badly battered by years—and eroded from reverent fondling—that it was hard to make out the image of a woman, with what looked like a mutie's outsized round head, cradling a baby in her arms.

Ricky knew it wasn't her head that was round. It was her halo.

On Puerto Rico, as on the mainland, the faith of the old times had mostly died away. The Armageddon that humanity had endured, the fire and plague followed by the cold and the dark, had brought judgment of a sort. But no promised Messiah. And the survivors who had emerged from the shelters after the skies cleared and the sun shone again, about thirty years on, were embittered and disillusioned with just about everything about the world that had betrayed and almost killed them. Especially its faith in the rival religions of science and God.

One they blamed for causing the devastation. The other they blamed for not preventing it.

Yet in some places, hints of the ancient beliefs clung on as superstition. Not least in the peaceful, prosperous, happy seacoast ville named for the lady on the medallion.

Ricky had been raised a rationalist, a scoffer, even by the standards of the day. His uncle regarded with cynicism anything he couldn't touch with his hands or measure with a micrometer or precision scales. But since they had been infants, both he and his beloved elder sister had worn the medallions given to them by their grandmother, who seemed to believe in every superstition.

So he whispered, "Blessed Maria, pray for me," and kissed the medallion. Just in case.

Then he let it drop back into his shirt. It wouldn't do to let the Virgin see what he was about to do.

Just in case.

Then he folded his left hand over the one that held the blaster, keeping the thumb well out if the way of the reciprocating slide and a forefinger hooked over the front of the trigger guard. He sucked down the deepest breath of his young life.

Then he swung around into the open doorway.

Chapter Twenty-Nine

The control room was small and mostly dark. A stocky man with a bush of kinky black hair sat hunched in a swivel chair, his round bearded face underlit by the glow of a computer screen. El Guapo bent over his shoulder, pointing to something on his display. A second guard stood back, his AKM slung over his shoulder, his face drooping in boredom.

That would quickly change.

With practiced speed and chill calm, Ricky lined up the three dots of his sights on the plump technician's head. He squeezed his whole hand, but fast, giving the trigger what his uncle's *pistolero* and *pistolera* friends had taught him as a compressed surprise break.

The yellow muzzle flash was as bright in the gloom as the blast was loud. The fuzzy head jerked. Dark droplets spattered the glowing screen.

Ricky was already swinging his muzzle right. When he fired again, the flash illuminated the most surprised look he had ever seen on a human face.

He saw the guard's head snap back. Even noted the beret flying off behind. Time seemed to have bogged down, be running slow. Ricky flash-aligned his sights and fired the second half of a double tap as the man folded. He didn't know if he hit him or not. It was the habit he'd been trained in and it was a good one.

He swung back to cover El Guapo. As he did, he noted the first tech. His normal practice would have been to give him a second shot, too, to be sure. But if the guy wasn't chilled, the way he had his cheek propped against the screen and his eyes staring half-lidded from his slack face, he was doing a fine job of acting for a man with a hole that big and blue in the side of his head.

As Ricky expected, the Handsome One had a tiger's reflexes. He reacted to the reality of his current situation fast enough to halt his right hand in its move for his the handblaster holstered at his hip and raise both hands. That meant Ricky didn't have to drop the hammer a fourth time.

Yet.

He wouldn't have chilled the would-be baron with that slug. He had his sights lined up on the middle of El Guapo's flat belly, about four inches above the brass U.S. Army belt buckle.

"Easy, kid," the man said, holding his hands by his head. "Easy now. Nice and easy. Let's talk."

"All right," Ricky said. "Talk."

His whole body was so tight he could barely pry words out of it. Squeezing the handblaster in a crushing grip was also part of the combat-pistol doctrine he'd been taught, but it was taking all his concentration to keep his arms from wobbling fatally. The blaster barrel did sway. But it never strayed far from his enemy's midsection.

"What do you want to talk about, my friend?" the horrifically scarred man asked. "You want me to tell you a bedtime story?"

El Guapo's tone was light, amused, as if he were in command of the situation. As if he had the blaster hand.

And he was bastard good at it. Ricky frowned in concentration to make his surging stomach remember that *he* held the blaster here.

"Yes," he forced out between teeth gritted so hard they squeaked like frightened mice. "Tell me a story. About my sister."

"Who? I know *lots* of sisters. I know them very well." His smirk widened. Ricky almost fired, but he didn't.

"Yami," he said. "Yamile Morales. Beautiful black-haired girl. Olive skin. Big dark eyes. About eighteen."

"We are Hispanic mostly here, you may have noticed. You just described ninety percent of the girls on the island. The beautiful ones, anyway. Care to be more specific?"

"The seaport ville you made an example of," Ricky said. Sweat streamed into his eyes, salt stinging them, threatening to cloud his vision. He blinked desperately to clear them. "Nuestra Señora. Mebbe a week ago. Your shark-head sec boss brought you one. Your shark-head sec boss who's at room temperature now downstairs, with his guts ripped open by the one-eyed man."

El Guapo shrugged. "If Tiburón let that happen to him," he said, "it was time I got a new chief of sec, anyway. Which I already reckoned, after he fucked up and let your friends in here. They are your friends, yes?"

"That doesn't matter now!"

"Whatever you say, son."

"I'm not your son!"

"Do you want to hear about your sister or not?"

"Yes."

El Guapo laughed. "I do remember her. You're right. She was very beautiful. Spirited, too. A fighter. Her teeth gave me a few more scars on my cheeks. Not that anyone would notice, of course. But in the end she gave it up sweet. They always do."

"You bastard!" Hot tears stung Ricky's eyes now.

"Of course," the Handsome One said. "What else would you expect? The island needs to be united. Needs to be lifted from the misery and anarchy in which it's been mired for centuries since the Nuke War. That takes a strong man with a strong hand. And the only way to show your strength is to act in a way that, inevitably, causes some people pain. Because, you see, people are stupes. For many, pain is the only language they understand.

"It's for their own good, you see. And surely—what's that?" His body jerked. His gaze slid past Ricky to the door behind him, and his eyes snapped wide.

Ricky's brain knew it was a ruse. But he wasn't a seasoned blaster. His body bought the head-fake.

He couldn't help himself, though he knew El Guapo was this very instant grabbing his own blaster to shoot him. Ricky looked over his shoulder at the indicated threat behind him....

But his arms, pushed out in front of him and locked

in an isosceles triangle, never wavered. He pulled the trigger blind, two times fast, then he ducked back though the door. But it wasn't necessary. With a groan El Guapo collapsed. His handblaster dropped to the floor with a clatter.

Ricky strode back to stand over the supine man. Despite falling for the trick he felt pride in his shooting: two red stains were spreading over the front of the army boss's khaki shirt. One was about an inch above that belt buckle, the other six inches up and to his right.

Ricky pointed the gun at El Guapo's face. The wasteland of red, angry scar tissue was even more twisted than usual with pain, and sweat was pooling in the gouges and furrows.

"Talk, you fucker! Where's my sister? What have you done with her? *Tell me!*"

"Or what?" Despite the agony wound tight around the words, the injured man's tone was bantering, almost light. "You'll give me the mercy of a quick death? Or…let me live?"

"Yes."

The bastard actually chuckled. He winced, sure— it had to feel like a knife was being twisted in his viscera—but Ricky had to admit the man had stones.

"Why not? I sold her, kid. A slaver from the mainland. He claimed he wanted her himself, but he couldn't fool me. He knows a baron with a taste for Spanish girls. Virgins especially. Pay triple-good jack."

"Virgin? But you said—"

"I…say a lot of shit. Anyway, *technically* virgin. You know?"

"You asshole!" Ricky shrieked. "I should chill you! I should blow your dick off!"

"You should, you know? Honestly. You should chill me."

And the gutshot man uttered a hearty laugh.

"But you won't. And that's a mistake. Because, see, this is nothing. I've been belly-shot before. Had worse happen to me—take a look at my face. Yeah, you hurt me like a bastard, and I'm gonna make you pay with interest, you little shit!"

For a moment rage darkened and contorted the man's disfigured features. But El Guapo mastered both. He was every scrap as strong as he imagined himself to be.

"Got meds," he said. "Antibiotics. We found a boatload of them in this strange old-days place. Infection won't get me. My men'll find me before internal bleeding finishes what you couldn't. I got healers who'll patch everything back together and not fuck up. If they want to keep their skins on, anyway."

"But not if I blast you first!" Ricky shouted. His hands were shaking all but uncontrollably. The Para-Ordnance was waving all around.

"But you won't. You don't have the balls. Because you're soft. Like the people of your shitty little ville. You won't finish me off. You can't."

"No," Ricky said. His voice was calm, and suddenly, so was he. "I won't." He stepped back and aside. "But *they* will."

Chirping with vengeful glee, a pack of *chupacabras* skipped through the door and swarmed the prostrate army chief. They ignored Ricky as if he weren't there.

For a moment, he stood and listened to the screams. Despite how it would have horrified his mother and his father, they were music to his ears. Nor did he look away from what the black talons and toothy mouths were doing to his enemy's flesh.

But he couldn't linger. His friends were hard-pressed. He knew they'd leave him if he didn't reach them soon.

He ran out the door and down the hall, the echoes of his footsteps pursuing him.

WHEN THE DOOR FLEW OPEN on a corridor swarming with EUN troops, the coldhearts' first reaction was to freeze. As anybody might, confronted with the half a dozen strangers in the middle of a secret underground redoubt.

Half a dozen heavily armed strangers.

Mildred saw brown faces turn toward them, some bearded, some smooth, all slack and round-eyed with surprise.

Most of the coldhearts in the gray corridor had their arms full of crates and containers. One dude with a beard and an obvious stiff-leg limp was pushing a dolly loaded with big green metal canisters of some sort. They were emerging from doors on both sides.

Apparently, the worthwhile scavvy was stored on this level.

And beyond them was the gateway. So near, so far.

Mildred and Ryan were in charge of taking down the

coldhearts with actual blasters in their hands. She was already lining up the sights of her Czech-made target revolver on one of the handful of coldhearts standing casual watch with longblasters slung. Then she saw the astonished faces dip down and look toward the floor, toward the round fragmentation grenade bouncing at them along the floor.

Mildred saw the flash, then the report hit her in the face like a hard slap. And then the people standing immediately around the small bomb were falling away.

She saw a boot arcing through the air, about six inches of leg still stuck out the top.

She'd flinched, though not as badly as her target had. She dropped her aim a fraction to center of mass and fired once. The others cut loose with a storm of fire as Doc yanked the pin from a second gren. Hard and fast, Ryan had said before kicking open the door.

And hard and fast was how their enemies went down.

WHEN HE WAS HALFWAY back down the stairs, Ricky heard a strange squealing commotion below. Pausing to stick his head over the rail, he saw horror blocking the next flight.

A pack of scorpion dogs was tearing at a supine man, though he was hard to recognize as human. The exposed skin of hands and face was mottled red and black and green, grotesquely swollen from a dozen stings. His torso and limbs were bloating the tough uniform fabric like balloons.

Yet, somehow, he wasn't dead yet. Or maybe that was

just the poison, making his body jerk. It was causing him to make some awful noises if it was, though.

Whatever contract he had managed to make with the *chupacabras*—for however long they'd choose to honor it—Ricky had no deal with the sting-tailed mutant canines, who apparently considered this their home, as well.

Ricky wasn't a major fan of heights, but he was not eager to experience the toxins from monster stingers as they exploded the blood cells in his veins. All while he was being eaten alive by feral dogs.

Around him, the *chupacabras* continued to swing from landing to landing like monkeys. They ignored him, but seemed to want no more of the scorpion dogs than he did.

If they can do it… Ricky thought. Then he scrambled over the rail and let himself hang by his hands.

He became acutely conscious of how his feet dangled over empty space that ended abruptly in concrete. If his straining hands slipped, he was done.

But he was committed now; no way he could pull himself back up. He could only hold the weight of himself, his weapons and his own pack for a few more seconds on the cold, hard rail. He made himself swing his legs back and forth. Once. Twice.

The third time his hands lost their grip. He swung his body toward the landing below by sheer force of will.

He brushed the rail with a heel on the way down, almost caught. His left ankle twisted painfully on landing, and he had to get both hands under him to keep his face from slamming into the perforated metal platform. That hurt his right wrist. But he made it, and didn't get a waffle face for his troubles. A couple of the dogs looked down at him, curiously, then went back to feeding noisily on their still-groaning victim.

With a great heave, Ricky pushed himself to his feet and hobbled down the stairs as fast as he could.

"ANY SIGN OF THE KID?" Ryan asked as J.B. ducked back around the corner of the gateway's outer chamber after loosing a burst from his Uzi at the coldhearts back up the corridor.

"Not a hair," the armorer said. He popped the magazine out of the well in his stubby weapon's grip. Hunkering down, he began thumbing loose cartridges from his pack into it.

Krysty stuck her arm and half her face around the jamb and fired three quick shots from her short-barreled handblaster.

"Looks like they've got reinforcements arriving, lover," she said. "There's nearly thirty of them out there, near as I can tell."

Squatting low in case somebody was in firing position where Krysty's head had vanished, Ryan peered around. He didn't bother trying to shoot his SIG.

Sure enough, more men in ragged camo and EUN armbands were crowding in doorways and huddling behind the heaps of scavvy and high-piled carts that dotted the corridor.

"Looks like they're nerving themselves up to charge,"

he said, pulling back to safety as a volley of blasterfire cracked past. "They're way beyond nuke-red pissed. We're not going to stop them this time."

"One more gren," Jak reported, tossing the item in one white hand like a matte steel apple. "Save and take with?"

"Never save your magic bullet, as Trader used to say," Ryan said. "Give it to J.B. When they look poised to go, give them that. It'll slow them at least a couple of seconds."

He glanced at the interior chamber with its six armaglass walls.

"Get ready to move inside, and triple-fast," he said. "As soon as we're in, I'm initiating the jump."

"Ryan!" Krysty said.

He looked at her. Her emerald eyes were wide.

"Seems hard to leave the kid now," J.B. said, gesturing with the gren.

"Yeah, well, hard times make for hard calls. Kid'll have to take his chances here. Not like we got any better to offer—"

"Hey!" a voice called from down the corridor. "Wait for me!"

"It's him, Ryan," J.B. said, peeking around the corner. "Running balls-out. With all the monsters on the whole rad-blasted island coming hard on his heels!"

"And they're not on our side!" the kid screamed.

Ryan leaned out over his friend. The boy was flying down the corridor toward the EUN troops, who had stopped what they were doing and turned to look. A whole flood of *chupacabras* were leaping and hissing right behind him. So were at least two packs of the scorpion dogs and what Ryan thought was an actual armor cat bounding and growling at the rear.

"Holy shit." He pulled back. "J.B., give them the gren to clear the kid's way. Everyone else in the mat-trans!"

AS HE THUNDERED TOWARD the EUN sec men in the corridor and crouching in doorways, Ricky's heart, already beating as if it was going to explode, jumped in his throat. The hated coldhearts were aiming their blasters.

But not at him. At a hundred monsters charging down on the goons with blood in their eyes.

Of course, being out in front of dozens of autoblasters when they cut loose at once wasn't an ace long-term survival strategy even if they weren't shooting at you. Especially with the kind of rat-ass fire discipline the late, unlamented and now partially digested El Guapo had managed to terrorize into them.

Ricky stared up the muzzle-brakes of a score of longblasters.

Mami, Papi, he said in his mind, I'm coming.

A flash went off right among the sec. A blastwave knocked five or six down shrieking. Blood and bloody chunks of flesh flew everywhere.

The rest ducked, unsure of how to respond to attack from both directions at once. A couple stood in Ricky's way like jacklighted mountain sheep.

He hauled out his handblaster and shot them out of

his way. Vaulting the writhing bodies, he raced down the corridor.

Behind him a pandemonium of snarls, barks and screams erupted. The screams quickly came to predominate.

Ricky skidded around the corner into the room where he'd seen the companions. They'd retreated into a weird, smaller room, with six walls made of some kind of glass.

Standing in the entrance, Ryan beckoned him. His mouth moved, as if he were calling his name. Ricky heard no sound.

Maybe his pulse was just too loud.

Something growled greedily right behind him. Ricky put on one last impossible burst of speed, although his lungs felt as if they were tearing themselves to pieces in his rib cage, and slid into the mat-trans unit. Immediately Ryan shut the door. A fine mist seemed to swirl from the ceiling, and it seemed to Ricky that the disks in the floor glowed.

Infinite blackness, shot through with red and purple lightning, enveloped him.

Ricky fell away from the world he knew....

* * * * *